SUICIDE IS SUSPECT

So far there had not been even a whisper of anything resembling a reason why Pettifer should have killed himself. He had apparently had no financial, health or marital problems, he was respected in his work and his medical practice flourished. Moreover, his wife was pregnant with their first child *and* only yesterday afternoon he had made a booking for an expensive holiday in a fortnight's time. Then there was the business of the car. As Lineham had said, why bother to get your car repaired, if you know you'll never use it again? What was more, each of the four people interviewed so far— wife, housekeeper, secretary and old friend—had violently repudiated the idea of suicide as being out of character, and each of the three women had individually insisted that Pettifer had seemed in especially good spirits yesterday.

No, there was no doubt about it, the whole thing simply didn't hang together. And in view of the man's medical knowledge it was out of the question that he could have been unaware of the danger of settling down in bed with a lethal supply of alcohol and drugs to hand. Impossible.

So, Thanet thought as he returned to his car, if suicide looked unlikely and accident were ruled out... Unconsciously his shoulders stiffened and his nostrils flared slightly, as if he had just scented danger on the wind.

Bantam Books offers the finest in classic and modern British murder mysteries.
Ask your bookseller for the books you have missed.

Agatha Christie

Death on the Nile
A Holiday for Murder
The Mousetrap and Other Plays
The Mysterious Affair at Styles
Poirot Investigates
Postern of Fate
The Secret Adversary
The Seven Dials Mystery
Sleeping Murder

Dorothy Simpson

Last Seen Alive
The Night She Died
Puppet for a Corpse
Six Feet Under
Close Her Eyes
coming soon: Element of Doubt

Sheila Radley

The Chief Inspector's Daughter
Death in the Morning
Fate Worse Than Death
Who Saw Him Die?

Elizabeth George

A Great Deliverance
coming soon: A Payment in Blood

Colin Dexter

Last Bus to Woodstock
The Riddle of the Third Mile
The Silent World of Nicholas Quinn
Service of All the Dead
The Dead of Jericho
The Secret of Annexe 3
Last Seen Wearing

John Greenwood

The Mind of Mr. Mosley
The Missing Mr. Mosley
Mosley by Moonlight
Murder, Mr. Mosley
Mists Over Mosley
What, Me, Mr. Mosley?

Ruth Rendell

A Dark-Adapted Eye
(writing as Barbara Vine)
A Fatal Inversion
(writing as Barbara Vine)

Marian Babson

Death in Fashion
Reel Murder
Murder, Murder Little Star
Murder on a Mystery Tour
Murder Sails at Midnight

Christianna Brand

Suddenly at His Residence
Heads You Lose

Dorothy Cannell

The Widows Club
coming soon: Down the Garden Path

Michael Dibdin

Ratking

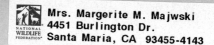

PUPPET FOR A CORPSE

DOROTHY SIMPSON

BANTAM BOOKS
Toronto • New York • London • Sydney • Auckland

*This edition contains the complete text
of the original hardcover edition.*
NOT ONE WORD HAS BEEN OMITTED.

PUPPET FOR A CORPSE

*A Bantam Book / published by arrangement with
The Scribner Book Companies Inc.*

PRINTING HISTORY
Charles Scribner's Sons edition published May 1983
A Mystery Guild Selection
Bantam edition / November 1985
3 printings through March 1989

ISBN 0-553-27774-X

Published simultaneously in the United States and Canada

PRINTED IN THE UNITED STATES OF AMERICA

O   12 11 10 9 8 7 6 5 4 3

FOR MY MOTHER

The regimen I adopt shall be for the benefit of my patients according to my ability and judgement, and not for their hurt or for any wrong. I will give no deadly drug to any, though it be asked of me, nor will I counsel such, and especially I will not aid a woman to procure abortion. Whatsoever house I enter, there will I go for the benefit of the sick, refraining from all wrongdoing or corruption, and especially from any act of seduction, of male or female, of bond or free. Whatsoever things I see or hear concerning the life of men, in my attendance on the sick or even apart therefrom, which ought not to be noised abroad, I will keep silence thereon, counting such things to be as sacred secrets.

Extract from the Hippocratic Oath

PUPPET FOR A CORPSE

1

The smell of burning toast drifted upstairs to the bathroom, where Detective Inspector Luke Thanet was
shaving. He grimaced at his foam-bedecked reflection,
laid his razor down on the wash-basin and went out on
to the landing.

The smell was stronger here and a faint bluish haze
was issuing from the half-open door of the kitchen, like
ectoplasm. The sound of a one-octave major scale,
haltingly played, indicated that Bridget was dutifully
doing her early-morning piano practice. Thanet was
loath to disturb her.

"Ben!" he bellowed. "Toast!"

A small figure clutching a comic shot out of the
sitting room and into the kitchen and Thanet heard the
clunk as the defective release mechanism on the toaster
was operated.

"Put some more in, will you, Ben?" he called. "And
watch it, this time."

He went back into the bathroom, took up his razor,
frowning slightly. Joan was presumably next door again,
administering an early-morning dose of comfort to their
neighbour, Mrs Markham. It was about time he put his
foot down. This had gone on long enough.

Joan had been working for eighteen months now as
an Assistant Probation Officer, prior to launching into
her formal training. She loved the job but it was very
demanding and, although Thanet tried to help as much
as he could, Bridget and Ben still needed a good deal of
attention. And at the moment they weren't getting it,
he reflected grimly as he rinsed and dried his face.
There was a limit to what one woman could do. It was

1

unreasonable of Mrs Markham still to be making such powerful bids for Joan's time and attention. Mr Markham had been dead for a year and, although Thanet had initially been full of sympathy for his widow, it annoyed him that she was now exacting from Joan the same degree of attention and service that she had expected from her husband.

When Thanet had dressed he went downstairs firmly resolved to speak to Joan about it. It was disconcerting to find that she still wasn't back.

"I can't find my leotard, Daddy," Bridget said, the moment he entered the kitchen.

She and Ben were munching their way through plates of Rice Krispies.

"I don't suppose it's far away." Thanet poured himself a cup of coffee and sat down. "When did you have it last?"

"Mummy was going to mend it for me. Daddy, I *must* have it for today. It's dance club and they're doing auditions for the Christmas pantomime." Bridget's grey eyes were beginning to glisten like pearls.

"Don't worry, Sprig." Thanet gave a reassuring smile, reached across to pat her hand. "I'll just eat this piece of toast and we'll go and look for it. Ben, how many times have I told you not to read your comic at the table! Anyone know if Mummy's had any breakfast yet?"

That was another thing, he thought grimly as they shook their heads. More often than not Joan was going off to work without even a cup of coffee these days.

Fifteen minutes later his decision to have it out with her had become full-blown determination. An exhaustive search had failed to turn up Bridget's leotard.

"Where can it *be*?" The tears were beginning to flow freely now.

He squatted to put his arms around her. "Hush, sweetheart, don't cry. It's bound to be here somewhere. Ben, run next door quickly and ask Mummy where she's put Sprig's leotard. Say she has to have it to take to school today. We really must go soon, or we'll be late." He hated to see the children go off to school distressed. His head was full of all the angry things he'd say to Joan when he had the opportunity. He had no intention of making a fuss in front of the children this morning though. He didn't want to upset Sprig further by having her witness an angry scene between her parents.

Joan came in with a rush, followed by Ben. "Sorry, darling," she said. "I just couldn't get away."

She avoided looking at him, he noticed.

"Don't worry, Sprig," she went on. "I know exactly where your leotard is. I've just got to put a stitch in it and . . ."

"You mean, you've still got to *repair* it?" Thanet could feel the anger building, fuelled by Bridget's distress and by the knowledge that they were already late, would now be delayed even further.

"It won't take a second," Joan said, disappearing into the sitting room. "I'll have it ready by the time you drive the car out of the garage," she called.

"Right, come on then, kids," said Thanet. Just as well it was his turn to take the children this morning. "Coats and scarves on, quickly now. We're late already."

True to her word Joan came running out with the leotard as Thanet was backing out of the garage. Thanet wound down his window to take it from her, handed it to Bridget.

Joan leant in to give him a quick peck on the cheek, blew kisses to the children. " 'Bye, darlings," she said. "See you this afternoon." One of Joan's friends earned pin-money by collecting Bridget and Ben from school with her own children. She would give them tea and keep them until Joan was free to pick them up.

Joan waved until the car was out of sight. Thanet watched her diminishing figure in the car mirror until he turned the corner. At the school he waited until Bridget and Ben were safely inside the playground and under the eye of a teacher before driving off.

"Beautiful day!" called another father, similarly engaged.

And it was, Thanet realised, noticing it properly for the first time, a perfect autumn day: unclouded sky and a sun whose strength was already dissipating that early-morning crispness which is a foretaste of frosts to come. His spirits began to rise, his mind to move forward to meet the day ahead. His undischarged anger was still there, underneath; but now, by some strange process, it was becoming translated into energy. By the time he reached the office he was brimming over with it and he began to hope that something really challenging would come in today. One of the things he liked about being a policeman was never knowing what would come along next.

It was a disappointment to find that his In tray held nothing of interest and after a cursory inspection he rose and crossed to the window. Down below in the street people and cars hurried by, intent on their destinations, seemingly imbued with a powerful sense of purpose. Thanet shifted restlessly from one foot to the other, envying them. He ached to be out there *doing* something.

Unfortunately, he told himself as he settled down at his desk, life is not in the habit of producing just what we want when we want it and for every exciting, challenging task there are usually a hundred dull ones to be tackled. He opened the first of the files awaiting his attention.

At once, as though Fate were giving him a pat on the head for Cultivating Correct Attitudes, the phone rang.

"Thanet here."

"DS Lineham, sir." Thanet grinned. Trust Mike already to be out on the job. "I'm at the house of a suicide, reported this morning. A Doctor Pettifer."

"It's Dr Pettifer *himself* who's committed suicide?" Thanet's tone betrayed something of the sense of shock, betrayal almost, which he experienced whenever he heard of a member of the medical profession killing himself.

"Yes, sir."

There was, Thanet thought, something almost obscene about the suicide of any man who had taken the Hippocratic Oath and dedicated himself to the saving of life. Unfortunately, the stress experienced these days by over-worked, over-burdened doctors took a heavy toll; the suicide rate in the profession, like alcoholism, was high.

"Apparently," added Lineham.

"What d'you mean, apparently?"

"Well, it all *looks* straightforward enough—an overdose helped on by alcohol, by the look of it. There's even a suicide note. But his wife's away and his housekeeper, well, she's hysterical, been with him since the year dot and swears he had no reason to do it . . ."

"That's what they all say," said Thanet. He knew only too well that the disbelief initially experienced by those closest to a suicide frequently equals and sometimes even exceeds their grief.

"Anyway, I thought I'd better give you a ring."

"I'll come along. I was just hoping for an excuse to get out of the office. It's that big Victorian house at the end of Brompton Lane, isn't it?"

"That's right. Pine Lodge. The one with the entrance pillars painted white."

"I'll be with you in ten minutes. Have you called a doctor?"

"The housekeeper says she doesn't know who his personal doctor was."

"Even though she's been with him for years?"

"I know it sounds odd, sir, but that's what she said. He was very healthy, apparently, and I suppose doctors tend to treat themselves for minor ailments . . . Anyway, I didn't feel it would be right to ring one of his partners. I thought we might give Doc Mallard a ring." Mallard was the local police surgeon.

"It's not usual, with a suicide," said Thanet. "But in the circumstances, yes, it's the best thing to do. I'll see if I can get hold of him. If not, I'll arrange something else from this end. See you shortly."

Mallard was soon contacted and Thanet arranged to meet him at Pine Lodge. Brompton Lane was in the prime residential area on the far side of Sturrenden, which was a thriving market town in the heart of Kent. Thanet had been born and brought up here, so naturally he knew most of the prominent people by sight. In the car he tried to recall what he knew of Pettifer, who was—had been—a striking figure: tall, thin, with a beaky nose and jutting chin, a distinctive, bony face. He hadn't looked an approachable man and had had the reputation of being a first-rate doctor whose patients were for that reason prepared to overlook his lack of a bedside manner.

And of course, Thanet thought, with a spurt of interest—he had been married to the actress, Gemma Shade! She was his second wife and much younger than he. Their marriage had been the talk of Sturrenden last year—or was it the year before? Thanet wasn't sure. Miss Shade's reputation as a serious actress was high and everyone had been astounded when she had chosen to marry a country GP. It had not fitted her somewhat exotic public image. Thanet wondered where she was this morning.

He was now nearing Brompton Lane and was aware of the growing knot of tension in his stomach; aware, too, that he was deliberately making his mind work in order to prevent himself thinking of the ordeal ahead. Not one of Thanet's colleagues knew how he dreaded the first sight of a corpse. There was something about that initial glimpse of the recently dead which moved him unbearably, especially when the death had been unnatural. Perhaps it was regret at the waste, perhaps a sense of being closer at this time than at any other to that central mystery of life, the moment when a living being loses his individuality, his identity, and becomes no more than a collection of discarded bones and flesh. At one time Thanet had been ashamed of such feelings, seeing them as unmanly, inappropriate to his calling; but slowly he had come to recognise that, paradoxically, they were one of his strengths, acting as a spur to his subsequent efforts. Acknowledging the value of what had been destroyed, he replenished his own sense of purpose.

There were the gateposts which Lineham had mentioned, painted white no doubt to act as landmarks for a tired GP trying to find his driveway in the dark after a night call.

Well, there would be no more night calls for Pettifer, Thanet reflected as he swung into the drive of neatly-raked gravel and parked beside Lineham's Renault 5.

Pettifer's sleep would never be disturbed again.

2

The Pettifer house was typical of so many Victorian family homes built towards the end of the nineteenth century. Constructed of rather ugly red brick it boasted large, square bay windows on either side of a shallow entrance porch and radiated an air of solidity and respectability. The figure of the uniformed constable planted outside the front door struck an incongruous note.

"Morning, Andrews," said Thanet. "DS Lineham inside?"

"In the kitchen, I believe, sir, with the housekeeper." He stood aside for Thanet to pass.

Thanet nodded and stepped into the house, closing the door behind him. The hall was wide, with doors to right and left and a broad staircase straight ahead rising to a half-landing illuminated by a stained-glass window similar to the panels on either side of the front door. A corridor alongside the staircase led presumably to the kitchen. The floor was patterned in black and white ceramic tiles and adorned by a truly magnificent Persian rug whose reds and blues gleamed in the dim light like semi-precious stones. On a carved antique oak blanket chest against the right-hand wall stood a deep pink bowl filled with Michaelmas daisies of all hues from pink to dark red, pale blue to indigo, echoing the rich colours of the carpet. The walls were hung with oil paintings, each with its own individual spotlight.

Thanet stood quite still, absorbing the atmosphere of the house. The place was well-ordered, no doubt about that, and there was both taste and money. Whose taste and whose money, he wondered. GPs didn't exactly starve, but neither did their incomes run to furnishings of this quality. And although Mrs Pettifer was well known, Thanet wouldn't have thought she was enough of a show-biz personality to be earning huge sums.

A door at the back of the house opened and closed and Detective Sergeant Lineham appeared, advancing along the narrow corridor beside the staircase.

"Ah, there you are, Mike," said Thanet. "Where is he?"

"In his bedroom. Are you ready to go up?" Lineham had worked with Thanet for several years now and was accustomed to Thanet's slow initial approach to a case, had even come to agree that those vital first impressions could be lost forever if there was too much haste.

"Lead the way," said Thanet, standing back to allow Lineham to precede him.

As he climbed the stairs he was aware of that knot in his stomach again, of the dryness in his mouth, his quickened breathing. He braced himself.

Lineham led the way not into one of the principal bedrooms but into a small room above the front door. It was simply furnished, spartan even, with a single bed, a bedside table and one small upright chair over the back of which Pettifer's dressing gown was neatly folded. There were no ornaments, no pictures, no concessions to luxury apart from one meagre bedside rug on the polished floorboards. Later, Thanet was to realise that this had originally been a dressing room for one of the principal bedrooms; one wall consisted entirely of built-in cupboards and there was a communicating door. For the moment, however, his attention was entirely focused on the occupant of the bed.

Doctor Pettifer had died peacefully—indeed it was difficult to believe that he was not simply asleep. He lay comfortably curled on his right side, chin resting on right hand, only his stillness and the unnatural pallor of his skin betraying his true condition.

"No doubt that he's dead?" Thanet murmured.

"None, sir. He's been gone for some hours. He's cooling fast."

Thanet laid his hand against Pettifer's cheek and found that it was cold, clammy to the touch. Lineham was right. Some time last night, then. He stepped back, clasping his hands behind his back. Better to be safe than sorry, touch nothing, just in case. Though he had to admit, everything looked innocuous enough, if suicide can ever be so described. Already his own tension was beginning to ease and he noted the empty pill container on the bedside table, the stained tumbler, the half-empty wine bottle. He stooped to peer at the label: Taylor's 1908 Vintage Port.

"Looks as though he went out in style," he said. "There was a note, you said?"

Lineham reached into his breast pocket, passed Thanet an envelope, handling it with care. "Addressed to his wife. Seems clear enough."

On the envelope was one word, *Gemma*. The letter was brief and to the point.

Darling,
 Forgive me for letting you down like this. Please, try and make it up to Andy for me, will you?
Ever yours,
Arnold

Thanet stared at the piece of paper. It seemed so . . . inadequate a message. But then no letter, no matter how long and tender, could possibly console a wife for being left in this way. The act of suicide was in itself explicit enough, the message inescapable: You don't matter enough to me to make my life worth living.

"Who's Andy?"

"Doctor Pettifer's son by his first marriage. He's away at boarding school."

Thanet frowned. "Poor kid. He'll have to be told, of course. Where is Mrs Pettifer?"

"In London, apparently. She's due back any minute, according to the housekeeper. Went up last evening, to have dinner with her agent and discuss a new play. She's Gemma Shade, the actress."

"Yes, I know. She stayed the night, then?"

"That was the arrangement."

"What time did she leave?"

"Mrs Price—the housekeeper—doesn't know. She was away last night too. It was her day off yesterday and she left soon after breakfast, to spend it with her sister out at Merrisham. When she came back this morning she found the curtains still drawn everywhere, no sign of Dr Pettifer having had breakfast, so she came up to investigate and found him like this. She's very upset. As I said, she's been with him for years."

"Bit odd, wasn't it, being away overnight? I'd have thought she'd have had to be back in time to prepare his breakfast, especially if Mrs Pettifer was away."

"In the normal way of things, she would have been. But she had special permission to spend the night at her sister's. There was something on in the village that they both particularly wanted to go to."

"Pity."

A car crunched on the gravel outside.

"That'll be Doc Mallard," said Thanet, crossing to the window. "Yes, there he is. Go down and meet him, will you?"

While Lineham was out of the room Thanet glanced around once more, noting for the first time the little pile of personal possessions on the seat of the upright chair. He moved across and glanced through them: wallet, thermometer, two bunches of keys, a couple of pens, some loose change and a diary. Thanet picked the latter up, found yesterday's date. *G London*, he read. *Mrs P to sister*. These were the only entries for this week. He flicked quickly through the rest of the diary but found nothing of interest. Most of the pages were blank, the few entries consisting chiefly of social engagements and Andy's beginning- and end-of-term dates.

Thanet put the diary back on the chair thoughtfully. It was interesting that Mrs Price's visit to her sister had been entered. Would a man normally note down the fact that his housekeeper was going to be away for the night? Surely not, unless he had a special reason for doing so—wanting the house to himself, for example. No, this had been no dramatic gesture carefully staged so that the suicide attempt would be discovered in time, Pettifer hauled back from the brink of death. Pettifer had meant to die, had timed the whole thing carefully. With both wife and housekeeper away until morning there would have been little chance of an unwelcome last-minute reprieve.

What a waste, Thanet thought, moving back to gaze down on the peaceful face of the dead man, what a waste. What could drive a man like Pettifer to kill himself? Despair, presumably, but over what? Thanet had met despair in many guises and in the most unexpected places, but suicide was something he had always found difficult to accept with equanimity. Was it not, after all, a form of murder—self-murder—surely no less heinous a crime than murder itself, if more understandable. And in one way, far more damaging to others: the murder victim is less likely to leave behind such a burden of guilt and self-reproach on his nearest and dearest. How close had Pettifer been to his wife? Thanet wondered. How significant was the fact that they had had separate bedrooms?

Mallard and Lineham entered the room, breaking into Thanet's train of thought. Mallard brushed his hand uneasily across his bald head as they greeted each other. He looked unusually grim. That was understandable. If Thanet found it hard to accept that a doctor had killed himself, how much more difficult it must be for a colleague. And, for all Thanet knew, the two men might have been friends. A tactful withdrawal was indicated.

"We'll wait downstairs," Thanet said. "There's not much room in here."

Mrs Price was huddled at the kitchen table, both hands clasped around a mug of steaming liquid, seeking comfort. The room was large, high-ceilinged and had an old-fashioned air, with a tall built-in dresser, a row of servants' bells labelled with the names of the different rooms and glass-fronted wall-cupboards painted institution green. Mrs Price matched her kingdom both in her ample proportions and in her slight dowdiness; her patterned crimplene dress and neatly waved brown hair would have passed unnoticed anywhere. She was, Thanet guessed, in her early sixties. As the two men entered the room she turned a dazed, tear-stained face towards them.

Thanet advanced, introduced himself, apologised for having to ask more questions. Courtesy paid off with all but the very few, he found. Mrs Price clearly found it reassuring. Thanet quickly learned that she had left the house at nine-thirty the previous morning and had travelled to her sister's by bus, arriving just before eleven-thirty. They had spent the afternoon at home and in the evening had attended a meeting in the village. This morning she had caught the workmen's bus at six-twenty in order to be back in time to clear up the breakfast dishes.

"I gather you don't usually spend the night away, on your day off?"

"No, but I specially wanted to go to this meeting and Doctor Pettifer said I could. If only I'd stayed home..."

"When did you ask him?"

"About three months ago." Mrs Price's cheeks were

pink. "I didn't often ask," she said defensively. "The last time was when . . ."

"Nobody's questioning your right to the occasional night off," Thanet said soothingly. "How did Dr Pettifer seem before you left, yesterday morning?"

"Fine. Real cheerful, he was," the housekeeper said promptly. "That's why I can't believe . . ." Her lips began to quiver and she dabbed at her eyes, blew her nose. "I *don't* believe it," she said vehemently, recovering herself. "The doctor would never've done it, never. Happy as a sandboy he was, yesterday. Well, I suppose that's putting it a bit strong. He never is . . . was . . . one to wear his heart on his sleeve, but I knew him and I could tell."

"How long have you been with him, Mrs Price?"

"Fifteen years," she said proudly. "Ever since Andy— that's his son—was a baby. And very happy I've been."

But there was a hint of reservation in that last statement. "So you must have run the house alone after the first Mrs Pettifer's death," he said, hazarding a guess as to where the trouble lay.

"That's right. For five years. Managed fine I did, too."

So he was right. Mrs Price had resented having to hand over the reins to a second Mrs Pettifer.

"Did you know that Mrs Pettifer was going up to London yesterday?"

"Yes, because of the meals. 'We'll both be out to lunch, and dinner'll just be for one,' she says to me, after breakfast yesterday morning. 'I'm going up to town this evening to see my agent and I shan't be back till tomorrow.' Well, I was a bit annoyed. I mean, I'd had this trip to my sister's arranged for months, like I said. 'But I'm going to be away tonight too,' I says. 'What about the doctor's breakfast tomorrow morning?' 'I expect he'll survive,' she says, as cool as you please. And now . . ." Mrs Price's eyes filled with tears.

"Oh, come, Mrs Price," Thanet said gently. "You

surely can't be saying that the doctor did what he did because you weren't here to cook his breakfast?"

The deliberate absurdity of the question made her smile. "No, but if I hadn't stayed away . . ."

"Mrs Price," Thanet said firmly. "Even if you had been here, what could you have done? I don't suppose that in the normal way of things you would see Dr Pettifer after he retired for the night?" He waited for her shake of the head. "There you are, then. And besides, you must remember this. If someone is really determined to kill himself, nothing will stop him. If anyone prevents him, he'll just try again. And from the way in which Dr Pettifer selected a night when he knew that both you and Mrs Pettifer would be away . . ." He paused to allow the point to sink in.

"It's no good, I still can't believe it," she said stubbornly. "He just wasn't the sort to give up, no matter what it was. When the first Mrs Pettifer was dying—she had cancer, and you know what that's like, she was ill for two years before she died—well, he never gave up hope, never gave up trying to save her. And just now, what with Mrs Pettifer being pregnant and all . . ."

"Mrs Pettifer is pregnant?"

"Six months gone, she is. The baby's due in the new year. He was that thrilled about it . . . And then there's Andy . . . Oh, who's going to tell Andy? Doted on his father, he did." And she dissolved into tears again.

"I think I can hear Doc Mallard coming down," said Lineham softly.

Thanet nodded, patted Mrs Price on the shoulder and went out into the hall, followed by Lineham. They met Mallard at the foot of the stairs. The police surgeon shook his head, his mouth tucked down at the corners.

"Doesn't seem much doubt about it, does there? The post mortem will verify it, of course, but that combination of alcohol and drugs . . . pretty typical of how a doctor would choose to go, if he wanted to. By far the most comfortable way to kill yourself, if you're set on it. Was there a note?"

Thanet nodded.

"That clinches it then, I should think. Why was I called in, by the way?"

"The housekeeper didn't know who his own doctor was and Mrs Pettifer is away. She's due back shortly."

"What a mess. She's pregnant, I believe."

"So the housekeeper said. Did you know him well?"

"Pettifer?" Mallard pursed his lips, shook his head. "Not really. I knew him, of course. Most doctors in a place the size of Sturrenden run into each other from time to time, at meetings and so on."

"What was he like?"

"Medically, his reputation was excellent. As a man, well, you'd have to ask his wife, or his partners. They operate from the Health Centre on the Maidstone Road."

So Mallard hadn't liked Pettifer, or at least had had reservations about him. Interesting, Thanet thought. "Have you heard of any reason why he might have done this? Rumours of depression, poor health, marital troubles, financial worries?"

"None. Truly, not a whisper. I won't say it's incomprehensible, because no one ever knows just what's going on inside someone else's mind, but in this case . . . Anyway," Mallard said, more briskly, "that's it, for the moment, as far as I'm concerned. I must get on."

"What time do you think he must have taken the overdose?" Thanet asked as he escorted Mallard to the car.

"Difficult to estimate exactly. Death would probably have been pretty swift. He would have known the appropriate dosage of whatever drug he used, of course, and the alcohol would have speeded things up enormously. He'd probably be dead within an hour or two. But there are various factors which would have delayed the cooling of the body—the fact that he was warmly tucked up in bed, that it was a mild night anyway . . . I'd guess he took it between ten and twelve last night."

15

Mallard's guess was good enough for him, Thanet thought as he watched the police surgeon drive away. Mallard's integrity and acumen were widely respected in the force. Thanet was fond of the older man, had known him since childhood. Pettifer's death had shaken Mallard, Thanet reflected as he returned to the house. The doctor's usual dry humour and testiness had been conspicuous by their absence.

Back in the kitchen he accepted the mug of coffee which Mrs Price had made while he was away. She looked calmer now, had perhaps found the tiny chore therapeutic.

"Well now, Mrs Price," Thanet said carefully, "the police surgeon has examined Dr Pettifer and I'm afraid it really does look as though he committed suicide. He even left a note, for Mrs Pettifer. Are you absolutely certain that you can't think of any reason why he should have done this?"

Mrs Price shook her head, her lips compressed in a stubborn line.

"No money worries?"

A vehement shake of the head this time. "There's never been any shortage of money in this house. Doctor Pettifer had a good practice and I've always understood that the first Mrs Pettifer left him everything when she died. And I believe she wasn't short of a penny."

"No . . . difficulties in his second marriage?"

Mrs Price folded her arms and glared at him. "No. Not that I'd tell you if there had been. I'm not one to gossip, but you can take it from me there weren't. I'd have been the first to know, living in the house. No, he worshipped the ground she walked on."

"And Mrs Pettifer?"

"She treated him well, I can't say different."

And, thought Thanet, it was clear that she would have liked to. It sounded as though there had been no problem there. All the same . . . "I did notice," he said delicately, "that Dr and Mrs Pettifer did not share a bedroom..."

"That," said Mrs Price, with an air of putting someone in his place, "was simply out of consideration for Mrs Pettifer. He didn't like her being disturbed at night. He was often called out, you know. So, ever since he knew she was expecting he's insisted on sleeping in the dressing room. So polite and considerate, he always was..."

Tears were imminent again and Thanet intervened quickly. "What about health? Did he have any problems there?"

"As strong as a horse, he was. Never a day's illness as long as I've been here. That's why I don't know who his doctor is, or if he's got one, even. Perhaps it's one of his partners. Oh, I'm not saying he didn't have the odd cold, that sort of thing, but he used to dose himself and there was never anything serious. I can't recall him ever being off work for more than a day or two in the last fifteen years. No, I tell a lie. He was laid up for a few days last year. He tripped over something and tore a muscle in his leg. But he didn't make a fuss about it. He put a lot of store by keeping fit. Didn't smoke, didn't drink—except at a dinner party, perhaps—and took regular exercise."

Dr Pettifer, Thanet thought, sounded dauntingly self-disciplined. "Any family worries? Parents? Son?"

"His parents are dead and Andy's as nice a boy as you'd hope to find, especially these days with all the tales you hear about youngsters. No"—and Mrs Price sat down suddenly, her eyes filling with tears yet again— "there's no reason, no reason at all, I tell you. It must have been an accident."

Thanet and Lineham said nothing. Who better qualified or more aware than a doctor, of the dangers of taking drugs and alcohol together? And there was the note. But there seemed little point in saying so. Mrs Price would have to come to terms with the tragedy in her own time.

Dorothy Simpson

"What time is Mrs Pettifer due back?" Thanet said.

"Around a quarter to ten. She's got a pre-natal appointment at ten-thirty this morning."

They all looked at the clock. Ten to ten. And, as if she had timed this entrance as carefully as one of her appearances on stage, the front door slammed and a woman's voice could be heard in the hall. Thanet and Lineham rose in unison.

It sounded as though Gemma Pettifer was home.

3

Thanet turned hurriedly to Mrs Price. "What is the name of Mrs Pettifer's doctor?" *Six months pregnant, I should have thought of this before.*

"Dr Barson."

"Get in touch with him right away," Thanet said to Lineham. "Mrs Pettifer will need him."

"There's a phone on the wall over there," said Mrs Price. "And if there's anything I can do..."

"Make some tea," Thanet said on his way to the door. "I expect she could do with some." Tea, he thought. The English panacea for all ills. What would this nation do without it?

Mrs Pettifer—or Gemma Shade, as her many fans would call her—was standing in the entrance hall facing an uncomfortable Constable Andrews.

"Accident?" she was saying. "What sort of an accident?"

"Ah, Inspector Thanet," Andrews said with relief. "This is..."

"Inspector?" she said, turning.

Thanet wondered if he had caught a hint of wariness in the questioning look she gave him. He had never seen her off-stage or at close quarters before and his

18

immediate reaction was one of surprise that she should look so ordinary. She was small and slight, with long brown hair caught back in an elastic band, and she was wearing a flowing Indian cotton dress which effectively concealed her fairly advanced state of pregnancy. He managed to manoeuvre her into a chair in the drawing room before breaking the news to her.

"Dead?" she said, staring up at him. "Of an overdose? *Arnold?*"

She was, he now saw, older than he had thought, in her mid-thirties, perhaps, but still a good ten years or so younger than her husband. Her one outstanding feature was her eyes, which were a clear willow green with very distinct irises. Thanet was conscious of an unusually strong surge of compassion.

"I'm afraid so," he said.

Her eyes slid away from his and she folded her hands protectively across her swollen belly, as if to reassure the child within that she at least had no intention of abandoning it. He could almost feel her trying to assimilate the facts of her husband's death and the significance of the word "overdose"—Pettifer's medical knowledge, the near-impossibility of its having been an accident...

"Suicide, you mean, then," she said at last.

"Yes. I'm sorry. There'll have to be an inquest, I'm afraid." He took out the note. "Your husband left a letter for you."

She stared at the proffered envelope for a moment before reaching out to take it between the tips of two fingers, warily. Then she glanced up at him, the green eyes accusing. "It's been opened," she said.

"Yes, I'm sorry. It's what one might call standard procedure in these circumstances."

"Standard procedure," she breathed scornfully as she took out the single sheet of paper. Her eyes took in the brief message in one single sweep. "And this is . . . all?" she said.

Thanet understood at once what she meant. She was

19

echoing what he had felt when he first read it and she was right. Those pitifully few words did seem a totally inadequate valediction. "I'm afraid so. And I shall have to ask for it back, temporarily."

She returned it to him, then shook her head. "It's no good. I still can't believe it."

"Why not?" said Thanet gently.

She frowned and stared down at her hands as if they held the answer. "All sorts of reasons," she said slowly. "As far as I knew he had no health problems—and surely I would have known, if there had been anything sufficiently serious for him to ... And then, he was so looking forward to the baby's arrival." She bit her lip. "Only yesterday, at breakfast, we were discussing names ..."

"Was that when you last saw him? At breakfast?"

The door opened and Lineham entered, bearing a cup of tea. Dr Barson, he announced, would be here shortly. Thanet repeated his question.

"No, that was at about six o'clock last night," she said, accepting the tea with a grateful nod, "when I tucked him up in bed, so to speak, with a hot drink and a couple of paracetamol. He said he thought he had a cold coming on ... and whenever that happened, which was rarely, he'd always have a hot bath, take a couple of paracetamol and put himself to bed."

She was still calm, remarkably calm really, Thanet thought. But he had seen this kind of reaction before. He guessed that at the moment she was being cushioned by a sense of unreality. Later on, when it hit her ... He sat down and said gently, "Do you feel up to telling me briefly about yesterday?"

"What do you want to know, exactly?"

"If you could run through the day, so that I could have some idea of your husband's movements ..."

Yesterday, it seemed, had been a day like any other, with no hint of the tragedy to come. Dr Pettifer had left for the Health Centre immediately after breakfast. After taking surgery he had done his usual round of late-morning visits before returning home to lunch, when he had behaved just as usual.

"He didn't seem at all depressed?"

"Not in the least, no."

"You really wouldn't say that there was anything out of the ordinary in his behaviour or his attitude?"

"No, nothing."

"And after lunch?"

After lunch Mrs Pettifer had gone up to her room for the afternoon rest upon which her husband had insisted during her pregnancy. Pettifer had returned from his second round of visits at around five-thirty. This was when he had first said that he thought he had an incipient cold. As his wife was going to be out for the evening he had decided to take a hot bath right away and go to bed early. Mrs Pettifer had waited until he was in bed and had then taken up the hot drink and paracetamol.

"And that was at about six o'clock, you say?"

"Yes, just before I left. My taxi was due at ten past six. I was supposed to be catching the six twenty-seven and when I went up I asked if he'd like me to cancel my engagement and stay at home. But he said no, that was quite unnecessary, that in any case it would be silly for me to keep him company in case I caught his cold. I suppose he knew I'd be disappointed if I didn't go. You see, I stopped work a couple of months ago, because of the baby, and he knew I'd found it difficult to adjust. I was so excited when my agent sent me this new part to consider, but then I simply couldn't make up my mind whether to accept it or not. That's why I was meeting him, to discuss it with him. So my husband . . ." She stopped.

"Yes."

She shrugged. "Nothing. As I say, he just said it was unnecessary for me to stay, that no doubt he'd be right as rain by morning."

This wasn't what she had been going to say, Thanet was certain of it, but he didn't feel he could press her at

21

the moment. He let it pass. "You gave him a hot drink, you say?"

"Yes. Cocoa." Her eyes widened. "He didn't . . . it wasn't in the cocoa that he took the . . ."

"No. You left the drink with him, then?"

"Yes. It was very hot and he was still sipping it when I left."

"And you also gave him some paracetamol, you said?"

"That's right. Two tablets. That's all he'd ever take."

"And you left the container on the bedside table?"

"No. The paracetamol are kept in the cabinet, in the bathroom. I took two out, put the container back."

"And you're sure they were paracetamol?"

"Certain."

"It's labelled, the container?"

"Of course. But there couldn't have been any mistake anyway. Both of us have . . . had a bit of a thing about drugs. Neither of us ever used anything but paracetamol, unless it was absolutely essential to take an antibiotic, perhaps, and we never keep any other drugs in that cabinet."

"Could you tell me if your husband would ever take a drink before he went to bed, to help him sleep, perhaps?"

"Alcohol, d'you mean? Good heavens, no! Never!"

Her astonishment was genuine, Thanet was sure of it. But remember, she's an actress, and a first-rate one at that, whispered the voice of caution. All the same, he could see no reason to disbelieve her. Mrs Price had said much the same thing. By now he thought he had a clear picture of what had happened. Pettifer had waited until he was certain that there was no possibility of his wife returning and had then disposed of the cocoa mug. (But why bother? And where was it now?) Then he had fetched the bottle of port, the glass and the necessary quantity of drugs and had returned to bed to seek eternal oblivion.

But why?

He must have had his reasons and they must have been cogent, powerful indeed—and yet, both wife and housekeeper had been blissfully unaware of their existence. What was more, Pettifer had played into that ignorance, had fostered and encouraged it, had kept the charade up right to the end. And why the fuss about something as trivial as a cold, if he had intended suicide? To enjoy, one last time, the luxury of being cosseted by his wife? Surely, someone who intended committing suicide would be past caring about such things?

"Oh, I don't understand it," Mrs Pettifer burst out. "I just don't understand it. He was so cheerful yesterday. How can he have . . . I know that by evening he thought he was getting a cold, but that was nothing, such a . . . trivial thing. He insisted that I should still go to London . . . I simply can't believe that all the time he was planning to . . ." She was becoming more and more agitated and now she stopped abruptly, blinked.

Here it comes, Thanet thought.

She struggled clumsily to her feet. "No!" she said, her voice rising. "It's not possible! Not Arnold. He'd never do such a thing. Never. He'd never leave me all alone, like this . . ." She sounded near panic now and with one brief gesture at her belly somehow managed to evoke all the bleak and lonely years ahead, bringing up the child alone.

Thanet rose as Lineham jumped up and took one or two uncertain steps towards her. The front door banged and voices could be heard outside in the hall. Lineham swung around and made for the door with evident relief. "That's probably the doctor."

Barson was tall, balding and wore pebble-lensed spectacles. One sweeping glance told him the situation. "Gemma," he said, hurrying across the room to take both her hands. "I am so very sorry."

His use of Mrs Pettifer's Christian name surprised Thanet a little, but he realised at once that it was only to be expected. Pettifer had no doubt known Barson well—he would, after all, scarcely have entrusted the

23

health of his wife and coming child to a mere acquaintance.

"I think Mrs Pettifer should rest," Barson said, with a hostile glance at Thanet. "She can't afford to take risks at this stage. So if you don't mind..."

"By all means." Thanet watched them go, Barson solicitously supporting her. The doctor's arrival had been fortuitously well-timed, coming as it had just at the moment when Mrs Pettifer's self-control had begun to crack.

The thought slid insidiously into his mind: too fortuitous? Had Mrs Pettifer heard the doctor's car, in the drive?

Somehow, with her going, Thanet felt a curious shift in his attitude towards her. Compassion for her plight was natural in the circumstances, but now, thinking back over the interview, it occurred to him that the strength of his reaction had been surprising. One of the hall-marks of a first-rate actor is the degree of response he is able to arouse in his audience. Had he, Thanet, just witnessed a truly superb performance, so carefully calculated, so understated that at no point had it crossed his mind that it could be anything other than genuine? Or was he being less than fair to Gemma Pettifer?

"Poor woman," said Lineham, as the door closed behind them.

"You think so?"

Lineham looked at him sharply. "Yes. Why, don't you?"

"Yes," Thanet said doubtfully. "Well, yes, of course I do. No one could help feeling sorry for her, in this situation."

"But?"

"But I've just got this niggling feeling... perhaps I'm being unfair. Perhaps being an actress means that in a situation like this people will constantly be questioning whether the emotions you display are genuine."

Experience had tempered Lineham's former naivety, the susceptibility to feminine charm which had on at least one occasion seriously impaired his judgement and impeded the progress of a case. And by now he had worked with Thanet long enough to have a healthy respect for his opinion. Whereas once he would have leaped to Gemma Pettifer's defence, now he simply said, "Don't you think she was genuine, then?"

"I'm just not one-hundred-per-cent convinced, that's all."

"Did she say anything specific that makes you doubtful?"

"No, nothing. Though she was evasive at one point, you'll have noticed."

"When she switched what she was going to say? Yes, I did notice that. I wondered why you didn't press the point."

"Things were going smoothly. I didn't want to rock the boat. I was concerned that if I put any pressure on her she might crack."

"Just as well you didn't, in view of the way it suddenly hit her."

"Mm, just as the doctor arrived." Thanet tried to sound neutral and failed. Lineham picked up the implication at once.

"You mean, that sudden break-up was deliberate? A performance, put on for our benefit?"

Thanet shook his head. "Let's leave it for the moment, Mike. It's all speculation really, so there's no point in wasting time discussing it." He grinned. "I think Dr Barson thought I'd been giving her the third degree. Anyway, let's see what we have to do now. We'll have to chase up that cocoa mug, check on the paracetamol container in the bathroom . . ."

"We're not just leaving it, then?"

"I don't see how we can, not until we get at least a glimmer of a reason why he did it. I agree, all the circumstantial evidence points to a clear-cut case of suicide—the method he chose, the suicide note, the way he carefully timed it to coincide with the absence of both wife and housekeeper . . . But I'm just not happy about it. If he did kill himself, he must have had a reason, and it's possible that it simply hasn't come to light yet. He might just have found out that he had cancer, for example. If so, anything of that nature will show up in the post mortem. Or he might have been about to go bankrupt, and felt he couldn't face the disgrace . . . I think we'll have to do a bit of discreet checking, treat it as a suspicious death for the moment, just in case. Better to be too careful than kick ourselves later for being slipshod."

"You want me to get the boys in, then?"

"Yes. I'll have a word with Mrs Pettifer. We'll have to take her finger-prints and Mrs Price's, for elimination purposes. Then you'd better get on to his bank. No need to press for details, just find out if his financial situation was healthy or not. And I'll go down to the Health Centre, have a word with his partners, in case something was awry there. One of them might possibly still be there, taking surgery. Let's hope they're not all off on their rounds by now."

"Do you want a search of the house?"

"I'll ask permission. But make it discreet. We really don't want to overplay things at the moment . . . You know, Mike, there is one thing that strikes me as odd. It's only just occurred to me."

"What?"

"Well, Doc Mallard said that he would estimate that Pettifer took the overdose some time between ten and twelve last night, and you know as well as I do that he's hardly ever wrong about something like that. Now, if that is so, why did Pettifer wait four or five hours after his wife left? Why not do it once he was sure she was out of the way?"

"Screwing up sufficient courage?"

"Possibly, I suppose. Perhaps that's why the port was there."

"You mean, he got drunk, first? Or perhaps something happened, between the time she left and the time he did it, to make him decide to."

"If so, it must have been something pretty drastic.

From what we've heard of him so far, he doesn't sound the sort of man to commit suicide on impulse without good reason."

The door opened and Dr Barson came into the room. "I'm afraid Mrs Pettifer refuses to settle down until she's seen you again, Inspector," he said tersely.

"Right. I wanted a brief word with her anyway." As they mounted the stairs together Thanet glanced speculatively at the doctor's stony expression. He needed this man's cooperation. "Perhaps I ought to explain, Doctor, that contrary to what you might think, I was consciously careful in what I said to Mrs Pettifer. She was perfectly calm until just a few moments before you arrived. Then it suddenly hit her. You can check with her, if you like."

They had reached the top of the stairs now and Barson stopped. He looked a little shamefaced as he said, "I'm sorry, Inspector. Evidently I've misjudged you. Naturally, when I say how upset Gemma was . . . I'm very fond of her, of both of them. I've known Arnold—Dr Pettifer—for years. Ever since we were medical students together, as a matter of fact."

Thanet privately breathed a prayer of gratitude that he had attempted to propitiate the man. His knowledge of Pettifer might be invaluable.

"What was he like?"

Barson pursed his lips. "D'you know, I always find that a difficult question to answer, and the better one knows someone, the more difficult it seems to be. One automatically begins to select all the good qualities, as if one were writing a reference. Let me see, now . . . Well, he was an excellent GP—thorough, hardworking, conscientious and a very good diagnostician. He had a rather unfortunate manner though, off-putting. He was very reserved, it was hard to get close to him. Although I've known him so long, I never really felt I understood what made him tick."

"Would you say this business was in his character?"

"Good God, no. Arnold was, above all, a sticker.

27

He'd never give up or opt out, however hard the going, certainly not for any reason I could imagine. I'm quite astounded by what's happened."

"You don't happen to know who his doctor was, do you?"

"I was, for what it's worth. I say 'for what it's worth' because, although he was theoretically on my list, in fact he never consulted me in all the years he's been on it, not once. He had excellent health, always, and I imagine he'd dose himself for any minor ailments. So if you're thinking he might have had a terminal illness . . . well, if he did, I certainly knew nothing about it. And *if* he did, of course the post mortem will show it."

"What if he just suspected he had it? People have been known to kill themselves because they were convinced they had cancer, for instance, when they really had nothing seriously wrong with them at all."

Barson shook his head emphatically. "Arnold would never have killed himself on a mere suspicion. No, if ill-health was the reason, it'll emerge soon enough, but frankly I think you're barking up the wrong tree."

"Have you been into his room this morning, to have a look at him?"

"Just briefly, yes. I didn't touch anything, of course." Barson frowned. "Vintage port and drugs. I must admit it's the way out most doctors would choose. By far the most comfortable. I understand there was a note, too."

Thanet showed it to him. Barson groaned. "Oh God— Andrew! I suppose his headmaster will have the unenviable task of breaking the news, poor devil. I'll ask Gemma if she'd like me to ring the school."

Mention of her name reminded them why they were standing here on the landing conversing in whispers and they began to move towards the door of Mrs Pettifer's room.

It was a complete contrast to her husband's monastic little cell. There was a fitted, butter-coloured carpet and the tall windows were hung with floor-length curtains patterned with sprays of wild flowers on a creamy background. The same fabric had been used in the curtains and drapes of the four-poster bed which dominated the room. Tiny, lacy cushions in many shapes and sizes were heaped at one end of the green velvet chaise-longue in the bay window and there was a clutter of silver, cut-glass and expensive-looking jars and bottles on the dressing table. A white satin peignoir trimmed with swansdown had been tossed carelessly across the foot of the lace bedspread. The effect was delicate, light, airy and overwhelmingly feminine. Thanet tried and failed to visualise Pettifer at home in this setting.

Gemma Pettifer was propped up against the lace-trimmed pillows, looking as fragile as a wax doll.

"You wanted to see me?" said Thanet.

"Yes. I've got something to show you. Perhaps it'll convince you." She reached for a large brown envelope on the bedside table. "Yesterday afternoon, my husband brought me a present. He'd picked it up on the way home, he said. I'm sure you'll be able to check that." And she spilled the contents of the envelope out on to the bedspread.

Thanet had no time for more than a glimpse of brightly coloured brochures before Mrs Pettifer selected a piece of paper and handed it to him.

"It was a surprise for me. He knew I'd always wanted to go."

Thanet stared down at the paper. It was a receipt from a travel agency. Yesterday afternoon, only a few hours before he had killed himself, Arnold Pettifer had paid £2,000 for a cruise to the Canaries, with a departure date in three weeks' time.

4

On the way to the Health Centre, Thanet found himself thinking about a man who had become something of a local legend.

Once upon a time (from 1948 to 1973, to be precise) there lived in Paddock Wood, in Kent, a doctor with a dream. The doctor was DJA Macdonald, the dream to gather together in his village and under one roof all the medical services which the people of his rural area could require. Women would no longer have to spend half a day trailing their children into Tonbridge or Maidstone for dental appointments, old age pensioners would no longer have to expend an alarming proportion of their pensions on bus fares and pregnant women would no longer have to find baby-sitters for their other children or endure the nausea-inducing bus journey into town for their pre-natal care. Doctor Macdonald was determined that his people were going to be the best-cared-for health patients in the whole of Kent, and the Woodlands Health Centre in Paddock Wood still thrives—a monument to his vision, patience and determination.

Since then a handful more of these excellent Centres have been established in Kent, but they are, of course, expensive to build and Doctor Macdonalds are few and far between. Sturrenden was fortunate in that its Centre was more or less complete before the economic recession came along to give the kiss of death to many a similar project. Thanet had never visited it before and he looked about with interest as he parked his car and approached the main entrance.

The building was single-storied, flat-roofed and built in the shape of a W, with specialist clinics such as dentistry, chiropody, speech therapy and pre-natal care in one of the long arms and a series of consulting and treatment rooms in the other. In the base of the W were the administrative offices, the reception area and the waiting room, which was cheerful, spacious and furnished with comfortable chairs upholstered in cream, chocolate, orange and black. Everywhere was spotlessly clean.

Thanet approached the Enquiries counter, where two

women were engrossed in some of the prodigious quantity of paperwork demanded by the National Health Service. Within a few minutes he was seated in a small, bright office with Mrs Barnet, the Administrative Secretary, a slim, trim woman in her mid-forties with neatly-waved greying blonde hair and a general air of reassuring capability. Her hazel eyes rounded as Thanet gently broke the news.

"Dead? Dr *Pet*tifer?" she said, a strangely formal echo of Mrs Pettifer's cry.

Thanet nodded. "And I'm afraid it looks as though he has committed suicide."

She sucked in her breath sharply, as if someone had just hit her hard in the solar plexus. She swallowed. "No," she said. "I don't believe it."

Thanet said nothing, waited.

"It's not possible," she said, after a few moments in which she was clearly trying to assimilate the news. "Not Dr Pettifer."

"Why not?"

"Well, because with some men, yes, you can imagine them doing it, killing themselves if they were desperate, but Dr Pettifer . . . it's just out of character, that's all. He's such a strong person, very . . . powerful, determined. If he's up against something he doesn't sit back and hope it'll go away, or just give up, he fights. And usually wins."

"You're saying, then, that it would be totally out of character for him to kill himself."

"That's right. Totally. And then, well, it was only yesterday he was in—here at the Centre, I mean. Today's his day off, you see, that's why we haven't missed him. Though . . ."

"What?"

"His car. It's still here. And I did wonder . . . I noticed it when I arrived this morning. I thought it must have broken down, that he'd had to leave it here overnight. I was half expecting him to give me a ring about it this morning."

31

"I'll check. What make is it?"

"A brown Rover. New."

"Right. But you were saying, about yesterday..."

"Well, he seemed so cheerful. Unusually so. He wasn't a very forthcoming person." Unconsciously Mrs Barnet had already slipped into the past tense. "He was a very good doctor, everybody respected him, but he could be a bit, well, off-hand I suppose you'd call it, in his manner. Oh, he wasn't rude or anything like that," she added hastily. "I hope I'm not giving the wrong impression. But yesterday, well, he was telling me all about this terrific meal he and Mrs Pettifer had had last week. It was their second wedding anniversary, apparently, and they'd been to the Sitting Duck out near Biddenden for a celebration dinner. That's what I mean by unusually cheerful. In the normal way of things he'd never have been so chatty."

"Did he have any health problems, to your knowledge?"

"I don't suppose I'd have known if he did, unless it was something very obvious, but not to my knowledge, no. He always seemed very healthy. Doctors often are. They build up an immunity, I suppose, being in constant contact with germs."

"Yes. Though I understand that in fact yesterday Dr Pettifer did think he had a cold coming on."

"Oh, really? Well, he certainly wouldn't have mentioned it to me, if he had. He wasn't one to make a fuss."

"You saw no sign of it, then?"

"No, but then in the early stages of a cold there often are no visible symptoms, are there?"

"No, I suppose not. What about the Health Centre? Were there any problems connected with his practice that might have been worrying him?"

She frowned. "I'm sure there weren't. I'd have known, if there had been. I'm not saying we don't get the odd problem cropping up, it would be a miracle if we didn't in a busy practice like this, but something serious enough for one of the doctors to kill himself . . . no, never."

"How many doctors are in practice here?"

There were, he learnt, three in addition to Pettifer. Dr Pettifer had originally been in practice with his father-in-law by his first marriage. When the old man died Dr Lowrie, now in his late fifties, had come into the practice, followed at intervals by Dr Fir, who was away at present on holiday, and Dr Braintree, who had come in only three years previously and was the baby of the practice. All three were married and only the Braintrees were childless.

The Centre was funded by the Area Health Authority and the medical practice was an independent one, paying rent to and sharing administrative costs with that authority. It was a flourishing practice, having around 11,500 patients on its books—rather a heavy work-load, Thanet learned: it was generally accepted that the standard number of patients per doctor should be around 2,500. Could overwork have been a contributory factor in Pettifer's death? he asked.

Mrs Barnet didn't think so.

"Is there any chance of having a word with either Dr Lowrie or Dr Braintree?"

"Not at the moment, I'm afraid. They're both out on visits. I'll have to contact them, of course, to tell them about Dr Pettifer . . . Oh, dear, they're so much under pressure at the moment. We were supposed to have had a locum to take over Dr Fir's work while he's on holiday, but unfortunately the man had a car accident the day before he was due to arrive and we weren't able to get a replacement at such short notice. And now, well, goodness knows how we're going to manage." She bit her lip. "That sounds awful, doesn't it, thinking of the Centre when there's poor Mrs Pettifer . . ."

"Life always has to go on," Thanet said gently.

"I suppose so . . . Anyway, let me see." She reached for a desk diary, flicked it open. "Ah, yes, I thought so. Dr Lowrie has to be back here at two, to meet someone

from the new Family Counselling service they're starting
in Sturrenden. When I speak to him I'll tell him you'd
like to have a word with him, shall I?"

"That would be kind."

"What arrangement shall I make, about your seeing
him?"

"Would it be possible for him to get back here a little
early, say at a quarter to two? Then I could see him
before his meeting."

"I'm sure that'll be all right."

Thanet thanked her and left.

In the car park a mechanic was tinkering with the
engine of a brown Rover. Parked alongside was a small
blue pick-up with CLOUGH'S FOR CARS on the side.
Thanet strolled across.

"Trouble?" he asked, pleasantly.

"Looks like it, don't it?" The mechanic barely glanced
up.

"Dr Pettifer's car, isn't it?"

A grunt of assent.

"Serious?"

"Give us a chance, mate. I only just got here, didn't
I?"

"Perhaps I'd better introduce myself. Detective Inspector Thanet, Sturrenden CID."

The man's back stiffened. He gave Thanet a wary
glance, then straightened up. "Oh?" He was in his
thirties, small, wiry and hairy.

"When did you hear that Dr Pettifer's car had broken
down?"

"Yesterday afternoon."

"What time?"

"Must've been about half past four, quarter to five.
Harry—Mr Clough, that is—come into the workshop
and told me."

"What, exactly, did he say?"

"Harry? He said Dr Pettifer'd just rung to say his car
wouldn't start."

"And?"

"Well, Harry said he couldn't send someone straight away because the other mechanic was off sick and I was trying to get this job finished for five o'clock, for another customer."

"Was Dr Pettifer put out?"

"Not according to Harry. Harry told him that if he'd like to hang on at the Centre I'd get there as soon as I could, but Dr Pettifer said it didn't really matter. He wasn't on call last night and wouldn't need the car, and he was off duty today and anyway if he needed a car he could always use his wife's."

"So what arrangement was made?"

"I'd get along as soon as I could this morning and deliver the car back to the house."

"How did you get the keys?"

"Dr Pettifer said he'd leave them at the desk."

The receptionist obviously hadn't bothered to mention them to Mrs Barnet, Thanet thought. No doubt there had been other, more urgent matters to attend to.

"Were you surprised that Dr Pettifer didn't want you to see to it right away?"

The man shrugged. "Didn't think about it one way or the other."

"You'll be delivering the car yourself?"

"Yeah."

"Well, when you do I should just park it and hand the keys to the constable at the door. Mrs Pettifer won't want to be bothered. I don't suppose you've heard, but Dr Pettifer was found dead this morning."

The man's face sagged and his mouth fell open slightly. "No kidding?"

"I'm afraid not."

"Heart attack?"

"You'll hear all the details in due course, no doubt. Perhaps you'd let your boss know."

"Sure." The man looked down at the spanner in his hand as if he wondered what it was doing there and then, as Thanet walked to his car, turned slowly to peer once more inside the raised bonnet.

Before driving away Thanet sat for a few minutes, thinking. What now? He wanted to talk to Lineham, but he didn't really have time to go to Pine Lodge and be back by one-forty-five. No, that wasn't strictly true. he did have time, just, but he wanted to be by himself for a while, to think and to assimilate all that he had learned this morning. He made up his mind. He would ring Lineham from a call box and then have a beer and sandwich in the nearest pub. As he drove out the mechanic straightened up and nodded farewell. Thanet raised a hand in response.

He found a phone box on the corner of the next street.

"Mike? Thanet here. Anything new?"

"I rang Pettifer's bank and there doesn't seem to be much point in going down there. The Manager was cagey, of course, but he was definite that Pettifer's financial position was what he called 'very healthy.'"

"Have the lads finished yet?"

"Just about. I checked up with the travel agents, by the way. Pettifer did call in to pay for that holiday yesterday afternoon. Just after five, apparently."

"Hmm. So what are you doing now?"

"Still looking around. I'm not sure how thorough you want me to be."

"Thorough. It really does look as though something is beginning to smell."

"Does it?"

Thanet smiled at the eagerness in Lineham's voice. The sergeant's unfailing enthusiasm for his work was one of his most endearing qualities. Thanet had seen so many good men grow blasé and cynical. He hoped it would never happen to Lineham. He told him about the car.

Lineham whistled. "Why bother to get your car repaired if you know you're never going to need it again?"

"Exactly. It isn't as though Mrs Pettifer would need

it. She's got a car of her own, apparently, as one might expect. Have you taken a look at Pettifer's desk yet?"

"I didn't think that came under the heading of 'discreet.'"

"Good. Leave it, then. I'd like to have a go at it myself. Where's Mrs Pettifer?"

"In bed."

"And Mrs Price?"

"Hasn't stirred out of the kitchen."

"Right. Well, try and find out from her—without making it obvious what you're doing—exactly where Mrs Pettifer stayed last night."

"So that's the way the wind blows, is it?"

"I'm not sure, and that's the truth. Or even if it's blowing at all. If you want to get in touch, I'll be back at the Health Centre at 1.45. I'm seeing one of Pettifer's partners then."

A couple of streets away Thanet found a promising little pub. He went in. There were perhaps half a dozen customers. Thanet ordered a cold beef sandwich and carried his beer across to a corner table. Another day he might have stayed at the bar and chatted. Today he wanted to be alone.

The beer was good, the beef sandwich superb—a great wedge of succulent pink meat between slabs of crusty, homemade bread. Thanet abandoned himself to the pleasure of this rare gastronomic treat and then lit his pipe and sat sipping his beer, staring into space and trying to get his thoughts into some sort of order.

As he had said to Lineham, all the circumstantial evidence seemed to point to suicide—the note, the timing, the method chosen—and yet... So far there had not been even a whisper of anything resembling a reason why Pettifer should have killed himself. He had apparently had no financial, health or marital problems, he was respected in his work and his medical practice flourished. Moreover, his wife was pregnant with their first child *and* only yesterday afternoon he had made a booking for an expensive holiday in three week's time.

Then there was the business of the car. As Lineham had said, why bother to get your car repaired, if you know you'll never use it again? What was more, each of the four people interviewed so far—wife, housekeeper, secretary and old friend—had violently repudiated the idea of suicide as being out of character, and each of the three women had individually insisted that Pettifer had seemed in especially good spirits yesterday.

No, there was no doubt about it, the whole thing simply didn't hang together. And in view of the man's medical knowledge it was out of the question that he could have been unaware of the danger of settling down in bed with a lethal supply of alcohol and drugs to hand. Impossible.

Thanet became aware that he was shaking his head and that some of the men at the bar had turned to stare at him. Had he been talking aloud? Embarrassed, he quickly drank off the rest of his beer and rose to leave.

So, he thought as he returned to his car, if suicide looked unlikely and accident were ruled out . . . Unconsciously his shoulders stiffened and his nostrils flared slightly, as if he had just scented danger on the wind.

5

Short and rather plump, with a bald head and gold-rimmed spectacles, Dr Lowrie was the antithesis of his dead partner. The laughter lines around eyes and mouth spoke of a warm and jovial disposition.

"Come in, come in, Inspector." Lowrie advanced, hand outstretched, and settled Thanet in a chair at right-angles to his desk. "This is a terrible thing, terrible. It's ridiculous, I suppose, but I can't help hoping that Mrs Barnet must have got it wrong."

Thanet shook his head. "I'm afraid not."

Lowrie frowned. "How, exactly, did it happen?" Briefly, Thanet gave the details. Lowrie listened in silence, with complete attention, eyes fixed on Thanet's face. Thanet awaited his reaction with interest. If Pettifer had indeed been murdered, then Lowrie must be regarded as a potential suspect. And if Lowrie was guilty, this was his cue to present reasons why Pettifer should have killed himself.

"Incredible," Lowrie said, shaking his head in disbelief. "Absolutely and completely incredible."

So Lowrie might be as innocent as he looked.

"I just can't believe it!" Lowrie jumped up, went to stand looking out of the window, hands clasped behind his back. He was silent for a few moments and then he turned. "Look, Inspector, as you can imagine we see a considerable amount of mental illness here." A brief sweep of the hand encompassed the consulting room, the Health Centre itself. "And we become pretty astute at spotting it. Approximately thirty per cent of our patients have anxiety-based or stress-related symptoms. Are you asking me to believe I wouldn't have noticed it in one of my own partners? Now if . . ." He broke off.

"Yes?"

Lowrie shook his head. "Nothing. The point is, I'm certain that if Pettifer had been suffering a degree of strain sufficiently acute for him to kill himself, for God's sake, I would have noticed."

"We often notice least changes in those we know best. Especially if we see them every day."

The doctor shook his head impatiently. "I know that. But I can't accept that it applies here. Dammit, I'm trained to notice that sort of thing. It becomes as automatic as breathing. And I knew Pettifer well. We've been partners for eighteen years. He just wasn't the sort of man to crack under pressure. In fact, he seemed to thrive on it. A challenge was meat and drink to him. If this place had gone up in flames, Pettifer would have been in the thick of it, calmly directing salvage and rescue operations." He shook his head again. "It's no good, I simply can't believe it." He gave a wry smile. "And don't think I'm not aware how often one hears those very words from the friends and relations of suicides. But in this case, I do assure you, they're justified."

"Are you suggesting that it was an accident, then?"

Lowrie stared at Thanet and then, slowly, returned to his desk and sat down. "My God," he said. "I see what you mean."

"Exactly. You really do think that it is out of the question, that it could have been an accident?"

"Oh, absolutely. No doctor in his right mind would go to bed with a supply of pills and a bottle of alcohol on his bedside table."

"Even if he had a cold? Mrs Pettifer said he thought he had one coming on."

"Not for any reason. We're too aware of the dangers of taking an extra pill—or pills—while in a drowsy or semi-conscious state. And of course, alcohol compounds the situation. Look, I know the point at issue is that Pettifer wasn't in his right mind, but I absolutely refuse to accept that. Though there's the note, of course . . ." Lowrie ran a hand distractedly over his bald pate. "I'm beginning to feel somewhat confused."

No more confused than I am, thought Thanet. "Anyway, you see my difficulty. I do ask, of course, that you treat this conversation as confidential. For the moment we are officially treating this as a case of suicide."

"Yes, yes, I see that you must. But . . . Look, Inspector— and of course it goes without saying that this is in confidence—let's not beat about the bush. We're now talking about murder, aren't we?"

"Possibly."

"I really find it difficult to believe that we are having this conversation. To associate Arnold with the idea of suicide is difficult enough, but murder . . ." He gave a little half-laugh. "Before I know where I am you'll be asking for my alibi."

Thanet said nothing, merely raised his eyebrows a fraction.

"Good God, man, you surely can't be thinking..." Lowrie's face was a study in outraged disbelief. Then, with a visible effort, he pulled himself together. "Well, I suppose that's reasonable enough. After all, I'm the one who's been insisting it couldn't have been suicide. As it happens, I'm lucky. Mrs Barnet and I both attended a meeting in Sturrenden last night. It didn't end until ten—and in case you're thinking I could have slipped out, I'll add that I was in the chair."

"And afterwards?"

"Someone who lives near her offered Mrs Barnet a lift and I went home with a colleague. My wife is away at present, visiting her mother, and I didn't feel like going home early to an empty house."

"And the colleague was...?"

"Dr Phillips. Do you know him?"

Thanet's own GP. "Yes... 'with,' you said...?"

"Well, not in the same car, obviously. But I followed his, all the way from the meeting—and stayed there until one in the morning. You can check with him, if you like."

So it looked as though Lowrie really was in the clear. "If it becomes necessary, I will. Though as I said, this is still officially a case of suicide. Meanwhile, perhaps I could enlist your help."

Lowrie sat back, steepled his fingers. "By all means. Anything I can do... My two o'clock appointment has been cancelled, so I'm at your disposal."

"Facts first then," said Thanet. "Mrs Barnet has given me a brief outline of the set-up here, so I won't need to bother you with that, but there was one point I wondered about. I gather that your quota of patients in this practice is rather high and that, especially with Dr Fir away at the moment and his locum unable to come at the last minute, the pressure of work has been considerable. Could overwork have been a contributory factor to Dr Pettifer's death, assuming that it was suicide?"

41

"I don't think so for a moment. Let me explain. Our quotas are high, yes, but different doctors have different methods and those methods determine the amount of time spent with patients. Pettifer was brisk, brief, thorough. He got through his surgeries far more quickly than any of the rest of us. So I really don't think he would have found the high quota a problem."

"You make him sound a bit inhuman."

"Do I? I didn't intend to. I suppose he could appear that way to someone who didn't know him. Certainly he wasn't easy to know. He was pretty reserved, didn't show his feelings much."

"In any case, you wouldn't say that there were any problems with the practice that could have bothered him sufficiently to prey on his mind."

"I'm pretty certain that if there had been I'd have been aware of them."

But there was a shadow at the back of Lowrie's eyes and Thanet recognised the neat evasion, stored it away for future investigation. He didn't want to antagonise Lowrie by pressing him at this point for information he was reluctant to give. There was one matter in which he particularly needed his cooperation.

"I was wondering, for example, if there could have been a patient, or relative of a patient, perhaps, who might have had a grudge against Dr Pettifer? One often hears of cases in which people feel they have been neglected or received the wrong treatment . . ."

"There certainly wasn't anything like that to my knowledge. And if there had been, I should think I'd have known. Such people are anything but quiet and unobtrusive. And surely it would have been impossible for anyone on the fringe of Pettifer's life to stage the circumstances in which he died?"

"Difficult, certainly. Impossible . . . well, I'm not so sure. Given sufficient intelligence and determination . . . I do think it's a possibility we can't afford to ignore. So I was wondering if you might be willing to glance through Dr Pettifer's records and check—I'm sorry, I know that this is a lot to ask, especially as you will now inevitably be under even greater pressure of work . . . I hesitate to offer you anyone to help. I know how important the question of confidentiality is to doctors and in any case the presence of one of my men here might give rise to undesirable speculation."

"Quite. Perhaps I'll ask Mrs Barnet to give me a hand. I can rely absolutely on her discretion . . . Very well, Inspector. But I'm afraid it might take a little time."

"I appreciate that. And thank you. Now, leaving that possibility aside, I must ask you to think again if there could have been any other problem—medical, financial or marital—which might have been preying on his mind."

"I have thought. And no, there wasn't, not to my knowledge. Financially, he was very comfortably off. He didn't depend on the practice for a living. His first wife was a wealthy woman and he inherited most of her estate. Some of it was of course left in trust for their son—adopted son, perhaps I should say."

"Adopted?"

"Yes. He's about fifteen now. Away at school. Nice boy, very. He'll be really cut up about this."

"So the baby which the present Mrs Pettifer is expecting would have been Pettifer's first child."

"Yes. Which makes the idea of suicide even more incomprehensible."

"He was pleased about it?"

"Like a dog with two tails." Lowrie smiled. "Interesting, really, when you think they'd both said in no uncertain terms that they had no intention of having any children."

"Really?"

"Most emphatically. And, frankly, I was a bit surprised how delighted he was about it. He never found it easy to relate to children, didn't even particularly like them, I should say. It was difficult for him to unbend sufficiently to get down to their level . . . But then, I suppose one's own child is different."

"He didn't get on with his adopted son, then? Andrew, isn't it?"

"Yes, Andrew. Oh, don't misunderstand me, he became very fond of the boy. I think he found it difficult when Andy was a baby, but then many men do. But over the years he grew very attached to him, in his own way. Perhaps he realised that the same thing would happen with the new baby. And, as I say, when it's one's own child... In any case, I suppose nothing should surprise me in that area anymore. I've seen it all. Childless couples who change their mind and have them, couples who don't want them and keep on having them and, worst of all, those who simply can't conceive. Pettifer's first wife, Diana, was one of those. Finally, they decided to adopt. Poor Diana, she had a pretty bad time of it one way and the other. She was only forty when she died."

"Cancer, wasn't it?"

"Yes. Of the stomach." Lowrie grimaced.

"I wonder how the boy feels about the new baby."

"Andy?" Lowrie frowned. "I'm not sure."

"Was he put out when his father married again?"

"He wasn't very happy about it." Lowrie sighed. "It would be less than honest of me if I didn't admit that he and his stepmother didn't get on. He's at a very vulnerable age, of course, and she has had no experience of children, let alone adolescents—who, as you no doubt know, can be the very devil even with the most loving and understanding of parents."

"So I believe." Thanet grinned. "The problems of parenthood never disappear, I'm told. They just change their nature. Er... What about Dr Pettifer's relationship with his wife?" He was aware that they were getting on to delicate ground here, wasn't sure how Lowrie would respond. But he needn't have worried.

"He idolised her," Lowrie said promptly. "Absolutely adored her. Let me put it this way. Pettifer may have appeared a cold fish to those who didn't know him, but those who did knew that he had two overriding passions—

his wife and his work. And I'd be hard put to it to say which mattered more to him. Certainly he has always been devoted to his work and his second marriage made no difference to his commitment to it, but there's no doubt that ever since he first set eyes on Gemma he's been head over heels in love with her. Extraordinary how a level-headed fellow like him can lose all sense of prudence or commonsense when he goes overboard. He proposed the first week he saw her on stage, you know. It was flowers, gifts, the old stage-door routine every night."

"You think it was an unwise choice, then?"

"Oh no. Not at all." Lowrie was emphatic. "They've been very happy together. I think Gemma found with him exactly what she needed—the security of marriage combined with the freedom to pursue her career."

"He didn't object to her doing so?"

"Not in the least. He was very proud of her reputation as an actress. She is a very fine one, you know."

"Yes. I've seen her. In *Away Day*, a few months ago. But the baby . . . It doesn't sound as though children would fit into her scheme of things."

"Well, as I said, he was over the moon about it. She . . . well, I think it took her longer to adjust to the idea. But once she had . . . No, they were both looking forward very much to the child's arrival. As I say, that's one of the reasons why I find the idea of suicide so impossible."

"What about Dr Pettifer's health? Was it good?"

"Disgustingly so. Mind, he took good care of it. He was something of an exercise fanatic. Did his daily dozen every morning, playing squash with Dr Fir twice a week . . . In all the years I've known him, he's never had anything more serious than a common cold. He didn't smoke, drank only occasionally, ate moderately and had perfect sight and hearing—no, there was a brief worry about his eyesight last year, but that came to nothing."

The telephone rang.

"Excuse me," said Lowrie. Then, "It's for you, Inspector."

It was Lineham. "Sorry to disturb you, sir. We've just had a phone call from Andrew Pettifer's school. He's absconded."

Thanet groaned. "I expect he's heading for home."

"That's what the headmaster thought."

"How long does it take to get here?"

"Depends how he travels. It's only thirty miles by road, so if he hitched a lift he could be here quite soon."

"Is that what they thought he'd do?"

"Yes. Public transport is tricky, apparently. The school's right out in the country."

"I'll get back. I'd more or less finished here anyway. See you shortly."

Thanet told Lowrie what had happened.

"Would you like me to come with you?" offered Lowrie, standing up.

Thanet considered. The boy would no doubt be distressed and it might be a good idea to have medical help at hand. And it would probably help for him to see a familiar face, especially in view of the fact that he didn't get on with his stepmother. There was the house-keeper of course, but perhaps a sympathetic but de-tached outsider... "Thank you," he said. "That's very kind."

"I must get in touch with Dr Braintree," Lowrie said, "to let him know what's happened. But I can easily do that from Pettifer's house. I do think it would be a good idea to be there when Andy arrives."

"Let's hope we'll be in time."

With a shared sense of urgency they hurried to the door.

6

Back at Pine Lodge, Thanet and Dr Lowrie were relieved to find that there was as yet no sign of Andrew. Lowrie at once commandeered the telephone and Lineham beckoned Thanet into the drawing room.

"I hope you don't mind, sir, but I haven't had the body removed yet."

"Why not?"

Lineham looked embarrassed. "The boy, Andrew...I didn't know what would be the right thing to do... Whether he'd be more upset to see his father dead or to find the body already gone."

"Adoptive father, as a matter of fact. Yes, I see your point." Thanet was surprised. Lineham did not usually demonstrate such sensitivity.

"Oh, Andrew's adopted? I didn't realise."

"Does it make any difference?"

"I don't know. I...When my own father was killed, well, for ages I didn't really believe he was dead. Years, even. I never *saw* him dead, you see." Lineham gave a little, awkward laugh. "Stupid, really. I mean, I was only six, much too young to be shown dead bodies anyway but, well, it didn't seem possible that he could be dead, somehow. He'd just said goodbye like any other morning, only that day he never came back. So today I thought...idiotic, I suppose. Andrew's practically grown up, isn't he? And if Dr Pettifer was only his adoptive father..."

"Only? Don't underestimate the power of a relationship like that, Mike. The very fact that the boy's absconded shows how upset he is. And although fifteen

sounds pretty grown up, it's a very vulnerable age. I
think you did the right thing." Although he was more
than twice that age now, Thanet could still remember
the intensity of it, the swings from black despair to
dizzy euphoria, the crippling uncertainties which the
adolescent has to endure in the search for his final
identity. "Anyway, did you manage to find out where
Mrs Pettifer stayed last night?"

"The Lombard Hotel, in Lombard Square. I checked."

"Any idea what time she arrived?"

"The receptionist couldn't be sure. The one I spoke
to wasn't on duty last night and even if she had been,
it's a pretty big hotel and busy, so I don't suppose she'd
have remembered. But she did say that judging by the
position of Mrs Pettifer's name in the register it would
have been early to mid-evening."

"I expect she checked in before meeting her agent for
dinner."

"Probably. Anyway, I didn't press it. She did say she
could try to find out more if I wished, but I said not to
worry at the moment. I didn't want to arouse too much
interest at this stage."

"Fine. What about the cocoa mug?"

"Mrs Price found it in the sink, this morning. She
automatically washed it up and put it away."

"Pity. Though I don't suppose it matters all that
much. But it does corroborate Mrs Pettifer's story.
What about the paracetamol container?"

"In the bathroom cabinet, as Mrs Pettifer said. Half
full."

Thanet strolled restlessly across to the window. A
little wind had sprung up and the branches of the tall
shrubs in the garden were swaying and dipping with
the sinuous grace of eastern dancers. Fallen leaves
stippled the lawn with random patterns of scarlet and
gold. "We must remember to ring Clough's garage later
on this afternoon, Mike, find out exactly what was
wrong with Dr Pettifer's car." Thanet stiffened. "There's
a boy turning into the drive. Quickly, tell Dr Lowrie."

He stood back and, feeling like an old lady who spies on her neighbours, watched Andrew Pettifer from behind a curtain.

The boy was tall and thin with the lankiness of adolescence. Hands in pockets, shoulders hunched, head down, feet kicking moodily at the gravel, he looked . . . defeated, Thanet thought. The boy paused to glance up at the house and scowled as he noticed for the first time the policeman on duty at the front door. He took his hands out of his pockets and straightened his shoulders before moving forward again.

There was a murmur of voices in the hall and Dr Lowrie put his head around the door. "I'm just going upstairs with Andrew."

Ten minutes later he led the boy into the drawing room, made the introductions.

"Dr Lowrie says my father left a note," Andrew said to Thanet through stiff lips. He was very pale.

Thanet, somewhat belatedly, had slipped the letter into a transparent polythene envelope. "I'm sorry," he said, as Andrew made to take it out, "could you leave it in the cover?"

The boy frowned, shot Thanet a resentful glance before scanning the brief message. Then he read it again. And again. And stilled.

Thanet found that he was holding his breath.

For a long moment the boy remained motionless and then, slowly, raised his head to stare at Thanet.

"My father didn't write this," he said flatly.

Tiny, almost imperceptible movements from Lineham and Dr Lowrie betrayed their tension as Thanet said carefully, "Oh? What makes you say that?"

"This." Andrew's finger stabbed at the plastic. "Whoever wrote this has spelt my name wrong." He put the letter down and feverishly began to empty out his pockets.

The three men waited in silence, too conscious of the significance of the moment to want to smile at the extraordinary collection of objects which mounted up on the low table: grubby handkerchief, notebook, diary, bits of string, a couple of screws, a magnifying glass, pens, pencils, a rubber, half a broken ruler, coins, wallet, golf ball, penknife and a number of tattered envelopes, each scrutinised and discarded. They all knew what he was looking for, of course: a letter from his father.

"Ah . . ." Andrew pounced at last on a crumpled sheet of paper. "I knew I had it somewhere." He glanced at it, murmured, "Yes," with satisfaction, then laid it on the table to smooth out the creases before handing it to Thanet together with the suicide note. "There you are," he said triumphantly. "He always spelt my name like that. With an E."

Thanet looked. "My dear Andie," the letter began. No possibility of typing error, it was handwritten. He glanced at the note left for Mrs Pettifer, in order to verify what he clearly remembered. "Make it up to Andy for me," Dr Pettifer had written.

"It's a very minute difference," Thanet said, handing both letters to Lineham. Though he was well aware that it could be a significant one.

Andrew was shaking his head vehemently as he stuffed his possessions back into his pockets. "He'd never have spelt my name with a Y," he said. "Never."

"With due respect, Andrew, your father could hardly have been in a normal state of mind at the time."

"I don't care what state of mind he was in. He just wouldn't have spelt it like that. He never, ever has. Anyway, you can check, surely, with the handwriting experts. They'll tell you."

"We will, of course," said Thanet.

"Look," said Andrew, suddenly fierce. "Don't humour me, right? Are you trying to say I don't know what my own father would have written? That's not the only example, you know," he said, pointing at the piece of paper in Thanet's hand. "I've got dozens more. Hundreds. I'll send you the lot if you like and then you'll have to believe me. Because you'll find that never, not in a single one of them, has my father ever spelled my name with a Y on the end. And the interesting thing is, of course, that no one else has seen those letters, no one else would know that, would they? And nobody else would realise, because they sound the same, don't they? They sound just the bloody same . . ." His voice had been rising and now, suddenly, it broke and the tears gushed forth, streamed down his face. He dashed them away angrily with the back of one hand, then went to stand looking out of the window, shoulders twitching as he struggled to regain control of himself.

Dr Lowrie took a step towards him and then checked, aware no doubt that any display of sympathy would simply make the battle more difficult.

There was an uncomfortable silence.

Finally, when Thanet judged that the boy was ready, he said, "You do realise the implications of what you're saying, don't you, Andrew?"

Andrew swung around, his eyes hard. "I'm not a complete fool, Inspector. And it seems to me you won't have far to look." His mouth twisted as he glanced up at the ceiling.

"Andy!" Dr Lowrie sounded shocked. "You can't realise what you're saying!" And to Thanet, "He's overwrought, doesn't realise the implications . . ."

"Please, Dr Lowrie!" Andrew broke in. "I'm sorry, I don't want to be rude, but I'm not a child of five, you know. OK, I know I'm not an adult, either, but I do think I'm old enough to have an opinion of my own, and frankly, that's it."

"What on earth is going on?"

They all turned to the door. Gemma Pettifer, in a delicately pretty blue robe with deep ruffles at neck and hem, was standing with folds of the soft material clutched just below her breast, emphasising her distended stomach. She looked slightly dazed and flushed with sleep. "I heard shouting . . . Oh, Andy," she said, noticing him for the first time. "My dear . . ." She

51

released her robe and advanced, hands outstretched, to greet him. "I'm so sorry," she said. "So very sorry..."

"And so you should be, you cow," shouted Andrew, backing away from her, his hard-won self-control flying out of the window. "Keep away from me!"

"*Andy!*" Dr Lowrie and Gemma Pettifer spoke in identical tones of horrified disbelief. Gemma checked in her advance and glanced uncertainly at the doctor, who put a hand protectively on her arm.

"Don't worry, my dear," he said hurriedly. "He's upset, naturally..."

"Upset? OF COURSE I'M BLOODY UPSET!" bellowed Andrew. "He was my father, wasn't he? MY FATHER, FOR CHRIST'S SAKE!"

"Your *adoptive* father, actually," said Gemma crisply, each precisely articulated word as deliberately hurtful as a slap on the face.

There was a shocked silence. He's right, Thanet found himself thinking furiously. She really is a cow. And, in any case, this has gone on long enough.

"Take Mrs Pettifer back upstairs, please, Sergeant," he said, seizing her elbow with one hand and Lineham's with the other and giving them both a sharp push towards the door.

Mrs Pettifer opened her mouth to protest and then, glancing at the stony faces of the three men, evidently thought better of it. In silence she gathered up the skirt of her robe and swept out of the room, followed by Lineham.

Thanet glanced at Andrew's still, white face and decided to leave Lowrie to comfort the boy as best he could. "I'm going to have a word with Mrs Price," he said. At the door he paused. "Andrew, I wasn't just humouring you, you know. If you're right, I'll get to the bottom of it somehow. That I promise you."

7

"I wish everyone was as well-organised as this," said Thanet.

He and Lineham were going through Dr Pettifer's desk. Accustomed as they were to the chaotic clutter which most people leave behind them, they were impressed by Pettifer's management of his affairs. There were no unpaid bills, no unanswered letters and not a single slip of paper, it seemed, out of place. A row of box files neatly labelled FUEL, INSURANCE, EDUCATION, HOUSEHOLD EXP stood on the ledge at the top of the old roll-top desk.

Thanet reached for the education file. Predictably, this related to Andrew and contained not only correspondence with the school but mementoes of the boy's childhood—hand-made Christmas and birthday cards, drawings and letters in crooked, childish script. Thanet picked up the last bundle of papers in the file: school reports. He slipped off the elastic band, skimmed through them. Andrew was a bright boy, it seemed, hardworking and popular. His mother's death had hit him hard:

. . . Andrew has been subdued and somewhat with-drawn this term and there is no doubt that it is taking him some time to recover from his mother's death. It is therefore not surprising that the standard of his work has slipped, but I am confident that in time he will regain his old sparkle and once more attain the excellent standards which he has achieved in the past.

*   *   *

How long would it take Andrew to regain that "sparkle" this time? Thanet wondered. There was a limit to the number of blows any one person could assimilate without suffering a permanent degree of damage. To be abandoned by not one but two sets of parents was hard indeed. Andrew now had no one of his own left—only a stepmother whom he clearly loathed. Thanet passed the report to Lineham.

Lineham read it, then snorted. "If Pettifer did kill himself, you really would have thought he'd have considered the effect it'd have on Andrew, wouldn't you? He must have been fond of the boy, or he wouldn't have kept all this stuff. Though if you think about it . . ."

"What?"

"Well, isn't it another argument against suicide? Being fond of the boy and realising the effect it would have on him?"

Thanet sighed. "I don't know. People can be overwhelmingly selfish when it comes to personal happiness—or unhappiness, for that matter. How are you getting on with those drawers?"

"Nothing interesting so far. Mostly supplies of stationery, that sort of thing. This one's locked, though," Lineham added, giving a sharp tug.

Thanet thought for a moment. "That bunch of keys upstairs in Dr Pettifer's room, on the chair. Are they still there?"

"Yes."

"Go and fetch them, will you?"

Lineham was back in a minute or so.

"Ah," Thanet said with satisfaction as one of the keys turned sweetly in the lock. "Now then, what have we here? Details of his financial position, by the look of it." Together they pored over the sheaf of papers: bank statements, lists of share-holdings and amounts of money invested, together with dates. Thanet whistled softly as he glanced down the immaculate records. "The bank manager wasn't exaggerating when he said, 'healthy,' was he?"

"Beats me why he bothered to work at all, with that lot," said Lineham.

"He was a dedicated doctor, that's why. Lowrie told us that."

"Catch me," said Lineham. "I'd be off to an island in the sun."

"Would you? I wonder. Haven't you come across any personal stuff at all?"

"Not yet, no."

"Funny. Let's take a look at the rest."

But neither of the remaining two drawers yielded anything of interest.

"Nothing personal at all, apart from the stuff about Andrew," said Thanet. "Nothing relating to his first marriage, for example."

"I did come across the marriage certificate in one of the other drawers. But that's all."

"If it wasn't for that, his first wife might never have existed. No letters, no photographs of her—for that matter, no photographs at all, except for that one." This was a large, framed photograph of Gemma Pettifer, a glossy studio portrait. "No family photographs, even . . . Surely everyone accumulates those? Is there anywhere else he could have kept them? A photograph album, perhaps?"

"We certainly haven't come across one. I know you're always interested in that sort of thing and keep my eyes open."

"Tell me, Mike . . . Have you got a desk at home?"

"Not a desk, exactly. A couple of drawers in a side table my mother gave us."

"Tidy?"

Lineham grinned. "Louise is always complaining there's so much stuff in them they won't shut properly. I go through them from time to time, weed things out a bit . . ." He stopped. "I see what you mean," he said slowly.

"Quite. Pettifer may have been tidy-minded, but even the best-organised of men have odds and ends lying about waiting to be filed or dealt with. There's nothing like that here. And together with the fact that there's nothing personal at all . . ."

"He's cleared it all out recently, you mean."

"Looks like it, doesn't it?"

"In which case . . ."

"It's back to suicide again," agreed Thanet.

They contemplated the desk in silence.

"If he did kill himself," Lineham said reluctantly, "then I suppose it would have been in character for him to have got rid of any personal stuff. I mean, from what we've heard of him, he wasn't the sort of man to relish the idea of someone poking about in his papers after he'd gone."

"I agree." Thanet stood up. "Let's go and have a word with Mrs Price."

The housekeeper's eyes narrowed at Thanet's question. "Now that you mention it, yes, Dr Pettifer did clear out his desk. I remember because he asked me for a plastic sack and later I saw him carry it down the garden and have a bonfire."

"When was this?"

"Let me see, it must be, oh, a good month ago, I should think."

"A month!"

"Easily, yes. Yes, I remember now, I was bottling the Victorias when he came through the kitchen and I always do that in the middle of September."

Five weeks ago, then.

"Where do you burn your rubbish?"

"At the bottom of the garden, behind the laurel hedge."

Little point in looking, after all this time, but Thanet and Lineham went to see for themselves just the same. The sky was overcast, the wind had dropped again and the air was still and heavy with moisture. Fallen leaves from a towering copper beech lay in great crimson swatches upon the dew-heavy grass and dahlias, chrysanthemums and Michaelmas daisies stood out with the brilliance and clarity of gem-stones in the fading light.

The laurel hedge was tall and thick, screening the vegetable garden from the house. A narrow concrete path bisected the neat rows of autumn cauliflowers and brussels sprouts and led to a metal incinerator beside a compost heap.

"Looks as though they've got a gardener," Lineham said, nodding at the weed-free soil.

"Pity. At this time of the year he'd have been burning rubbish regularly a couple of times a week."

They contemplated the incinerator, empty of all but a few charred twigs.

"Five weeks ago!" Lineham said. "Could anybody plan his own suicide as far ahead as that?"

"Perhaps there's no connection." But Thanet couldn't really believe that. No man totally destroys his past if he can visualise a future. Thanet shook his head, hard, as if to try to dissipate his confusion. "Come on," he said. "I've got to have a breathing space, try to sort things out a bit, in my mind." His need to get away was physical too. His nostrils suddenly seemed full of the stench of decay, the autumn garden permeated with a sense of mortality.

"We'll go back to the office and do our reports, like good little boys," he said. "Getting things down on paper might help."

But he doubted it.

8

Before he reached the front door, Thanet could hear the television blaring forth. He frowned. Joan never watched television until after supper, nor did she ever turn the volume up so high. The children must still be up and Joan with Mrs Markham again.

He glanced angrily at the house next door before letting himself in, his morning's resolution to have it out with Joan resurrecting itself and hardening. He was further incensed to find both Bridget and Ben watching a completely unsuitable documentary on violence in Northern Ireland.

"Come on, you two," he said, dropping his coat on a chair and crossing at once to switch off the set. "It's long past your bedtime."

They must have been tired because there were no cries of protest. They simply turned dazed faces towards him and scrambled to their feet, putting up their arms to embrace him.

"Mummy next door?" he said.

They nodded and Ben reached into the pocket of his jeans.

"I saved this for you, Daddy."

Thanet smiled and accepted the sticky, unwrapped sweet, liberally coated with fluff. "Thank you, Ben," he said gravely. "Lovely. D'you mind if I save it for after supper?"

Ben shook his head and Thanet placed the sweet ceremoniously on the mantelpiece. Then they all went upstairs, hand in hand.

Ben was in bed and Thanet was kneeling on the bathroom floor drying Bridget when he heard the front door slam. A moment later Joan came upstairs in a rush.

"I'm sorry , darling," she said, stooping to kiss the top of his head, "I just couldn't get away."

"Do you realise," Thanet said, keeping his anger damped down and his voice as conversational as possible for Bridget's sake, "that those were the first words you spoke to me this morning, too?"

Joan compressed her lips. Neither the anger nor the reproach had escaped her. "Ben in bed?"

"Yes."

58

"I'll just go along and say goodnight, then I'll get supper. It's all prepared, it won't be long."

Thanet realised why when he saw what it was: sausage and chips. Again. Gone were the halcyon days of steak and kidney puddings, delectable desserts. Before she started working full-time Joan had been an excellent cook and the evening meal had been one of the highlights of Thanet's day. Now his anger on the children's behalf was fuelled by the thought that if Joan hadn't spent so much time next door he wouldn't be eating such a dreary meal. It was about time she got her priorities right, he told himself furiously.

"You'll give yourself indigestion if you go on eating as fast as that," Joan said.

The rebuke was the last straw. Thanet looked at his plate, then laid down his knife and fork. "D'you know what the children were doing when I came in this evening?"

"Watching television, I imagine." Joan's tone was defensive.

"Precisely. Watching boys not much older than Sprig hurling petrol bombs at soldiers in the streets of Belfast . . ."

Joan bit her lip. "I didn't realise. I'm sorry."

"I'm sorry, I'm sorry, I'm sorry! That's all you ever seem to say these days!"

"Only because you're always going on at me," Joan retaliated.

"Now wait a minute. You mean, you don't really feel sorry at all? If it weren't for my attitude, you wouldn't? Is that what you're saying?"

"No. Not exactly. Well, I don't know . . . Oh, darling, that's not true. I do know what you're complaining about and you're right, I know that too. I know I shouldn't be spending so much time with Mrs Markham, but I just don't seem to be able to get out of it."

Her capitulation disarmed him. "But why not?" he said, more gently. "I really just don't understand why not."

"Well, because she's so... pathetic. So helpless. I told you, her husband used to do everything for her. Do you realise she's never had to pay a household bill in her life, or keep any kind of budget... He used to organise the finances, say what they could or couldn't afford in the way of holiday, clothes, outings... She's absolutely lost without him. She just doesn't know how to begin to organise her own life."

"Then, without wishing to sound hard, isn't it about time she learned?"

"But that's what I'm trying to help her to do!"

"Are you? Are you, really? Come on, darling, be honest with yourself." Thanet's anger had evaporated now but he knew that it was important, for all their sakes, that he and Joan should settle this issue one way or the other. "Can you truthfully say she's much more independent now than she was a year ago?"

Joan sighed. "I suppose not. But what can I do, Luke? I try, I really do try very hard to get her to do things herself, but she just says, 'Could you do it, dear, you're so much quicker at it than I am.' Or, 'What a pity it takes so long to get to the library. It's such a long walk to the bus stop and then you have to wait around in the cold for so long...,' and before I know where I am I'm offering to change her books for her on the way home..."

"But don't you see? That's just what she's manoeuvring for."

"Yes, I do see, but I seem incapable of reacting in any other way. I get so cross with myself about it."

Thanet leant across the table to take Joan's hand. "Look, darling, you must see that we can't go on like this indefinitely. I'm not just being selfish, though to be honest I do resent the fact that she seems to be seeing more of you than I am at the moment, but the children need you too, just as much if not more than she does. Look at that business of Sprig's leotard this morning. She was in such a state... I hate seeing her go off to school like that."

"Yes, I know. So do I."

"And then, it's taking too much out of you. You really have enough on your plate, with a full-time job as well as a family to look after and a house to run . . . Try to look at it this way. All the while you're prepared to do things for her, why should she bother? It's much easier and more convenient for her to get you to do them. Don't you see, there's only one way for her to learn how to cope for herself and that's for her to do it. Alone. Otherwise, well, I can see no end to it, can you?"

"I suppose not . . . Yes, you're right, I know that . . . All right, I'll try. I really mean it. I'll just have to be a lot tougher, that's all." Joan rose and began to clear the table.

"Leave that. I'll do it, and the washing up. You go and sit down. you look exhausted. Coffee?"

She smiled gratefully. "All right. Thank you, darling. Yes, I'd love some."

Thanet waited until they were both sipping their coffee before saying, "Tell me, as a matter of interest, how you would spell the nickname for Andrew."

"A-N-D-Y, I suppose. Why?"

"Just wondered. You wouldn't put an I-E on the end, instead of Y?"

"No. I've never heard of it spelt like that. Why?" she asked again.

"Did you hear about Dr Pettifer?"

"No, what?"

He told her. He always had told her—everything—and since she had started work as a probation officer he had continued to do so, not without trepidation. When Joan had decided that this was the career she wanted, Thanet had tried to dissuade her. The views and attitudes of police and probation officers frequently clash and he had been afraid that this conflict of professional interests would spill over into their private life and they would gradually drift apart. But it had not taken him long to realise that they would be even more likely to do so if he prevented her from doing what she obviously very much wanted to do. So, instead, he had made a conscious effort to maintain between them the mutual trust and confidence which had always been the bedrock of their relationship. He still thought that one day the crunch would come, that they would find themselves on opposite sides of the fence over some fundamental issue, but was satisfied that this way they would be better equipped to deal with it if and when they had to.

Joan listened as she always did, with complete attention, her grey eyes solemn, the lamplight gilding her short, springing, honey-coloured curls.

"So that's why you asked me how I'd spell Andy," she said, when he had finished. "Poor boy, he really does sound most dreadfully upset. And if he can't stand Mrs Pettifer... Where is he now?"

"He went to Dr Lowrie's for the night. He'll probably go back to school tomorrow. Lowrie seemed to think it would be better if he didn't have too much time to brood."

"Yes, I can see that. Do you think he could have been mistaken, over the mis-spelling of his name?"

"Well, the note he showed us certainly bore out what he said. He was very overwrought, of course, poor kid. And, as I said to him, it was possible his father might have made a mistake, in the circumstances."

"You're having the handwriting checked?"

"Yes. But it'll be a day or two before we get an answer. You know how cautious they are. We mustn't complain—they have to be. But in circumstances like this when we need to have something that'll clinch the matter..."

"So what do you think, really? Do you think it was suicide?"

"I don't know." Thanet ran a hand through his hair. "I just don't know." And he didn't. One moment he would veer towards believing that Pettifer had indeed killed himself, the next he would be telling himself that there was too much evidence to the contrary. He said so. "I feel positively schizophrenic about it. The whole thing just doesn't make sense, doesn't hang together. If you look at the set-up of the suicide itself then, yes, it does look as though he did. All three doctors I've spoken to so far—Dr Barson, Doc Mallard and Dr Lowrie—all agree that the method he chose was the way most medical men would opt for, the most comfortable way to go if you know the right dosage of drugs and don't overdo the alcohol . . . Then there's the note, if it's genuine, and the timing, the fact that both his wife and his housekeeper were away overnight—a rather unusual circumstance, I gather . . ."

"Though that could work the other way," Joan suggested. "If it was murder and someone had been waiting for the ideal moment and knew Dr Pettifer'd be alone in the house last night . . ."

"True. But then, there's the fact that he left all his business affairs in such incredibly good order, that he'd cleared his desk of all his personal stuff . . ."

"But five weeks ago, you said. Surely nobody would cold-bloodedly plan his own suicide five weeks ahead and then go on behaving as though he didn't have a care in the world?"

"That's what Lineham said. And I agree, of course. You see what I mean? There's an objection at every turn."

"Perhaps there's some other reason you just don't know about yet. Perhaps he'd just found out he had terminal cancer . . ."

"If so, it'll show up in the post mortem tomorrow. But by all accounts he certainly wasn't acting like a man who'd just had a death sentence passed on him. On the contrary, everyone seems to agree he was in the best of spirits yesterday—exceptionally so, in fact."

"He certainly seems to have behaved very oddly for a man who was about to kill himself—paying for that cruise, for instance, only hours before he died."

"Exactly. Then there's the business of the car. As

Lineham said, why bother to get your car repaired if you know you're never going to need it again?"

"What did you say was wrong with it?"

"It's a bit technical," Thanet said dubiously.

Joan grinned. "Try me," she said. "Put it down to my thirst for information."

"Well, it was nothing very serious. Apparently—let's see if I can get it right—over the coil in the new Rover there's a damp-proof cap which is connected to the distributor by a high-tension lead. Engine vibration had loosened the cap and the connection was broken, so the car wouldn't start. It was only a little thing, but one which is not immediately obvious when you lift the bonnet. Clough said that Dr Pettifer knew a little bit about cars and could probably have found the fault himself if he'd been prepared to spend a bit of time looking for it, but I suppose he was in a hurry, knowing that his wife was going to London last night. I expect he wanted to get home before she left."

"Or he might have wanted to catch the travel agents before they closed."

"That's a point, yes, if he'd arranged to call in yesterday afternoon. But, as you say, he wasn't exactly behaving like a man who knew there'd be no tomorrow."

"Luke, are you saying you think there might be some truth in Andrew's accusation of Mrs Pettifer?"

"I just don't know. It was difficult to take it seriously at the time because he was in such a state. I simply thought his grief and anger had to find a focus and she happened to be it. But the way things are going, we certainly can't afford to dismiss the possibility."

"But then, you say she herself is also insisting it couldn't have been suicide. Why should she do that, if she killed him? Surely the last thing she'd want to do is stir up any doubts whatsoever?"

"Unless it's a double bluff—she's aware that there are discrepancies which might make us doubt that it could have been suicide and therefore she's trying to put herself in the clear by insisting it couldn't have been."

"Don't!" said Joan, clutching her head. "I see what you mean. I'm getting as confused as you are."

"And then, what motive could she have? Everyone seems to agree that they were as happy as the day is long."

"Oh, come on, darling. It's unlike you to accept that as true, just because everyone says so. You know how deceptive appearances can be. Just think how often you hear people say, 'I'm astounded. I always thought they were the ideal couple,' about a marriage that's split up."

"That's true."

"She could have been after his money," Joan suggested. "You say he was very well off."

"But why? She's got everything she wants, surely, materially speaking . . . A lovely home, a housekeeper to run it for her, a car of her own . . ."

"Then perhaps she wanted something else?"

"What, for example?"

"Her freedom?"

"Freedom to do what? Her husband was one hundred per cent behind her in her career. To go to a lover, I suppose you mean."

"Well, it's possible, surely? Someone in her position . . . Actors and actresses do seem to change partners fairly frequently, after all."

"I'd thought of it, of course," Thanet said, "but somehow I didn't consider it as a serious possibility. Now, why was that? Perhaps it's because she's pregnant." He grinned sheepishly. "All right, all right, I know. How naive can you get?"

"The sanctity of motherhood," Joan teased.

"Don't rub it in . . . I'll get on to Jennings at West End Central tomorrow, ask him to make a few enquiries at the hotel Mrs Pettifer stayed at."

"Just a minute," Joan said suddenly. "I've just remembered . . . Talking about her being pregnant . . . It rings a bell. Yes, I'm sure there was an article about her in one of the Sunday Colour Supplements. The *Telegraph*, I think."

"Really? I certainly don't remember that. Would we still have it?"

"I'm not sure. I'm trying to think how long ago it was. A few weeks, certainly."

"So the Cubs might not have taken it yet?" Once a month the local Cub Scout group collected newspapers, storing them up to sell at so much a ton for troop funds and charity.

"I'll see if I can find it," said Thanet, heading for the door. The old newspapers were stored in boxes in the garage.

"It's got a picture of her on the front cover," Joan called after him.

Thanet almost missed it, Gemma looked so different. "She doesn't look a bit like that close to," he said, brandishing the photographs at Joan.

"In what way?"

"Not nearly so glamorous. I hardly recognised her."

Joan laughed. "I bet you'd hardly recognise me if someone spent an hour or two on my make-up and gave me a dress like that to wear."

Gemma was wearing a sumptuous, exotic creation in scarlet and gold brocade

"I prefer you as you are," said Thanet, kissing the tip of Joan's nose. "Come on, let's see what they have to say about her."

The article was entitled *THE MOST GIFTED AC-TRESS OF OUR TIME*, and in the best journalistic tradition contrived to be both entertaining and informative.

Gemma, it claimed, set herself very high standards and did not spare herself in her efforts to attain them. She took her work very seriously indeed and had always been highly ambitious—which was, the article said, scarcely surprising in view of her background. She had been brought up in a children's home, having been abandoned on a doorstep. ("How *can* people?" murmured Joan.) According to her former Housemother, now retired, Gemma had always had a formidable capacity for hard work and a single-minded determination to succeed. Even while she was still at school it had become obvious that, on stage, she also possessed that rare power to grip and inspire an audience and send people away from a theatre feeling that they have for a brief while lived more intensely, that their experience has been enlarged by the performance they have just witnessed.

Gemma Shade's subsequent career, Thanet read, had more than fulfilled that early promise and her rise to the top had been truly meteoric. Her audiences were regularly moved to wonder and disbelief at the intensity of her portrayal, her ability to become the vessel through which the personality of another takes on a new and vibrant life.

"Ah, this is the bit I was thinking of," said Joan:

Most of us are able to change our minds in private without loss of face. Not so for public figures, and it is to Miss Shade's credit that she has not been afraid, in recent years, to admit to changing hers. She had always said that she would never get married and would never have children. "I'm too self-centred," she used to say gaily, "ever to want to arrange my life around that of another person."

Now married for two years and pregnant, reminded of these words Miss Shade just smiles and says, "Well, perhaps I've grown up a bit since then." And she has, she says, been exceptionally lucky; her doctor husband is completely in favour of her continuing her stage career. And the baby, due in January? "The best New Year present either of us could wish for," she says. "I can't wait to become a mother."

It has been said that maturity improves the quality of an actress's work. If so, Miss Shade's many admirers must contemplate the prospect of her future performances with something approaching awe.

"Interesting woman," commented Joan.

"Yes, well, don't expect me to pronounce on that. My conversation with her was somewhat limited by circumstance."

"What are you going to do, then? Will you go ahead with the inquest?"

"Fortunately, we've got a few days' grace before we need to make a final decision on that. Meanwhile, perhaps the post mortem result will help. If not, well, we'll just have to plod on until we're satisfied one way or the other."

"Of course, even if Dr Pettifer didn't kill himself, it doesn't necessarily mean that she did it. There must be a dozen reasons why he could have been murdered."

"Such as?"

"Well... two or three, anyway. Doctors are so vulnerable in some ways. He could have mortally offended some psychotic patient... or been held to blame for a patient's death by some close relation... For that matter, he could even have been having an affair and been killed by a jealous husband. Come on, darling, cheer up. It's early days yet."

"True." Tactfully, he did not say that all these and other possibilities had already crossed his mind. Instead, acknowledging her attempt to console him, he smiled, put up his hand to caress her face.

"What would I do without you?" he said.

9

"Inspector Jennings, West End Central, on the phone for you, sir."

"Hullo, Peter? Luke here."

"About this actress..."

"Gemma Shade. Yes."

"I checked with security at the Lombard. I know the chap there, he's an ex-copper. And you were right."

"I was?"

"Yep. Miss Shade had company on Monday night. Sorry we've been so long, but it took a bit of winkling out, apparently. The chambermaid in question was new and had got her room numbers muddled up and was afraid that if she admitted it she'd be in trouble. Anyway, the long and the short of it is, she took Miss Shade early morning tea by mistake and got herself bawled out by lover-boy."

"Ah . . . Did your chap find out who he was?"

"Have a heart. He's not a bloody miracle-worker. Remember, Miss Shade's boyfriend wasn't even there, officially."

"Any description?"

"Youngish and fair-haired, that's all. There was one thing, though . . ."

"Yes?"

"The girl, the chambermaid, said he looked kind of familiar. So I was wondering. Seeing as his lady love's an actress . . ."

"He might be an actor, you mean?"

"Well, it's poss., isn't it?"

"Yes." Thanet thought hard. Jennings could well be right. In which case, it was more than likely that Gemma Pettifer's lover had been in the cast of her last production. And, if she hadn't worked for the last couple of months . . .

"Luke? You still there?"

"Yes. Sorry. Thinking."

"God! You'll be solving cases next!"

"That'll be the day. Look, Peter, if you wanted to find out the gossip about the cast of a play, how would you go about it?"

"Current production?"

"No. Came off a couple of months ago."

"Here in London?"

"In the West End. *Away Day* at the Haymarket, to be precise."

"I'd ask Westwell."

"Who's he?"

"One of our DSs here. Theatre buff."

"Is he there at the moment?"

"Sure. D'you want me to put him on?"

"Please. And Peter, thanks."

"Don't forget you owe me a pint next time I see you."

"I might even make it two."

"The work must be getting to your brain. Hang on."

Thanet grinned. He and Jennings had been friends for years, had helped each other on a number of occasions. He covered the mouth of the receiver while he waited. "She spent the night with a lover," he said to Lineham.

"So I gathered." Lineham made a moue of disgust. "At six months pregnant."

"You don't switch off sex just because you're having a baby, you know," Thanet said with a grin.

"I didn't mean that. I meant . . ."

"Just a moment . . ." Thanet turned back to the phone.

"Inspector Thanet? DS Westwell here."

Thanet explained what he wanted to know.

"*Away Day* . . ." said Westwell thoughtfully. "I missed that, myself."

"So how would you go about finding out if Gemma Shade had an affair with a member of the cast?"

"Well, in the normal way of things I'd give the security bloke a ring, but unfortunately there's a new chap at the Haymarket. Only been there a month."

"What happened to the last one?"

"He died. Nothing suspicious, a heart attack. So that's out. I should think your next best bet would be the theatre manager, but frankly, I doubt if you'd get him to talk."

"And if that fails?"

"You'd have to go for other members of the cast, I suppose."

"And how would I go about finding them?"

"Sorry, I don't know. But I could find out for you, if you like."

Thanet would have loved to accept this offer, but couldn't bring himself to do so. Asking for help was one thing, making a nuisance of himself another. "Thanks, but it looks as though I'll have to come up to London myself. Tell Inspector Jennings he might get his beer sooner than he thinks. If I can get through the red tape quickly enough, I'll be up this afternoon."

There was a grin in Westwell's voice as he said, "Right, sir."

"Sir," said Lineham doubtfully as Thanet put the phone down.

"Yes? . . . Well, come on, man, spit it out." Lineham still occasionally reverted to the diffidence which had once so infuriated Thanet.

"Well, don't you think perhaps you're taking a lot for granted?"

"In assuming first that Mrs Pettifer's lover is an actor and second that he was in her last play with her, you mean?"

Lineham nodded.

"Certainly I am. But as there doesn't seem to be even the slightest whisper of a scandal down here it does seem logical—especially in view of the fact that the chambermaid thought he looked familiar—to assume that he might be an actor. We've got to start somewhere, after all. Can you suggest another way?"

"Tackle Mrs Pettifer."

"I told you, Mike, I don't like the idea. Not yet."

It was now late the following morning and the only interesting snippet of information that had so far come in was that Gemma Pettifer's prints had been found on the drinking glass, tablet container and port bottle on Pettifer's bedside table. Even more interesting was the absence of Pettifer's prints from the first two. Lineham had been all for rushing off to see her at once, but Thanet, more cautious, had held back.

"But surely, now we know she had a motive..."

"No." Thanet's tone was final. "It's too early yet. We've got to find out more. And remember, it works both ways. Agreed, this could give her a motive for murder, but it could also give him a reason for suicide."

"You mean, he could have found out..."

"He adored that woman, Mike, idolised her. And that's always dangerous. When you discover that your idol has feet of clay... Who knows how a man like Pettifer would have reacted?"

"But there's absolutely no indication he did find out."

"True... And I must admit, thinking about it, I can't see that it would have been in character for him to opt out like that, give up without a fight... It's no good, Mike, it's pointless speculating like this. We've got to have more facts. If only we could have had the PM results today..." The post mortem had had to be postponed until next day. Although there were two pathologists in the area, one of them was ill and the other not only hopelessly overworked but booked to spend all afternoon giving evidence at inquests.

"Or if the handwriting experts had come up with something..."

"But they haven't. So, tickle them up a bit, will you, Mike? Then get someone on to tracking down the history of that bottle of port. I want to know where, when and by whom it was bought. Meanwhile I'll get on to Scotland Yard, see if we can get permission to go and poke about in West End Central."

Thanet was still on the phone when Mallard came in.

"What's up?" he asked, when Thanet had finished. "I heard downstairs that you're working on the Pettifer Case. What case? I thought it was a straightforward suicide."

"It's not as simple as that, I'm afraid, Doc."

Quickly, Thanet ran through the mounting list of inexplicable facts. "And then we just heard this morning that Mrs Pettifer was having an affair—that she spent Monday night with her lover."

Mallard grimaced. "Oh, dear. That's another illusion

down the drain. I always thought they were a most devoted couple. Anyway, that surely explains the whole thing."

"What do you mean?"

"That he killed himself because he found out. He practically worshipped the ground she walked on, you know."

"Not good enough, Doc," said Thanet, shaking his head. "There's too much to be explained away."

"I agree that Pettifer didn't seem the type to throw in the sponge without a fight . . . Though there is another argument for its having been suicide, you know."

"Oh?"

"One school of thought sees suicide as an act of aggression, an expression of anger, rather than despair."

"That's interesting. I'll have to think about that."

"So, what now?"

"We've got to find out more. That's why I want to go up to . . ."

The phone rang. Thanet picked it up. West End Central, he mouthed at the others. "Yes, DI Thanet here . . ."

Mallard raised his hand in a gesture of farewell and left.

Once again, Thanet explained what he wanted to do in London. Finally, "It's all fixed," he said to Lineham, putting the phone down. "We're to report in at two. There's no reserved parking space in Savile Row, so it'll be easier to go by train." He glanced at the clock: twenty to twelve. "If we hurry we'll just catch the twelve-ten."

"There's plenty of time, surely."

"I want to pick up something from home, on the way."

The detour took a quarter of an hour and Thanet blessed Joan's orderly mind as he went straight to the drawer where she always kept souvenirs of holidays and outings and picked out the theatre programme of *Away Day*. In the train he produced it.

"You didn't tell me you'd seen *Away Day*."

"I wanted to check something first, in case my memory was playing me tricks. Ah, yes . . ." He offered the programme to Lineham. "See what you think."

Lineham flicked quickly through the photographs of the cast. There had been four main characters, two men and two women. "I'd plump for him." Lineham's finger stabbed at the classical features and golden curls of a young actor called Rowan Lee. "He fits the chambermaid's description."

"That's what I thought."

"So that's why you were so set on this trip."

"All right, Mike. Don't sound so aggrieved. I must admit he immediately sprang to mind. But as I said, I wanted to check before saying anything."

"Looks a bit young for her, doesn't he?"

Lee appeared to be in his mid-twenties, a good ten years younger than Gemma Pettifer.

"Perhaps he's older than he looks. You can never tell with these studio portraits. Or it might have been taken some years ago."

"So, are we going to try and see him today?"

"No, I think not. I don't want to risk his contacting Mrs Pettifer. If she's innocent I don't want her unnecessarily upset, and if she's not then when I tackle her I want it to be a complete surprise."

"What exactly are we going to do this afternoon, then?"

"At the moment what I'm really after is confirmation. It's quite possible that we're barking up the wrong tree. So what I want is someone prepared to gossip."

"Deborah Chivers, then."

This was the other woman in the cast.

"If we can get hold of her, yes."

"She could be working this afternoon. It's Wednesday, matinée day."

"I know. She could be anywhere, for that matter. Let's hope she's not off touring the provinces. We'll just have to see."

After the brief courtesy visit to West End Central headquarters in Savile Row they took the tube to Piccadilly Circus and walked down the Haymarket towards the Theatre Royal. They paused for a few mo-

ments to admire the classical façade with its six soaring
white columns before crossing the road to the main
entrance.

"It's supposed to be one of the oldest and classiest
theatres in London," Thanet said as they pushed open
the swing doors.

The foyer was elegant—milk-white walls with gold
mouldings and gilt-framed mirrors, gleaming brass hand-
rails and white leather chairs. The matinée performance
must have started, for the place was deserted but for a
young man in the box office.

Thanet approached him. "Could I speak to the manager, please?"

"You'll have to go around to the stage door. It's at the
back of the theatre, in Suffolk Street. Go out of the
main door, turn left and left again."

Suffolk Street was a cul-de-sac of tall white buildings
with black wrought-iron balconies at first-floor level.
The stage door was at the far end. Lineham edged his
way behind Thanet into the tiny space in front of the
Enquiries counter while Thanet repeated his request.

"D'you want the theatre manager or the production
manager?"

"The theatre manager, I should think."

"I'm afraid he's out, sir." The porter was friendly,
middle-aged and balding, with grey hair and grey moustache. He looked very snug in his tiny room, which
couldn't have been much more than seven feet square.
A real home from home, thought Thanet, noting the
square of carpet on the floor, the comfortable tub
armchair, the electric kettle. There was even a portable
television set.

"Perhaps you could help me, then." Thanet introduced himself. "I suppose you get to know the cast
pretty well, while they're playing here?"

"Well, I do and I don't. Depends how long a run it is,
how friendly they are and so on."

"But you might have a good idea of, shall we say,

what the relationships between the various members of the cast might be?"

The wary gleam in the man's eye told Thanet that the question had been correctly interpreted. "Oh, I don't know about that, sir. Bit outside my province, that is. I just deal with all the practical stuff, the nuts and bolts, you might say."

Thanet was adept at recognising a lost cause. "Perhaps the production manager could help me, then. Is he in at the moment?"

"That would be Mr Wemsley. Yes, he is. Would you like me to give him a call?"

The young man who came up the stairs behind them in response to Thanet's request looked more like a business executive than Thanet's idea of someone in the theatre world. What did you expect? Thanet asked himself in amusement. Purple suede trousers and shaggy sweater? He introduced himself, taking care to emphasise that his enquiries had no connection with either the current production or the theatre.

Wemsley's anxious frown faded. "Come down to my office." He led the way through the little black metal swing gate and down some uncarpeted stairs. In the office a loudspeaker in the corner was relaying the play on stage.

They all sat down.

"Now then, how exactly can I help you?"

"Well, as I said, we're from Kent CID. We're trying to trace some of the members of the cast of a recent production at this theatre. Of *Away Day*, to be precise."

"Then it's the theatre manager you want," said Wemsley promptly. "And I'm afraid he's out. I'm only here for the duration of this particular production, you see. He's permanent."

"When will he be back?"

"Not for another hour or more. But I've just thought... Are you trying to find out who the cast of *Away Day* were, or do you know the names of the people you want to see?"

"Oh, we know who they are." Thanet took the programme from his pocket.

"Then there's no problem. We can look them up in *Spotlight* . . . It's a directory of actors and actresses," Wemsley explained to their blank looks. "I've got one here." He reached out for a small stack of books, opened one at random. "You see?" he said, holding it out. "It gives details of professional careers and—this is what you want—agents' names and addresses. Mind you, trying to get a client's address from an agent is harder than trying to get the proverbial blood out of a stone, but as it's the police who're asking you should be all right."

"May I see?"

Ten minutes later they left the theatre with a list of the names, addresses and telephone numbers of the agents of all three other members of the cast of *Away Day*.

"Easier than we thought, eh, Mike?" said Thanet, patting his pocket with satisfaction.

"Bit of luck," Lineham agreed. "Where now?"

"Deborah Chivers' agent first. And as we don't want to waste most of the afternoon fathoming out how to get from A to B by public transport, we'll do it in style." He raised his hand as he spotted an empty cab and they both watched in admiration as the driver manoeuvred his way expertly through the one-way traffic to the kerb.

The spacious foyer of Jacob Solly, Theatrical Agent, was luxuriously furnished with a thick cream carpet and green leather armchairs, most of which were occupied. There was an atmosphere of bored expectancy. Successful clients smiled condescendingly down from the glossy blown-up photographs which adorned the walls. There were a few choice specimens of potted palms and giant ferns which, like the glamorous blonde in the green silk trouser suit behind the reception desk, had clearly been chosen for their sculptural qualities.

Assessing eyes followed Thanet and Lineham across the room.

"Can I help you?" The blonde's smile was as artificial as her eyelashes. She had already dismissed them as being of no interest. Thanet felt a malicious satisfaction at her response to his introduction.

"Er..." Her eyes darted nervously from telephone to waiting clients to the door marked PRIVATE behind her. It was as if a statue had suddenly become prey to human emotion. She swallowed. "I'm afraid Mr Solly is engaged just now," she said. "But I'll go and see... Could you sit down for a moment?"

Interested eyes followed Thanet's and Lineham's every movement. Thanet read speculation, resentment, hostility in them. What a life, he thought, staring composedly back. Quickly, he counted. There were fifteen people in the room, of various ages, shapes and sizes. He winked boldly at a woman with a particularly outraged stare and grinned as she hastily began to study her hands. Lineham shifted uncomfortably on the seat beside him.

The blonde emerged briskly from the door marked PRIVATE and approached Thanet. He tried not to recoil too obviously from the overpowering waft of perfume which assailed his nostrils as she bent to murmur, "Mr Solly is free now. This way, please."

Thanet and Lineham looked about them with interest at the room into which they were ushered. By contrast with the foyer this was a cosy masculine cave, with shaggy brown carpet and chestnut-coloured leather armchairs. The brown hessian-covered walls were crammed with theatre posters and more glossy photographs of famous clients. Behind a status-enhancing desk of teak and leather sat a short, plump man in cream suede jacket and silky polo-necked sweater. The shimmer of gold on his fingers was echoed in his smile.

"Come in, come in, Inspector." He rose, extended a soft damp palm to each man in turn.

With difficulty Thanet restrained himself from wiping his hand on the side of his trousers.

Courtesies exchanged, Solly sat back, folded his hands on the solid mound of his belly and said, "Now then. How, exactly, can I help you?"

"We're trying to trace a client of yours," Thanet said. "Deborah Chivers."

"Ah . . ." Solly pursed his moist, full lips and frowned. "Would it be proper to ask in what connection . . . Debbie hasn't been a naughty girl, I hope?" he asked archly.

Thanet hoped his wince didn't show. "No, not at all. We're just hoping that she might be able to give us some information about someone who is involved in a case we're working on."

"Debbie isn't actually . . . uh . . . involved in the case herself?"

"No. Not at all."

Solly sat up with a bounce. "Forgive me, Inspector. I am being remiss in my duty as a host. I won't insult you by offering you alcohol at this hour, but a cup of coffee, perhaps? Or tea?" The gold fillings glinted.

"Thank you, no. I'm afraid our time in London is limited."

"Yes, of course. Well, I see no reason why we shouldn't oblige." He pressed a button. "Make a note of Deborah Chivers' address for the Inspector, will you, Marilyn?"

"Do you think there's any likelihood that she might be at home, if we went to see her this afternoon?" Thanet asked.

"Well, she's resting at the moment," Solly said. A flash of gold again. "Our euphemism for 'out of work,' as I'm sure you're aware, Inspector. So it's possible. I'll give her a ring if you like, and find out." And swiftly, before Thanet could demur, "Get Debbie on the blower for me, will you, Marilyn? Yes, now."

It was pointless to protest. Solly clearly had every intention of warning Deborah Chivers of their impending visit. If he didn't do it now, he'd do it when they'd left, so he might as well be useful to Thanet in the process, perhaps save him a wasted journey.

"Debbie? Solly here, my love. Yes . . . No, afraid not.

79

Not at the moment. I might have something on ice, though. No, I can't say a word just now, in case it doesn't come off. No, you'll just have to be patient, darling. No, something quite different. Now don't be alarmed, but I've got two charming policemen here who want to have a word with you. Yes . . . No, you haven't done anything wrong, love. Just some information they think you might have in connection with some case they're working on. No, no idea. Honestly. The point is, they'd like to come and see you. Right away, I gather. They're only in London for the day. No, truly, darling, absolutely no idea. Anyway, I'll tell them you'll be in this afternoon, shall I? Right. Yes, I'll be in touch soon, I hope. Yes. 'Bye for now. And you, sweetie." He put the phone down. "Any time you like," he said to Thanet.

"Thank you."

Marilyn came in, handed a slip of paper to Thanet and swayed out, buttocks visibly caressed by green silk.

"Uh . . . this way out." Solly ushered them through a door in the far corner of his office.

"Where does she live?" Lineham asked as they emerged on to the street.

Thanet glanced at the piece of paper in his hand. "Maida Vale. It looks as though we'll have to get clearance again. We'd better find a telephone . . . Then," he added recklessly, "we'll take another taxi."

Lineham grinned. "I'd like to see the Super's face when he gets our expenses sheet," he said.

10

The house in front of which the taxi drew up was in a Georgian terrace which had, like so many London streets, suffered the indignity of neglect and was now in the process of becoming fashionable again.

Many of the houses sported newly-pointed brick-work, gleaming white window frames and front doors painted in glossy, sophisticated colours. These, Thanet guessed, were privately owned, testaments to the loving care of their occupants. Number four was clearly rented out and looked like a poor relation, with peeling paint and a general air of neglect. Thanet peered at the row of bells. CHIVERS was the bottom one. He pressed it.

When the door opened Thanet's first impression was of a younger version of Servalan in "Blake's Seven" (one of Bridget's favourite programmes). Deborah Chivers had the same pointed chin, beautiful high wide cheek-bones and immaculate cap of glossy black hair cut so short it might almost have been painted on. A deliberate imitation? he wondered. Certainly the effect was dramatic and made even more striking by the girl's clothes: black corduroy-velvet knee-breeches, ribbed tights and a sheer white cotton blouse with a froth of ruffles at neck and wrist. Had she made a special effort on their behalf? Probably not, he decided. Deborah Chivers cared very much how she looked and would habitually make every effort to achieve the effect she wanted.

"Hi," she said. "You the fuzz?"

Thanet was tempted to say, "Sure am, baby," but thought the better of it. He introduced himself formally, showed her his identification.

She was amused. "It *was* a joke," she said. "Come on down."

She turned to lead the way, plunging with the abandon of familiarity into a short, dark stairwell leading to the basement. Thanet and Lineham followed more cautiously. At the bottom she threw open a door.

"*Maison* Chivers," she said. "Make yourself at home." She plumped down cross-legged on to a huge, squashy black floor cushion.

The two policemen instinctively looked around for more conventional forms of seating and found none. Gingerly Thanet lowered himself on to a scarlet cushion. Red for danger, he thought with amusement. If the boys in the office could see me now! From the corner of his eye he noted that Lineham had chosen a yellow perch and with straight face had already taken out notebook and pencil and settled down with an air of calm expectancy. Ten out of ten for self-possession, Thanet thought. Studiously ignoring the mischievous gleam in the girl's eye, he looked about him.

The room was large and was obviously bedroom, sitting room, study, workroom and kitchen, all rolled into one, though attempts had been made to hide the fact. Thanet recognised the type of bed which folds up and pretends to be a bookcase and guessed that the kitchen was hidden away in the far corner behind a wooden screen on which had been pasted dozens of theatre programmes. The brick and plank bookshelves were well stocked, mostly with paperbacks, and there was evidence of industry: under the window was a long worktable covered with drawings and sketches, jars of poster paint and a scattering of pencils and brushes. Pinned up on a large cork board beside the window were more sketches, each with a moustache of multi-coloured wools tacked to it. The girl must be some kind of fashion designer. His eyes swivelled to a clothes rack on castors standing against the wall. Hanging on it were half a dozen women's sweaters which at first he had taken to be the girl's own clothes.

"That's right." The girl was smiling at this lightning scrutiny, aware of his conclusion. "It's my sideline. I sell them to boutiques." She scrambled to her feet, unhooked one of the sweaters and held it against her. "Like it?" It was one of the scenic sweaters currently in fashion.

Thanet did. Very much. "It reminds me of the Dordogne." He and Joan had spent their honeymoon there and had loved it.

She was pleased. "As a matter of fact, it is the Dordogne. Some friends of mine have a cottage there and I spent a few weeks with them, last summer. I'm surprised you recognised it." She stroked the sweater. "I adore doing these. They really are fun. I'll be sorry when the craze is over." She replaced the sweater on the rack and returned to her cushion.

"You do this in between plays?" Thanet said.

Her mouth tugged down at the corners. " 'Fraid so. It's a terrible profession, acting. Too many people chasing too few jobs. Most of us are driven to doing something else, in between. You name it, actors do it, to eat. Unless of course you're up in the stars and then you don't have to worry. I should be so lucky."

"But the last play you were in. That was a good part, surely?"

"*Away Day*? Yes, that was a good one, right enough. But unfortunately it didn't quite catch the public fancy enough to have a long run. So, it was back to the old knitting needles." She grinned. "Is this part of your softening-up technique, Inspector?"

He liked her directness. He smiled back at her. "Yes and no."

"Why yes and why not?"

"Well, I find that people are always more cooperative, if I can get on good terms with them. But it so happens that *Away Day* is very much what I want to talk to you about."

"OK. So we're on good terms. What about *Away Day*?"

"To be more precise, I want to talk to you about Gemma Shade."

Deborah Chivers had particularly expressive eyes, he thought. They were a clear, pure blue, the colour of southern skies. Now he could have sworn that they darkened by several shades.

"What about Gemma?" she asked warily. "What's she done?"

"Nothing, to my knowledge," said Thanet truthfully.

"But we do rather need to know a little more about her life on the stage."

"Why come to me? Why not ask her agent?"

Thanet sighed. There was no point in beating about the bush with this girl. "Because her agent might be biased."

Deborah gave a great shout of laughter and rocked to and fro on her cushion, hugging her knees. "Biased! Oh, boy, that really takes the biscuit! Believe me, if you want an *un*biased view of Gemma Shade, I'm the last person you should have come to!"

"Why?" said Thanet softly.

Deborah stopped grinning and sat up. "Because she pinched my man, the old witch. And believe me, Inspector, it hurt. It still does."

"Wouldn't she be, well, a bit old for him? Unless, of course, he's much older than you."

"Just a year, that's all. He's twenty-three. Oh, yes, she's too old for him, right enough. But that makes no difference to her, I'm afraid. Gemma Shade likes them young, always has. It's common knowledge in the profession. And she doesn't waste time worrying about whether they're someone else's property, either."

"That would be Rowan Lee you're talking about?"

She winced. "Yes."

"Do you happen to know if she's still seeing him?"

"I don't *know* . . . but yes, I think so. The word is, he's still unavailable, so I guess she hasn't finished with him yet. You'd think she'd have more . . . dignity, now that she looks like the back of a bus."

"The baby, you mean."

"Yes."

"How long ago did this affair begin?"

"Hey, look, why the interest in Gemma's love-life? This isn't going to get Rowan into trouble, is it?"

"I told you, it's Miss Shade we're interested in. So please, how long ago?"

Deborah didn't notice the evasion. The opportunity

to talk freely about Gemma was clearly too good to be missed. "Soon after we opened. Say . . . eight or nine months ago."

"What's she like as a person? Leaving aside this predilection she has . . ."

Deborah shrugged. "As I said, I'm not really the best person to ask. But she's a first-rate actress, I'm bound to say that even though I can't stand her. But she's, well, I suppose the best word for it is greedy. She wants everything—fame, fortune, money, adulation, lovers, husband . . ."

"I read somewhere that she'd always said she didn't ever want to get married."

"That was before the Doc turned up. And, as you may or may not know, he is loaded. And his . . . well, wooing is the right word for it, old-fashioned as it may sound— his courtship of Gemma, then, was really something, or so I've been told. That was before I worked with her, of course."

"But if she prefers younger men?"

"For fun, yes. But, let's face it, they're usually broke. So when it came to choosing a husband . . ."

"You really don't like her, do you?"

"No, I don't. And I don't mind admitting it. I don't care for people who trample over other people, just use them and throw them on the rubbish heap when they're finished with them . . ."

"So it didn't surprise you that she married Doctor Pettifer?"

"Well, I told you, I didn't know her at the time, though I knew *of* her, of course. But, in retrospect, no, it doesn't. She lost nothing in terms of career, freedom, and gained in terms of security. I know he's older than she is, but that simply means he'll die first and she'll have more stashed away for her old age."

Obviously she hadn't heard about Dr Pettifer's death. Thanet sensed Lineham shift uncomfortably beside him and knew that the sergeant was expecting him now to break the news to her. But it wasn't the right moment.

To do so would disrupt the whole tenor of the conversation, bias and distort her response. He couldn't afford to have that happen.

"I must say," Deborah was saying, "I was surprised she didn't have an abortion when she found out she was pregnant."

"Why?"

"Because nothing, nothing whatsoever matters more to that woman than her career. And also because, well, a friend of mine was in the same production as Gemma when the doctor came a-courting, and she says that Gemma told her that one of the reasons why she had decided to accept his proposal was because he didn't expect her to become a breeding machine, was how she put it. In fact, he didn't like children, was positively anti having them and had made quite sure she felt the same before he proposed. 'So I'll be spared that, thank God,' she said. Gemma, I mean. So you see..."

"Yes," Thanet said. "Yes. That is interesting." He shrugged. "Well, they obviously changed their minds."

"And the other thing that always surprised me was that Gemma had married a GP. I mean, boy, is she neurotic about illness!"

"Can't stand blood, you mean? That sort of thing?"

"Oh, no. Miles worse than that. If you had a cough or a cold you couldn't go within half a mile of her—in fact, unless it was an actual performance, she'd refuse to go on stage with you. And as for anything infectious, like measles or mumps... She just couldn't *bear* anything to do with being ill. D'you know, while we were doing *Away Day* one of the young stage hands had an accident, broke her thigh. We were all very sorry for her because it was her first job in the West End and as you can imagine she was heartbroken about having to drop out. Her family lives up north, so we all took it in turns to go and visit her in hospital, to cheer her up. Except Gemma. She made all sorts of excuses and then, in the end, said straight out that she couldn't bear illness, she couldn't stand hospitals and nothing, but nothing, would induce her to go near one." Deborah grimaced. "So you can see why it surprised me, when I found out she'd married a doctor."

"Perhaps she thought he'd keep her healthy," said Lineham with a grin.

Deborah looked surprised. It was the first time he had spoken and now she gave his youthful good looks an assessing, appreciative stare.

Thanet was amused to see his sergeant flush. Lineham had always been susceptible to a pretty girl, had never been at his best in dealing with them. Thanet and Joan had sometimes wondered how he had ever plucked up sufficient courage to ask Louise, his wife, out in the first place.

"That's a thought," Deborah said. "D'you know, you could just be right. It would tickle her to think she had her own private physician."

Thanet wondered if it was only Gemma who evoked this kind of acid response in the girl. A pity, if not, to be soured, so young. Certainly she'd shown no sign of it until Gemma's name was mentioned. And if she really had been in love with young Lee, it was scarcely surprising that she should feel bitter towards the older woman.

"Well, thank you, Miss Chivers," he said, struggling to rise with dignity from his floor cushion. "You've been most helpful. There's just one other thing . . ."

"Yes?" She came to her feet gracefully, in one supple, fluid movement, smiling and looking up at him expectantly.

He cast a slightly embarrassed glance at Lineham. "Those sweaters you make. Er . . . How much do you charge for them?"

"Thirty pounds," she said promptly. "And that's a fair price. In the shops, individually-designed hand-made ones like this go for double that. And that's not just sales talk, you can check for yourself. I can cut the costs because I haven't the overheads, of course. Why? Do you fancy one?"

"My wife would."

"Come and have a look." She beckoned him across to the rack with a tiny jerk of her head. "What size is she?"

"Er . . . medium. Not fat, not thin . . ."

She laughed. "A typical male answer!" Quickly she flicked through them, extracting three in all. "These should fit, then. Do you like any of them?"

One of them reminded Thanet of the beach where he and Joan had spent many golden afternoons. There were those towering cliffs behind which the sun had sunk each day in a final dazzle of splendour, there were the silken waters of the Dordogne river lapping at the rocks which plunged sheer into the water. On one occasion he and Joan had swum right across to touch them . . . There, too, in the foreground was the wide, pebbly beach overhung by trees. Why, that looked like the very spot where . . .

"That wouldn't be Meyraguet, by any chance?" he asked.

Her eyes lit up. "Yes, it is! D'you know it?"

"Very well indeed." That settled it. "My wife would love that one. I'll take it. You won't mind a cheque?"

Rivulets of light rippled across the burnished cap of hair as she shook her head. "Not at all. No tax evasion for me. Believe it or not, Operation Knitting Needles is entirely legit. Blame my Methodist upbringing." She folded the sweater carefully into tissue paper and gift-wrapped it.

In the taxi Thanet sank back against the upholstery and glanced at the colourful parcel with delight. He couldn't wait to see Joan's face . . . He turned to Lineham.

"Now then," he said briskly. "Tell me what you thought of Miss Chivers."

11

The children spotted the gaily-wrapped parcel the moment Thanet stepped through the door.

"A present!" they cried. "Who's it for, Daddy? Who's it for?"

Thanet was glad to see that tonight everything seemed normal. Both of them were bathed and in their nightclothes—Joan always allowed them to stay up until six-thirty to wait for their father—and there were savoury smells issuing from the kitchen.

He laid a finger across his lips. "Shh . . . It's for Mummy. Come on."

They followed him in a conspiratorial silence into the kitchen. The radio was on and Joan obviously hadn't heard him arrive home. She was chopping something on the work surface near the cooker, with her back to him.

He tiptoed up behind her, exaggerating his movements for the children's entertainment. Then, lifting his arm above her head, he slowly lowered the parcel to dangle in front of her face. She gave a little cry and the children shrieked with delight.

"What do I get for bringing home the goodies?" he said, smiling.

"It's for me?" Surprise, pleasure, anticipation, appreciation chased each other across Joan's face. "Thank you, darling!" She reached up to kiss him, wiping her hands on her apron, then took the parcel and moved across to the table. Thanet and the children followed her to watch as she began to unwrap it.

"Oh," she breathed, as the sweater emerged from its

folds of tissue paper. "Oh, darling, it's beautiful. Really beautiful. Wherever did you find it?"

"In London," Thanet said smugly.

"D'you know," Joan said, holding it up at arm's length to study it. "It reminds me of the Dordogne."

"It is the Dordogne. The girl who made it spent the summer there, last year." He paused. "Does it look familiar?" he asked, smiling.

She considered, head tilted to one side. "Well . . . Meyraguet? Darling, it isn't Meyraguet, is it?"

His face told her she had guessed correctly.

"Meyraguet . . ." she breathed, studying it. When she turned to him again her eyes had the sheen of tears. "What a lovely, lovely present," she said, flinging her arms around him.

He hugged her back, delighted. "Thought you'd like it," he murmured.

"Every time I wear it, it'll remind me . . ."

They exchanged reminiscent smiles. Their honeymoon had been memorable. Joan kissed him again, enthusiastically. The children beamed. Why didn't he do this sort of thing more often? Thanet asked himself.

After supper, though, he noticed that Joan seemed a little subdued.

"What's the matter?" he asked.

She pulled a face. "Louise rang me this morning, asked if I'd meet her at lunchtime."

Thanet groaned. He was fond of Lineham's wife, though she was a little over-powering for his own taste. He could guess what was wrong. "Mother-in-law trouble again?"

"I'm afraid so. Honestly, Luke, I really do wonder what will happen there, in the end. After that business of the wedding, I rather hoped Mike's mother had learned her lesson."

Lineham's wedding had twice been delayed by his mother having mild heart attacks. At the third attempt he had told her that even if she had another attack he

would, in fairness to Louise, have to go ahead regard-
less. She did and he had.

"What happened this time?" Thanet asked.

"Well, apparently they had some friends round to
supper last night. Fortunately they knew them well,
otherwise . . . well, anyway, Mike's mother kept on ring-
ing up."

"Did she know they were entertaining?"

"Yes. She rang first at eight, just as they were sitting
down to table, saying she didn't feel well, and the soup
got cold while they were waiting for Mike to finish the
phone call. Then she rang again just as they were all
settling down to coffee, after the meal. And then, to cap
it all, she rang yet again just after Mike and Louise had
got into bed and, I gather, had begun to make love.
And that time Mike actually got dressed and went over
to see her!"

"You can see why Louise was mad!"

"I should say. But what she finds so frustrating is that
Mike won't talk about it, won't even acknowledge that
they have a problem."

"I'm not surprised really. Louise can be pretty force-
ful at times too, you know. I should think he often feels
like a worm between two blackbirds."

"I thought you liked Louise!"

"Oh, I do. I do. But I wouldn't want to be married to
her."

"She says Mike doesn't even seem to realise how his
mother manipulates him, and this makes her furious."

"Poor Mike. But you can understand why he refuses
to talk about it, can't you?"

"Why?"

"Well, what good would it do? I bet that, by 'talk
about it,' Louise really means 'get him to see her point
of view, put her first.' Nothing else would really satisfy
her, now would it?"

"I suppose not." Joan sounded doubtful.

"I'm sure of it. She's not the compromising type.
And, looking at it from Mike's point of view, you can

understand him feeling that his mother has at least got some claim on him. Louise, after all, has him all the time, but his mother calls on him only occasionally. I can see why Louise gets angry but let's face it, she did know what she was letting herself in for, before she married him. And I don't know whether she'd be any happier if Mike did stop jumping when his mother claims his attention. As I see it, he'd then feel so guilty he'd be as miserable as sin anyway. And she wouldn't like that either, now would she?"

"You do sound unsympathetic, darling, I must say."

"If I do, I'm sorry. But I wouldn't call it unsympathetic, I'd call it realistic. Frankly, I think that neither Mike's mother nor Louise are going to change their spots at this stage. In fact, I can't really see the situation altering until one of them dies."

"Luke!"

"I'm sorry, love, but come on, don't you agree with me, underneath?"

Joan bit her lip. "I'm just being an ostrich, really. Yes, I suppose I do. It's just that, well, seeing Louise so miserable . . ."

"It's something she will have to come to terms with, I'm afraid."

"She wondered if you might perhaps have a word with Mike . . . ?"

"Me? Not on your life. Mike and I have got a damned good working relationship and I don't want to ruin it. Besides, you must see it really isn't my place to start butting in on his private life without an invitation."

"So you haven't any bright ideas?"

"Just one. If she really feels that the problem is serious—and it does sound as though it's getting that way—then by far the best thing to do is to go to the Marriage Guidance Council."

"Isn't that a bit drastic?"

"Not at all. I should think prevention is better than cure and besides, the only counsellor I've ever met really impressed me. You remember, Mrs Thorpe, in the Julie Holmes case?"

"Yes, I do remember, now you mention it. All right. I'll give Louise a ring tomorrow, see if I can tactfully suggest it."

Marriages, marriages, Thanet thought as he lay awake in bed, later. Who could ever tell what went on behind all those closed front doors? No one but the couples themselves—no, even that was a fallacy. Usually, the two people in a marriage were the last to be able to understand what was happening to them. It took a major upheaval, a crisis, a painful reassessment of self to do that. He remembered his own near-danger point, a couple of years ago, when he and Joan had clashed over her desire to abandon her contented-housewife rôle for a more satisfying job. But they had been lucky. He had been jogged into awareness by the case in which he had been involved at the time and besides, that had been only a temporary dilemma. Lineham and Louise were a different matter; their problem was permanent, rooted in their different character and backgrounds. Any solution they found would be hard-won and painfully achieved. He didn't envy them that.

His mind drifted back to the Pettifer case. Now there was an intriguing marriage. His forehead furrowed as he lay staring up into the darkness, thinking of each partner in turn.

Pettifer, now. A strange man, stern and proud, a man who set high standards not only for himself but, Thanet guessed, for those about him too, reserved in his manner yet capable of a passionate wooing... His twin obsessions: his wife and his work. No doubt about how he would have felt had he known that she had been— was still being—unfaithful to him.

If he had known.

Had he?

Thanet considered. There was, so far, not one single scrap of evidence to indicate that he had. They would have to find out, because if he had... Well, what if he

had? How would he have reacted? He might have cut
his wife out of his will, for a start. Thanet made a
mental note to check, in the morning. In any case
Pettifer must have been desperately hurt, wounded and
then angry, yes, overwhelmingly angry. But what would
he have *done*? Would he have killed himself?

Thanet thought. He remembered what Doc Mallard
had said about suicide—that one school of thought saw
it as an act of anger, of aggression rather than despair.
Could this have applied in Pettifer's case? Perhaps it
would depend on how Pettifer read his wife's character.
According to Deborah Chivers, Gemma had no moral
scruples whatsoever. True, Deborah was biased, as she
herself had freely admitted—but then, Thanet himself
had seen how cruel Gemma could be, in that incident
with Andrew. But Pettifer, blinded by love, might well
have seen her differently. If, then, he had thought her
to be a woman of conscience who would be overwhelmed
by guilt and remorse and blame herself for her husband's suicide, could he conceivably have decided to
revenge himself upon her in this way?

Thanet found himself shaking his head. No. Everything he had so far learnt about Pettifer contradicted
the idea. He could imagine Pettifer fighting back—
confronting his wife's lover, perhaps, or accusing her
outright, or repudiating her even, with an icy coldness
which masked his pain. But this . . . No, suicide as the
final act of aggression was surely the ultimate gesture of
a coward, of a man who felt he couldn't get his own
back on life any other way than by voluntarily surrendering
it. And Pettifer, by common consensus, had been a
fighter, a man who squared up to life and lived it on his
own terms.

Conclusion, then: Pettifer had not known of his wife's
infidelity.

And this was the only possible reason for suicide that
had turned up—yet, Thanet reminded himself. The
post-mortem result was still to come.

Then there was Gemma Pettifer—Gemma Shade.

The fact that she had two names seemed symbolic of her dual identity: at home in Sturrenden the happily married woman (with a touch of glamour, admittedly, for no one ever quite forgot her public persona), the respectable doctor's wife. And in the theatre world the cat in heat, the older woman with a taste for young men and a reputation for getting what she wanted irrespective of the damage it caused to those who got in her way. "Greedy" was the word Deborah had used, and if so it was understandable, considering the insecurity of Gemma's early life. Deborah had found it astonishing that Gemma should have chosen to marry a country GP, but Thanet felt he could understand it. Medicine was a solid, respectable profession and Pettifer had been able to offer the added advantages of wealth and maturity. Add to that the fact that he had been prepared to allow Gemma complete freedom to pursue her career (and therefore, unknown to him, her lovers) and the proposition must have been irresistible to her.

So, taking the hypothesis that Gemma had killed him, why should she have decided to throw all that security away? Had she become bored with Pettifer? Or, conversely, had she truly fallen in love with Lee? Suppose that, as in the classic murder triangle, she and Lee had wanted not only to be together but to get their hands on Pettifer's considerable wealth—and had conspired together to do so . . . How had they done it, in view of the fact that Pettifer had not taken the overdose for several hours after Gemma left? Obviously, Thanet decided, they must have returned to Sturrenden later on in the evening, after Gemma's dinner with her agent.

He considered the mechanics of the idea. Gemma would have given Pettifer a sufficiently strong drug in the cocoa to send him off into a sound sleep. Then, later, she and Lee would return—by car perhaps. By then Pettifer would be deep in a drugged sleep and it would be a relatively simple matter to administer the overdose . . . But if that was how it had been done, how

could Gemma possibly have known that Pettifer would
conveniently develop a cold, thereby providing her
with the opportunity to slip him the first dose?

For a moment Thanet's mind, poised between sleep
and wakefulness, skittered off into a wildly imaginative
explanation wherein Gemma somehow managed to get
hold of cold germs and administer them to her husband
at appropriate intervals before the night of the planned
murder...

With an effort Thanet dragged his thoughts back into
logical channels. Don't be ridiculous, he told himself. It
wasn't necessary for Pettifer to have had a cold at all, for
Gemma to be able to give him that initial dose. She
could originally have planned to give it to him in his tea
and then, when he conveniently developed the cold
symptoms, decided to use them to her own advantage.
For that matter, the whole thing could have been
*un*planned, could have been set in motion by that cold
of his. Seeing her chance, Gemma could have acted on
impulse, grabbed it with both hands.

Though, of course, they had only Gemma's word for it
that Pettifer had had any cold symptoms at all. For
some reason this seemed a significant thought, though
Thanet couldn't for the life of him see why. He felt
consciousness slipping away as he endeavoured to concentrate on it. It was no good. It would have to wait
until morning.

Morning... Tomorrow... Tomorrow he would have
to tackle Gemma, confront her with her adultery...

He wasn't looking forward to that.

12

When Thanet arrived at the office next morning he
found Lineham engrossed in a report.

"What's that?" Thanet asked.

"Handwriting report."

"Anything interesting?"

"Not really." Lineham handed it over.

Thanet scanned it quickly, read it again more careful-ly and finally tossed it on to the desk in disgust. "A second opinion! That'll mean another couple of days at least, before we'll know for certain."

"We might not know even then," Lineham pointed out. "There's no guarantee that the second report'll be any more conclusive than the first."

"True." Thanet ran a hand through his hair. "I really was hoping that today we'd have a definite pointer one way or the other. I'm sick of working in a vacuum like this. Is the PM definitely scheduled for today?"

"They're doing it now. They started at eight-thirty so they should be finished soon."

"Good."

"There are three interesting bits of information that have come in, though. First, the bottle of port. Accord-ing to Mrs Price, Mrs Pettifer gave it to her husband for his birthday. And the wine merchant confirms, we've checked. He remembers because Mrs Pettifer asked his advice in selecting it."

"So it's not surprising her prints are on that, at least."

"The next thing is, I thought it might be useful to know the terms of Dr Pettifer's will—I thought, if he did know his wife was being unfaithful to him, he might well have decided to cut her out."

"And?"

"He made a new will on his marriage. There's money left in trust for Andrew, of course, but all the rest goes to Mrs Pettifer. That will still stands and no changes had been discusssed."

"Now that is interesting. What's the third thing?"

"Just before you came in this morning I had a call from PC Sparks."

"Yes, I know him." Sparks was promising material. Thanet had had his eye on him for some time.

"He'd heard that we're taking a bit more than a routine interest in Dr Pettifer's death and the long and the short of it is, he and PC May were on patrol duty in that area the night Pettifer died and around midnight there was a car parked near the entrance to the house next door to Pine Lodge. They noticed it because it was an interesting model, an old Morgan sports car. They didn't think anything of it at the time, just assumed it belonged to someone visiting in the area. They just commented briefly in passing and more or less forgot about it."

"Did they get the number?"

"Afraid not."

"Pity. Colour?"

"Dark, that's all."

Thanet reached for his pipe, began to fill it. "Sparks could be right, of course, there could be a perfectly innocent explanation for its being there, but . . ."

"I was thinking, just before you arrived . . . If Mrs Pettifer and her boyfriend were in this together . . ."

"He could have driven her down from London, you mean? Yes, the thought had crossed my mind. We'd better ring Miss Chivers. She'd probably know what sort of car Lee has at the moment, if he's got one."

"I tried, sir. But she's out for the day, apparently."

"I expect the Met could find out for us, without too much difficulty. We'll give them a ring in a minute."

"Anyway, as I say, I was thinking," Lineham said. "Just say she'd been biding her time, waiting for the right moment . . ." Eagerly he presented the scenario which Thanet had worked out in bed the night before. ". . . By midnight Pettifer would have been sufficiently muzzy not to cotton on to what was happening when she roused him to give him the overdose," he finished triumphantly.

Thanet had been lighting his pipe as he listened patiently and now he waited for a moment before he commented, pressing his match box over the bowl to get it drawing properly. Eventually, satisfied, he put the matches back in his pocket and sat back in his chair, waving away the coils of smoke that were obscuring his view of Lineham. "But if she did all that, why be stupid enough to put the whole scheme in jeopardy by taking Lee back to her hotel and spending the night with him? I know they took care not to be seen, but they must have realised the risk was there."

Lineham looked crestfallen. "True."

"And why be so idiotic as to leave her fingerprints all over the glass and so on. *Everyone* knows about fingerprints these days. And why be so vehement in insisting it couldn't have been suicide? Why show us that cruise booking, for instance? Why not just keep mum and hope we'd swallow the idea of suicide—hook, line and sinker?"

"Because she knew we'd be bound to find out he had no reason to kill himself and we'd get suspicious anyway? So she thought she'd put herself in the clear by getting in first?" Lineham pulled a face. "No, it's too feeble, isn't it?"

"It is, rather. But don't think I'm dismissing her entirely. We both know how apparently insuperable objections have a habit of melting away. We just haven't enough information at the moment. Perhaps the PM results will help." Thanet looked at his watch. "Surely they won't be long now . . . While we're waiting, could you give Mrs Pettifer a ring, tell her we'll be out to see her shortly?"

Lineham had only just replaced the receiver when the phone rang. He snatched it up, listened.

"Doc Mallard," he said, handing it to Thanet.

Thanet listened intently for a minute or so and then said, "Yes. Yes, I see. They're positive about that? Right. Oh, just one other point. Was there any sign of a head cold? Yes, a head cold . . . I see. Thanks. 'Bye." He put the phone down. "Doc Mallard was particularly interested, so he went along to watch. It's been confirmed that Pettifer died of an overdose, but of course the stomach contents have yet to be analysed."

"Did he have anything wrong with him?"

"As far as his health was concerned? No, nothing. He was unusually fit and there was no sign of organic disease."

"Nothing creepy, like leukaemia, which might not show up?"

"Well, apparently, if it were sufficiently advanced, leukaemia would show up—in an increase in the size of the spleen. In any case, Doc Mallard was his usual scrupulous self and got them to do an immediate blood test, in case the disease was in its very early stages. And there was nothing... I think we'd better play safe, Mike, arrange that the stomach contents are sent to London rather than to County Hall, just in case we have got a murder on our hands. Incidentally, there was one interesting point. There was no sign of a head cold, either."

"How could they tell?"

"There'd be something called hyperaemia—reddening— of the nasal passages. Odd... only last night I was thinking, no one else noticed that he had any sign of a cold—I specifically asked."

"But why on earth should Mrs Pettifer say he had a cold if he didn't"

"I really can't imagine."

"Perhaps he was putting it on, to prevent her going to London."

"But she said he positively insisted she still went."

They stared at each other, baffled.

"It's only a trivial thing of course," Thanet said at last, "but it's like so many other things in this case. It just doesn't make sense. Ah, well, perhaps it'll all become clear in the fullness of time. It's pointless to sit about here speculating any longer. Let's go out to see her. We'll just make those phone calls first. You get on to the Met, ask them if they can discreetly find out what sort of car Lee drives—I still don't want him alerted, by the way—and I'll make the arrangements to have the stomach contents sent to London."

On the way to Pine Lodge, Thanet stared moodily out of the window. Yesterday's crisp, bright weather had vanished overnight and the sky was a uniform, leaden grey. A steady drizzle was falling, slicking the pavements and blurring the silhouettes of roof-tops. The faces of passers-by were dour, as if the dreariness of the day had seeped into their souls.

"Why do they think we've got zebra crossings?" muttered Lineham, braking sharply as a pedestrian dashed out from the kerb.

Thanet glanced at the sergeant, his attention caught by some undertone in his voice. Lineham was driving with a frowning concentration, his eyes bleak. Thanet remembered what Joan had said last night. Perhaps he should at least give Lineham the opportunity to talk, if he wanted to.

"Anything wrong, Mike?"

Lineham glanced at him uneasily, shook his head. "I was only thinking about Mrs Pettifer."

Thanet had to accept the statement at its face value. He couldn't press the point. The opening had been there, if Lineham had wished to take it.

"What about her?"

"I really can't make her out."

"No. Ditto. Perhaps it's something to do with what we were saying the other day, that with actors we're constantly wondering if they're putting on a performance or not. And in view of what we've learnt about her since then, it's difficult to believe that she was completely sincere. And yet . . ."

"What?"

"I'm not sure," Thanet said slowly. "It's just that, well, that show of grief . . . There was something odd about it." He thought back, trying to put his finger on the elusive impression. "It's almost," he said at last, "as if she was surprised at herself, at the way she was reacting."

"I don't see what you're getting at."

Thanet grinned. "That's not surprising. I'm not really

sure myself. If only we knew whether or not Pettifer knew she'd been unfaithful to him."

"It does seem to be the only possible reason he could have had, for killing himself."

"But surely, Mike, if he had known, someone would have noticed? Mrs Price, for instance. She knew him well and she was there, in the house, all the time. Even if Pettifer had put on a brave front at work, to salvage his pride perhaps, surely Mrs Price would have seen some hint of the true state of affairs? But obviously she didn't. If she had, I'd have thought she'd be only too ready to say so. It's obvious she still disapproves of Mrs Pettifer."

"Perhaps that's why Pettifer felt it necessary to put up a front at home, too."

"I don't follow you."

"Well, Pettifer must have been aware that Mrs Price didn't like his wife, disapproved of his second marriage, and I imagine he would have resented her attitude. I should think he would have felt it was none of her business. So, if he found out that she was right and he was wrong, then he would have found it very difficult to lose face by behaving in front of her in such a way as to show her his disillusionment."

"Possibly. Even so, I can't help feeling it would have shown, in little ways—in a tone of voice, a look, a gesture."

"Maybe."

Thanet sighed. "What we really need is the opinion of someone in front of whom the Pettifers wouldn't have been on their guard, someone whose opinion wouldn't have mattered to them, or who could have observed them without their realising it."

"Next thing we know, you'll be subpoenaing the flies on the wall," Lineham said with a grin.

Thanet laughed. "A fly on the wall would be perfect. Incidentally, while I'm talking to Mrs Pettifer, I'd like you to nip up and take a look at her room."

"Won't she object?"

"I don't see why. After all, she's the one who's insisting he couldn't have killed himself. She can scarcely complain that we're being too thorough. We'll ask permission, of course, but frankly I can't see how she can refuse it. Did you search Andrew's room the other day, by the way?"

"Just a quick look, that's all."

"Go over it again, then."

"You don't think he's involved, do you?"

"Just being careful," Thanet said evasively. "Ah, here we are."

Mrs Price showed them into the drawing room. Gemma Pettifer was lying on the brocade sofa. There was a typescript propped up against the mound of her belly, but she wasn't reading. Thanet had the impression that they were disturbing some profound reverie; the expression on Gemma's face as she looked towards them was uncomprehending, her eyes glazed. She made no attempt to rise.

"Inspector Thanet, Mrs Pettifer," Mrs Price repeated, raising her voice a little.

Gemma's eyes cleared and now there was recognition in them. "Oh, Inspector, forgive me." Awkwardly she swung her feet to the floor.

"Please," he said quickly, "don't get up. There's no need."

"Do sit down." Her glance included Lineham.

"I wonder . . . my sergeant wasn't able to finish looking around upstairs, the other day," Thanet said. "Do you think . . ."

"In my bedroom, you mean? By all means."

"And in Andrew's room too, if you don't mind."

"Andrew's?" Her eyebrows arched. "Well, yes, of course, if it's necessary. Though I don't quite see . . ."

"Just routine," said Thanet. Oh, the usefulness of that blanket expression!

Lineham went out and Thanet sat down, taking his time and deliberately choosing a deep, comfortable armchair. Out of the corner of his eye he saw her relax,

103

the lines of her body settling back into the cushioned depths of the sofa. Briefly, he reviewed in his mind what he had learned about this woman from Deborah Chivers. If the younger woman was to be believed, Gemma was self-centred, careless of other people's feelings, had a penchant for younger men... Not a pretty catalogue. Once again, he cursed the cloud of uncertainty which hovered over the manner of Pettifer's death, the resulting ambivalence which he, Thanet, felt towards Gemma Pettifer. Should he treat her as a grieving widow, or as a potential murderess? This wasn't going to be easy.

She was watching him expectantly. "Well?" she said with a faint smile. "What can I do for you, Inspector?"

He decided on strict neutrality. If she thought him unsympathetic, it couldn't be helped.

"The post mortem on your husband was carried out this morning," he began and saw her flinch. "And it may interest you to know that there was no sign of illness."

"I'm not surprised. I told you, he was very fit, took very good care of his health..."

"So there's no possible reason for suicide there."

"But that's what I've been telling you!" she cried impatiently, swinging her feet to the floor and leaning forward intently. "There wasn't any reason, none at all. That's why..."

"Mrs Pettifer," Thanet interrupted. "I think I ought to tell you... We know about Mr Lee."

"Oh." She was silent for a few moments, folding her hands together and staring down at them. Then she raised her head to flash him a look of defiance. "But that makes no difference. My husband had no idea that Mr Lee and I..."

"... were lovers?" Thanet finished for her. "How can you be sure of that?"

She raised her hands in a helpless gesture. "I just am, that's all."

"But what makes you so certain?"

"Oh, come, Inspector. You're married, aren't you? If

you'd found out that your wife was being unfaithful, do you mean to say that your attitude towards her would have remained completely unchanged?"

A palpable hit there, Thanet admitted silently. Because, of course, it wouldn't have. "What I would or would not do in such circumstances is beside the point, Mrs Pettifer," he said calmly. "The point at issue is what your husband would or would not have done. It is, as I'm sure you will agree, a matter of temperament."

"So?"

"I understand that your husband was rather a reserved man. If he had found out about your . . . affair, might he not simply have said nothing, brooded on it in private and, eventually, unable to live with the knowledge, have killed himself?"

"No!" It was a cry of pain.

Acting? wondered Thanet. If only he could make up his mind.

"Not with me," she was saying. "Not with me. He couldn't have hidden his feelings from me."

Nothing was going to make her budge, he could see that. Even to herself she could not begin to admit the possibility that he might have known of her disloyalty. Perhaps she really had cared for him, after all. And above all, if she had killed him, why seize on this as the perfect reason for his having committed suicide, thereby putting her in the clear?

"And then there's the baby," she said, unconsciously taking up Thanet's line of thought. "He was so looking forward to the baby coming. Andy's adopted, you know, it would have been Arnold's first child. It took his breath away, when I first told him about it."

"He was surprised?"

"Surprised and delighted." She gave a reminiscent little smile. "He thought, you see, that I didn't want any . . . I'd made a bit of a thing about it, earlier on. Well, I was much younger then . . . Before he asked me to marry him he went to great pains to make sure I knew he wouldn't expect me to produce any children.

He knew how much my career meant to me, you see. And he was very proud of me..."

"What made you change your mind? About having children, I mean?"

She shrugged. "I didn't actually make a conscious decision. But, underneath, I must have decided I wanted one. They say that if you forget to take the Pill, it shows that subconsciously you're wanting to conceive. So when I did... When you suddenly realise that the baby's not an abstract thing, it's actually there inside you, growing bigger with every day that passes... And if you've no real justification for killing it, for having an abortion... And anyway, I'm established in my profession now. I can pick and choose my parts. Taking time off to have a child isn't going to set me back. And motherhood's an important part of being a woman, isn't it? For all I know, it'll extend my powers as an actress into a whole new dimension."

Thanet's sympathy—which had, despite his resolution to remain impartial, been growing by the minute—dissolved abruptly. A more self-centred reason for having a child he couldn't imagine.

"Would it surprise you," he said, aware that he was being rude in cutting her off like this, and not caring, "to know that according to the pathologist your husband had no cold symptoms whatsoever?"

And this did astonish her (or was she just acting, dammit?). Her eyes widened and her mouth dropped open slightly. "It certainly does."

"Why?"

"Well, because he *said* he had a cold coming on. And he wasn't the sort of man to mention it unless he was pretty certain. I mean, usually I had to more or less make him go to bed, if there was anything wrong with him."

"And that night?"

"That's why I'm surprised at what you say. That night he scarcely needed any persuading at all. He went off to bed like a lamb." She was frowning, looking as baffled as Thanet felt. "It's crazy. If he'd been the sort of man to play up like that in order to stop me going out, I could understand it. But he wasn't. Just the opposite, in fact. As I told you, when I suggested I cancel my engagement, he wouldn't hear of it. Insisted I still went..." Suddenly her face crumpled and she buried it in her hands. "It's all like a nightmare," she said. "I keep thinking I'll wake up and he'll be there..."

Thanet could have sworn the emotion was genuine. He waited for a few moments, then said, "When your husband came home that night, did he say anything about his car?"

He thought her shoulders tensed before she raised her head. "Oh, yes," she said, "I meant to mention that to you. It was odd, wasn't it? I didn't even realise his car wasn't in the garage until Clough's left the keys with the policeman at the door."

"You didn't know your husband had left his car at the Centre?"

She shook her head. "He didn't say anything about it, so I assumed he'd driven home as usual. I rang Clough's, after the car was delivered here next morning, and they told me he'd asked them to fix it and bring it back here next day."

"I believe you said you took a taxi to the station?"

"That's right. I always do when I stay in town overnight. I don't like leaving my car in the station car park all night. Otherwise I'd have noticed my husband's car wasn't there when I went into the garage."

"Did he normally mention it, if something went wrong with his car?"

"Yes. Of course, there wasn't much time to talk, that evening. I could see as soon as he arrived home that he was looking under the weather. Though now that you say there was nothing wrong with him..." She put up her hands, began to massage her temples with her fingertips. "It's all so confusing..."

There was a knock at the door and Lineham came in,

carrying a crumpled sheet of paper. "Sorry to interrupt, sir, but I thought you'd like to see this."

Thanet glanced at him sharply. There had been an undercurrent of emotion in Lineham's voice which Thanet couldn't quite identify. He took the proffered sheet of paper and his scalp prickled as he read it. The handwriting was different from that of the suicide note:

My darling, darling Gemma,
    You looked so beautiful last night, I can't get you out of my mind. Lying here on my bed I close my eyes and pretend that you are beside me, that I can touch—

Thanet glanced at Gemma Pettifer, who was watching him expectantly. "Would you excuse us for a moment?"

13

In the hall, he and Lineham conversed in whispers.

"Where did you find this?"

"In Andrew's room. Under one of the pedestals of his desk."

A draft, then, Thanet guessed, crumpled up and discarded and, unknown to Andrew, kicked out of sight. So, had the final version ever been sent?

"What do you think, sir? Are we going to show it to her?"

Thanet shook his head. "Not just yet."

"But why not? I know she's pregnant and we have to be careful, but why should that always let her off the hook? If she really has seduced him, why should she get away with it?"

"I'm not thinking of her, Mike. Just consider for a

moment how Andrew would feel if there isn't any truth in this, if this letter is just part of an adolescent fantasy . . . and we showed it to her."

Lineham's face showed that he had taken the point. "I see what you mean. What are we going to do, then?"

"Nothing for the moment."

Thanet went back into the drawing room. When he said that he and Lineham were leaving now, Gemma Pettifer frowned.

"That piece of paper your sergeant brought in. What was it?"

"I'm afraid I can't tell you that." Thanet was polite, but firm.

"Where did he find it, then? Surely I have a right to know that, at least."

"In Andrew's room."

"Andrew's room?" The stress on the first syllable said: But what possible interest could there be in anything found in Andrew's room?

"Yes. And now I'm afraid we really must go."

Lineham was waiting in the car.

"Well, Mike, what do you think?" Thanet asked, as he fastened his seat belt. "Fact or fantasy?"

"Thinking it over . . . fantasy."

"Why?"

"Well, he is only fifteen . . ."

"Oh, come on, Mike, don't be naive. You know as well as I do that these things happen."

"Yes." Lineham paused. "I suppose, if I'm honest, I just don't want it to be true. I felt sorry for Andrew the other day and I don't like the idea of his being in her clutches." He gave a shamefaced grin. "There speaks the detached investigator."

"Full marks for insight, anyway." Thanet was pleased. In his view a readiness to question his own motives and to understand his own reactions were hallmarks of the good detective. "Anyway, as it happens, I'm inclined to agree with you. I may be wrong, of course, but having seen Andrew I just can't visualise him having a torrid affair with his adoptive mother. Fantasising about one, yes . . . though it does explain his attitude to her the other day. Let's go and have a bite to eat, while we think about it."

Lineham waited until they had settled down in a quiet corner of the pub with their beer and pasties before saying, "What did you mean, about the letter explaining Andrew's attitude to Gemma?"

"Well, I think we were all a bit taken aback at that outburst of his, weren't we? But now, well, I can see that if he's had secret hankerings after Gemma he might well feel very guilty about them, angry with himself for having them."

"And he might have directed that anger against her instead?"

"Mmm," said Thanet, his mouth full of pasty. He chewed, swallowed. "He might even imagine that it had something to do with his father's death."

"You mean, that his father might have suspected that he and Gemma were having an affair and killed himself because of that?"

"I wouldn't think he'd have been as specific as that. If he had, he'd no doubt have seen how unlikely that was. No, I'd think it would be much more a generalised feeling of guilt, an irrational idea that he might somehow have contributed towards his father's depression. And if he did feel that, then this would account for his vehemence in insisting that it couldn't have been suicide."

"Because if it wasn't, he couldn't have helped bring it about?"

"Exactly."

"You're not suggesting he made up that bit about the spelling of his name?"

"Oh, no. He produced evidence to back up what he said, remember. No, he was sincere enough. I'm just saying that we must be careful how much weight we place upon Andrew's opinion in view of what we now know he feels about Gemma."

"Of course, as you said, it could be true, though, couldn't it? They really could be having an affair, couldn't they? After all, we know how much she likes young men . . ."

"According to Deborah Chivers."

"Well, yes, according to Deborah Chivers. But Lee's a good ten years younger than Mrs Pettifer, so there is some evidence to support the idea. And as her life has been so much more restricted lately, with the baby coming . . . She could just have thought Andrew would be a convenient stop-gap until she was able to get back to having regular fun and games in London, couldn't she?"

Thanet grinned. "You really don't like her, do you, Mike? I thought you were very taken with her at first."

"That was before I got to know more about her." Briefly, Lineham's eyes were shadowed.

Was Lineham also expressing his disillusionment with Louise? Thanet wondered.

"Anyway, I agree with you. It's a possibility we can't ignore. If they were lovers and Pettifer found out, he could have threatened to throw them both out, refuse to pay for Andrew's education . . ."

"What a prospect!" Lineham said gloomily. "Imagine arresting a fifteen-year-old schoolboy and a pregnant actress twice his age—his adoptive mother at that. The Press would have a field day."

"I don't think we'd better dwell on that one."

"How did Mrs Pettifer react when you told her we knew about her affair with Lee?"

Thanet told him.

"She was really upset at the idea that her husband might have known?"

"Quite independently of the possibility that that might have been why he committed suicide, yes . . . Or she seemed to be. That's the trouble. With her I can never make up my mind whether she's genuine or not . . . I really do wish we could find out if he did know."

"I don't see how we can."

111

"Wait a minute. You know what I was saying about an independent witness... I've just remembered. Mrs Barnet, the secretary at the Centre, mentioned some restaurant where Pettifer had taken his wife for an anniversary dinner recently—the Sitting Duck, that was it. Out Biddenden way. Do you know it?"

"I know *of* it. It's a bit beyond my pocket."

"It just occurs to me that if it's a fairly small place the owner might remember them. It might be worth going to see him, ask him how they seemed together."

"Yes."

"You sound doubtful, Mike."

"I'm not sure there'd be much point. After all, it is a public place. If Pettifer was so determined to keep up a front that even his housekeeper didn't know, I can't see that it would help."

"It just might. If Mrs Pettifer is lying and he did know about Lee, they might not have been so concerned to pretend that everything in the garden was lovely in front of a lot of strangers."

"You'd like me to go out there this afternoon, then?"

"I think so. Yes."

"Right." Lineham hesitated and then said, "You know, sir, it's only just occurred to me that for some reason we just aren't bothering to look very hard at anyone but Mrs Pettifer."

"What do you mean?"

"Well, assuming for a moment that it was murder, not suicide, then in the normal way of things, yes, I agree we'd look first at the wife. But, at the same time, we'd be investigating other possibilities—friends, business associates and so on... I know Dr Lowrie is checking the files for disturbed patients but apart from that we seem to be concentrating entirely on Mrs Pettifer."

Thanet was staring at him fixedly.

"Sir?" Lineham said uncertainly.

"You're right, Mike," Thanet said softly. "By God, you're right. Now, why is that?" He felt on the verge of recognising an important truth. It was there, hovering just beyond his grasp....

"Well," said Lineham, taking him literally. He began to tick the points off on his fingers. "One, there are the fingerprints. Did you ask her to explain them, by the way?"

Thanet was only half listening. "What? No. I'm holding back on that, for the moment."

"Two, we find she's got a lover and therefore a motive. Three, we're beginning to wonder whether we can believe a word she said—there's the business of the cold, for example... And that's about it."

They stared at each other blankly.

"You're right, Mike. It just isn't enough for us to be focusing exclusively on her. I can't think how it's happened. I started off with an open mind. When I saw Dr Lowrie, for instance, one of the first things I did was check his alibi. Though I haven't bothered to verify it... What the hell's the matter with me? Talk about slipping... Thanks, Mike. Come on, drink up." Thanet stood up abruptly.

"Where are we going?" Lineham asked, in the car.

"Back to the office first. We're going to do a bit of catching up on lost time, so we'll need two cars. Now let's see..." Thanet took out his notebook. "We'll make a list. First, there's Andrew..."

"Andrew?"

"Of course. If only for elimination purposes. I don't like the idea, he's upset enough as it is... And I certainly don't think we ought to speak to him directly at this stage—after all, he is at boarding school. It should be easy enough to check his whereabouts on Monday night. Then there's Mrs Price. And the partners—Doctors Lowrie, Braintree and Fir. Fir's away on holiday at the moment, but we'd better verify that. And lastly, there's Lee. That's about it, isn't it?"

"Unless Dr Lowrie has turned anyone up in the files."

"I should have thought he'd been in touch with us, if

he had. Right, we'll split them up between us, leaving Lee out for the moment. I want to wait until we find out whether that Morgan was his or not, first. So you take Andrew and Mrs Price, I'll take the doctors."

"What about the Sitting Duck? Shall I try and fit that in on the way back?"

"Yes." Thanet closed his notebook with a snap. "That's it, then . . . You know, Mike, there's one thing I keep coming back to, over and over again . . ."

"What's that?"

"This business of children. It really puzzles me."

"In what way?"

"Well, I think Mrs Pettifer's attitude is understandable, just about. Initially she didn't want them because they would interfere with her career. When she found she was pregnant she'd reached the top of her profession, felt she could afford the time off. Also, she had realised there was a bonus to producing a child—she would enlarge her experience of life with a capital L. But him . . . well, you don't make sure your prospective bride doesn't want children unless you're pretty well against having them yourself."

"Unless, as she said, he thought she wouldn't marry him unless he made it clear he didn't want a conventional wife and would be one-hundred-per-cent behind her continuing her career?"

"True. But there was no need to make an issue of it, was there? I mean, if he'd asked her to marry him and she'd refused on the grounds that it could interfere with her career, you could understand him *then* saying, well, I don't expect you to be a conventional wife, there'll be no need to have children and so on . . . But the impression I had—certainly from Deborah Chivers—was that he wanted to make sure Gemma didn't want them *before* he asked her to marry him."

Lineham was shaking his head. "I don't agree. I should have thought that, if you didn't like children and didn't want them, it's the very thing you *would* want to check out before you proposed. And remember, Pettifer was no spring chicken either. Apart from his dislike of children he might well have felt he just couldn't face the prospect of nappies, disturbed nights and disruption of routine all over again. People often do feel that, when they're getting on towards middle age."

"Yes, I agree. But surely it's therefore all the more strange that, when she did tell him she was pregnant, he was over the moon about it."

"Oh, I don't know. People do change their minds about such things. After all, he was supposed to be devoted to her. He probably didn't want to upset her."

"Possibly. But I had the impression, from her, that it wasn't something they'd ever discussed, he was just presented with a *fait accompli*. I shouldn't have thought, from what we've heard about him, that he'd have been too pleased about that."

"Even so, if he doted on her . . ."

"I suppose you're right. That's how it must have been."

Back at the office there was as yet no word about Lee's car. Lineham set off at once for Merrisham to interview Mrs Price's sister and Thanet settled down to do some checking. First he rang his own doctor, Dr Phillips, who confirmed Lowrie's alibi in every detail. Satisfied, Thanet moved on to Dr Fir. Mrs Barnet at the Centre provided the information that, last Saturday, two days before Dr Pettifer's death, Dr Fir and his family had left on a 10 a.m. British Airways flight from Heathrow for a three-week stay with his brother-in-law in New Zealand. It proved relatively simple to establish that the Firs had indeed left on their scheduled flight and would have arrived in New Zealand on Monday morning. So unless Fir had abandoned his family half-way and flown back to England . . . Too far-fetched, Thanet decided. Temporarily he shelved Fir as a suspect. Which left Braintree.

Thanet sat back and thought. He was still angry with himself that he had allowed himself to be so . . . blinkered, was the word, in focusing exclusively on Mrs Pettifer.

He was glad that Lineham had seen what was happening, but humiliated that he had not been aware of it himself. How had it come about? He felt ruffled, as edgy as a cat that has been stroked the wrong way. He gave a wry grin. It's your ego that's been dented, he told himself. How *had* it come about though, he asked himself again. During that interview with Dr Lowrie he had certainly had an open mind . . . His eyes narrowed. He had just remembered Lowrie's evasiveness when asked if there had been any problems with the practice. It was remiss of him not to have followed that up before now. Perhaps, before seeing Braintree, it might be fruitful to see Lowrie again . . . .

A second phone call to Mrs Barnet informed him that it was Dr Lowrie's afternoon off, but that Thanet could find him at the Inn in the Forest until three o'clock. Swimming.

On the way he wondered how Lowrie was getting on with checking Pettifer's files. The way he felt at the moment even a psychopath or two couldn't add much to his confusion.

14

Dr Lowrie was also floundering, though physically not metaphorically.

It was a brave man, thought Thanet, who decided to learn to swim in his late fifties. Most people would be afraid of looking foolish. He sat down in one of the white wrought-iron chairs tastefully arranged in the raised seating area at one end of the pool and waited for Lowrie to finish his lesson.

The Inn in the Forest had once been an undistinguished Victorian country house, its ugliness redeemed

only by the beauty of its setting. Surrounded on three
sides by dense deciduous woods (which at this time of
the year were a kaleidoscope of colour) and on the
fourth by a lake, its potential as a money-spinner had
quickly been spotted by one of the major hotel chains.
Architects, consultants and environmentalists had been
called in and almost before one could say "planning
consent" the builders had arrived. Now, one would find
it almost impossible to detect the presence of the
original building in the shell of concrete, rustic wood
and glass which had been constructed around it—and
for those who liked canned comfort and a variety of
entertainment on tap, it was a holiday paradise. Sailing,
swimming, windsurfing, tennis, table-tennis, snooker, a
choice of discos and no fewer than four restaurants
ranging from the formal to the tastefully sleazy: it
offered them all, confident that few prospective customers would spurn all of its attractions.

And although he hated to admit it, Thanet thought,
gazing around, they would have been right, for the one
redeeming feature in his eyes was the indoor swimming
pool. It overlooked the lake, seemed almost, by some
trick of perspective, to merge into it. Flanked by tall,
curved white concrete wings which supported a high,
glass bubble of a roof, it contrived despite its almost
aggressive modernity to blend with the lake, the sky,
the trees in a way which gave those who swam in it the
illusion of being at one with nature. Entrance fees to
this pool were high—ten times as much as those for the
pool at the new sports centre in Sturrenden—but the
setting was so delightful, the water so well-heated and
the pool so uncrowded that a swimming session here
was truly a delight and local people would bring their
children as an occasional special treat. Thanet and his
family had been twice, enjoying a picnic afterwards at
the lakeside.

Thanet sat back in his chair and allowed himself to
sink into a pleasant torpor induced by the warm, steamy
atmosphere and the knowledge that there really was

117

nothing to do but wait. Beyond the tall sliding glass doors lightly misted with condensation the colours of the forest trees were blurred, hazy as in an Impressionist painting and as Thanet relaxed the cries of those in the pool blurred too, became distanced as he began to drift towards sleep.

A child's sudden shriek aroused him and he sat up with a start. Dr Lowrie was still in the pool practising the leg movements for the breast stroke, grasping the instructor's long pole to keep afloat. As Thanet watched, the lesson ended and Lowrie waded to the steps and hauled himself out, gasping. Thanet half rose and called his name in a low voice. Lowrie looked up, raised his hand in response and went to retrieve a towel from the far end of the seating area before coming to join Thanet. They greeted each other, Lowrie towelling himself vigorously, his fat little paunch wobbling.

"I'm quite happy to wait while you get dressed," Thanet said.

"No, no. I'll be going in again later, when I've had a breather. I only have time to come once a week, so I have to make the most of it. Marvellous exercise, swimming." Lowrie sat down, towel slung around his shoulders and patted his stomach ruefully. "Though you might not think so, looking at this. Anno Domini, too much good food and too little exercise, I'm afraid. That's why I decided to take up swimming. I only started recently. Marvellous exercise," he repeated. "You use up 480 calories per hour, you know."

Thanet privately thought that he would prefer to deny himself four or five slices of bread a week, the equivalent in caloric value. Lowrie, with the enthusiasm of the newly converted, was still talking about the benefits of his chosen form of exercise: "... muscle tone ... heart rate ... reduction in weight ..." punctuated Thanet's consideration of which subject to broach first. There was a lot to talk about.

He decided to begin on neutral ground and, when Lowrie eventually said, "But you haven't come to hear me talk about swimming," responded with, "I was wondering how you were getting on with checking through Dr Pettifer's files."

The jovial lines in Lowrie's face sagged. "I thought that might be why you're here. You're still working on the theory that he might have been murdered, then?"

"At present, yes."

"Are you sure? I mean, is it definite? Have you any conclusive evidence?"

"No. Not as yet. All imponderables, I'm afraid. But we can't afford to let the matter rest, just in case. Too much time would be lost."

"What about the post mortem?"

"Nothing significant. He was a healthy man, as you said. As a matter of interest, did you see him on the afternoon of the day he died?"

"Briefly, yes. Why?"

"Any sign of a cold?"

Lowrie considered. "Not as far as I remember, no."

"And the files?"

"Ah, yes." Lowrie sighed. "Well, I've been working on them every night, right through into the early hours . . ."

"You really should have allowed us to send someone to help you."

"No, I couldn't have done that, not under the circumstances. If we'd been certain it wasn't suicide, perhaps I would have felt justified, but as it was I felt I didn't even want Mrs Barnet to help. Anyway, I've been right through them now. I was going to give you a ring later on this afternoon. I'm afraid there's no one who seems to be even a remote possibility. I told you I didn't think there would be."

"Why not?"

"Two main reasons, I suppose. First, as I said before, if there had been anyone with a strong enough grievance against Pettifer to want to murder him, then I really can't believe that I wouldn't have heard about it. I simply couldn't see him attacking out of the blue.

From what I've heard—and I must admit I haven't had any experience of such a situation, thank God—such people usually kick up a terrible stink. Secondly, even if such a person did attempt murder, I can't see him using the drink-and-drugs method. It's too quiet, too—comfortable. He'd be wanting not only to release his own feelings of violence, but to make Pettifer suffer in the manner of his death, in payment for the suffering he'd caused. Wouldn't you agree?"

"Yes I do. So I suppose that's that. I apologise for wasting your time."

Lowrie shrugged. "I can see that it had to be done."

Thanet took his pipe from his pocket, held it up. "Do you mind?"

"Go ahead."

Thanet took out his tobacco pouch and began to fill the bowl. The next topic was a delicate one. How best to broach it without making Lowrie clam up, that was the question. He gave the little doctor an assessing glance, caught his eye.

"Come on, Inspector. Out with it. I can see you're wondering how to put what you want to ask me next."

Thanet gave a wry smile. "That was below the belt, Dr Lowrie. I'm the one who's supposed to be reading you, not the other way around."

"Long practice," said Lowrie, with a hint of smugness. "An essential weapon in the GP's armoury. You wouldn't believe how inarticulate some patients can be."

"I'll be frank, then. When I last saw you I asked if there were any problems with the practice which might have preyed on Pettifer's mind. I had the impression you were holding something back."

"I see." Lowrie looked away, through the tall glass doors and across the lake, as if the answer to his dilemma were hidden in the distant trees. "Well," he said at last, "I suppose there's no reason why I shouldn't tell you. If I don't, you won't rest until you find out from someone else... The truth is, Pettifer was very autocratic, and this caused certain tensions."

Introducing the first and only complete hardcover collection of Agatha Christie's mysteries

Now you can enjoy the
greatest mysteries ever written
in a magnificent
Home Library Edition.

Discover Agatha Christie's world of mystery, adventure and intrigue

Agatha Christie's timeless tales of mystery and suspense offer something for every reader —mystery fan or not— young and old alike. And now, you can build a complete hardcover library of her world-famous mysteries by subscribing to The Agatha Christie Mystery Collection.

This exciting Collection is your passport to a world where mystery reigns supreme. Volume after volume, you and your family will enjoy mystery reading at its very best.

You'll meet Agatha Christie's world-famous detectives like Hercule Poirot, Jane Marple, and the likeable Tommy and Tuppence Beresford.

In your readings, you'll visit Egypt, Paris, England and other exciting destinations where murder is always on the itinerary. And wherever you travel, you'll become deeply involved in some of the most ingenious and diabolical plots ever invented ... "cliff-hangers" that only Dame Agatha could create!

It all adds up to mystery reading that's so good ... it's almost criminal. And it's yours every month with The Agatha Christie Mystery Collection.

Solve the greatest mysteries of all time. The Collection contains all of Agatha Christie's classic works including *Murder on the Orient Express, Death on the Nile, And Then There Were None, The ABC Murders* and her ever-popular whodunit, *The Murder of Roger Ackroyd.*

Each handsome hardcover volume is Smythe sewn and printed on high quality acid-free paper so it can withstand even the most murderous treatment. Bound in Sussex-blue simulated leather with gold titling, The Agatha Christie Mystery Collection will make a tasteful addition to your living room, or den.

Ride the Orient Express for 10 days without obligation.
To introduce you to the Collection, we're inviting you to examine the classic mystery, *Murder on the Orient Express*, without risk or obligation. If you're not completely satisfied, just return it within 10 days and owe nothing.

However, if you're like the millions of other readers who love Agatha Christie's thrilling tales of mystery and suspense, keep *Murder on the Orient Express* and pay just $9.95 plus postage and handling.

You will then automatically receive future volumes once a month as they are published on a fully returnable, 10-day free-examination basis. No minimum purchase is required, and you may cancel your subscription at any time.

This unique collection is not sold in stores. It's available only through this special offer. So don't miss out, begin your subscription now. Just mail this card today.

☐ **Yes!** Please send me *Murder on the Orient Express* for a 10-day free-examination and enter my subscription to <u>The Agatha Christie Mystery Collection</u>. If I keep *Murder on the Orient Express*, I will pay just $9.95 plus postage and handling and receive one additional volume each month on a fully returnable 10-day free-examination basis. There is no minimum number of volumes to buy, and I may cancel my subscription at any time.   70110

Name_____

Address_____

City_____ State_____ Zip_____

QB123
Send No Money...
But Act Today!

BUSINESS REPLY MAIL

FIRST CLASS   PERMIT NO. 2154   HICKSVILLE, N.Y.

Postage will be paid by addressee:

The Agatha Christie
Mystery Collection
Bantam Books
P.O. Box 956
Hicksville, N.Y. 11802

"What sort of tensions?"

"Well, take policy decisions, for example. We all have different ideas on how the practice should be run and Pettifer tended to steamroller them. The situation wasn't in the least unusual. You'd find it in many group practices."

"Can you give me an example of the sort of decision you're talking about?"

"Well, take a very simple issue like the number of patients in the practice. As you know, we have around 11,500. Now, in an expanding area like Sturrenden you have a problem. Theoretically the quota of patients per doctor is supposed to be 2,500—don't ask me why, the powers that be have decided that—so in a practice with four partners that would mean ten thousand patients in toto. So, what happens when you get to eleven thousand? Do you close your list? If not, where do you stop?"

"And what did Dr Pettifer want to do?"

"Go on expanding. Let me explain. We all work in different ways. A man like Pettifer is brisk, thorough, a very good doctor diagnostically, as I said, but not very interested in his patients as people, tending to see them as walking case histories. Therefore he could get through his surgeries pretty briskly and be away on his visits by ten in the morning. Whereas Dr Braintree, for example, the youngest of the partners, is very interested in the psychosomatic origins of his patients' illnesses and therefore tends to spend much longer with them. So in any dispute over increasing our quotas—and, believe me, the question is a perennial headache—Pettifer would be for, Braintree against. And Pettifer, of course, would win."

"And you?"

"Would tend toward supporting Braintree. But it would make no difference. Pettifer had perfected the technique of overruling others with the minimum of fuss. He would listen but refuse to budge. If we became heated, he would become the opposite—ice-cold.

It never failed. But I can assure you, Inspector, that none of us ever felt sufficiently strongly about it to want to kill him off to get our own way."

Until now Lowrie had been completely frank, Thanet was sure of it, but suddenly he was convinced that he was lying—or at least skirting around the truth.

"Not about that, perhaps . . . but about something else?"

Lowrie tugged his towel more closely around his shoulders and sighed. "I suppose if I don't tell you, someone else will, and I'd rather you heard it from me and got the facts straight. There had been some trouble between Braintree and Pettifer."

"What kind of trouble?"

Braintree had apparently been precipitated into the classic doctor's nightmare. A prescription of his had been misread, too strong a dosage of a drug had been administered, and a patient had almost died. Despite the fact that the mistake had been as much the dispenser's as the doctor's, Pettifer had been furious, had refused to listen to reason. In his view the whole affair was inexcusable. Doctors' handwriting might be notoriously illegible, but it was criminally irresponsible not to ensure that quantities and strengths of dosage were crystal clear. Braintree, who tended in any case to be over-sensitive and who, to cap it all, was having serious marital problems, had had a minor nervous breakdown as a consequence and had only recently started seeing a low quota of patients again after a gap of nine months.

"So you can imagine, Pettifer hasn't been too popular lately. But I repeat, emphatically, that none of us hated him enough to kill him."

"Not even Braintree?"

"Strangely enough, Braintree least of all. In an odd way he even has reason to be grateful to Pettifer. Braintree's breakdown has brought him and his wife much closer. Perhaps they needed something as dramatic as that to bring them to their senses. They seem much happier together now."

"You haven't once mentioned Dr Fir. How about him? How did he get on with Dr Pettifer?"

"Well enough. If I haven't mentioned him it's because he's a very equable type who gets on well with most people . . . Look, I'm not trying to avoid the issue, but I am getting rather chilly. Have we nearly finished because if not I think I'd better get dressed."

"I'm afraid there are still one or two points I'd like to discuss with you . . . Sorry. You won't get your second dip after all, will you?"

Lowrie stood up. "In that case . . . I won't be long."

He headed for the changing rooms, a short, plump and slightly comic figure in his brief bathing trunks. Thanet watched him go with something approaching affection. He saw so many people in the course of his work and most of them were either nervous, aggressive or devious. Many were outright liars and almost all were on the defensive. It was a pleasure to come across a witness like Dr Lowrie, who was both frank and perceptive as well as cooperative.

Although, he reminded himself as he went across to the hot-drinks dispenser to fetch two cups of coffee, the most dangerous witness of all was the one who could convincingly present himself as credible while having something to conceal . . .

"I thought you could do with a hot drink," he said when Lowrie returned.

"That's very kind of you."

Thanet waited until Lowrie had sipped at his coffee before saying, "Would it surprise you, doctor, to learn that Mrs Pettifer has a lover?"

Lowrie hadn't known, Thanet was sure of it. Astonishment, disbelief, enlightenment flitted in swift succession across the little doctor's chubby features.

"But in that case . . . why all this talk about murder?"

"What do you mean?" Though Thanet knew, of course.

"Well, it's obvious, isn't it? I told you before, Inspector, Pettifer worshipped that wife of his. If he'd found

123

out she was being unfaithful to him...it's the one reason I could accept for his having committed suicide."

"Ah, but did he?" Thanet said softly. "Find out, I mean?"

Lowrie grimaced. "I see what you mean." He was silent for a while, thinking. "No," he said reluctantly at last. "I'd like to say yes, it would simplify matters so much, wouldn't it? But I must admit that, no, I don't think he did. If he had... No. He didn't know, I'm sure of it. Which of course leaves us back at square one, doesn't it? Except that...." Lowrie's eyes dilated slightly. "Oh," he said. "Oh, dear... This is beginning to look rather unpleasant, isn't it?"

"Shall we say, it opens up certain avenues of speculation. Which, forgive me, I really don't feel free to discuss with you... I wonder, Doctor Lowrie, if you could tell me a little more about Pettifer's attitude to children—or perhaps I should say, to fatherhood?"

"I'm not sure that I can add much to what I said last time."

"I just find it rather surprising that, although he made it clear he didn't want any children, he was apparently delighted when his wife told him she was pregnant."

"I don't think it was so much a matter of his not wanting any as trying to assure her he wouldn't expect her to give up her career to have them. Anyway, I told you, people react in peculiar ways to the prospect of parenthood. When a child is no longer a hypothesis but a reality... I suppose it's gut reaction rather than an intellectual response. The idea of being reproduced... there's something irresistible about it, to a man who's never had a child of his own."

"What was his attitude to the fact that his first wife couldn't have any?"

"Pretty phlegmatic. To have shown disappointment would, to him, have been disloyalty. Poor Diana, she really went through the mill over it. Had endless tests, a couple of minor operations, you know the sort of thing . . . And yet, strangely enough, I wouldn't have called her the maternal type, either."

"He was fond of her?"

"Fond is a good word. They got on well, had a good relationship, but a man like Pettifer only goes over-board once in a lifetime. That's why it hit him so hard when it happened. I don't think he could ever have visualised feeling as he did about Gemma."

"Why did he marry the first time, then, do you think?"

"It was really almost a business arrangement, I should say. An arranged marriage, though with the consent and cooperation of both parties. Diana was an only child and her father was at that time the senior partner in the practice, and on the verge of retirement. He wanted to see her settled, she wanted a home and a husband and Pettifer . . . well, I suppose he saw the advantages of the match when it was offered him on a plate. And as I said, I think he was genuinely fond of Diana. Fond enough to go along with it when she eventually decided she wanted to adopt." Lowrie gave an indulgent smile. "His mother-in-law, Diana's mother, was a character. When his father-in-law died and she moved away, I really missed her for a time."

"She's still alive?"

"So far as I know. She was much younger than her husband. I have a feeling she went to live with her mother, Diana's grandmother. The old lady must be pretty ancient by now, if she's still with us."

"Where did they go, do you know?"

"Somewhere near Headcorn, I believe. I think I remember hearing something about converting an oast house."

"What was her name?"

"Blaidon. Dr Blaidon, her husband, was the founder member of the practice. At that time it was based in Pine Lodge."

"I had the impression that Dr Pettifer's first wife was a wealthy woman."

"That's right. Her grandfather made a small fortune in the grain business, but her father wasn't interested in carrying it on. He'd always wanted to be a doctor and so Diana's grandfather agreed to set him up in this practice. Dr Blaidon and Pettifer were alike in that having a generous private income didn't stop them from working just as hard as if their living depended on it."

"I wonder how many of us would do that, if we had the choice," Thanet said with a smile, getting to his feet.

"Not I, for one," Lowrie responded. "Oh, I might have once, but now . . . well, it won't be too long before I retire and I must say I'm looking forward to it."

They parted amicably.

The interview with Dr Lowrie had taken rather longer than Thanet had thought it would. He decided to call at the office to see if Lineham was back before trying to get hold of Dr Braintree.

Lineham was on the telephone.

"The adoption agency," he said, when he had finished the call. "I got the address from Dr Pettifer's files. I thought it might be worth checking to see what they thought of the Pettifers as adoptive parents."

"Good idea. And . . . ?"

"If Pettifer wasn't too keen, he certainly didn't show it. They were considered an eminently suitable couple."

"Hmm . . . Well, it was worth a phone call, anyway. What else have you found out?"

"It looks as though Andrew's in the clear, you'll be glad to hear. He was playing in an away match in Sussex on Monday afternoon. The coach didn't get back until eight-thirty, then it was supper, baths and bed. He shares a room with two other boys and one of them was sick at about eleven o'clock that night. Andrew fetched the school matron and helped transfer some of the boy's stuff to the sanitorium."

"Good." It was no more than Thanet had expected, but he was still relieved. "What about Mrs Price?"

Lineham grinned broadly. "D'you know what she was up to? Lecturing, if you please!"

"Lecturing?"

"Well, in a manner of speaking. She was giving a talk to the Merrisham Women's Institute on 'Herbs in the Modern Kitchen.'"

"Good for her. I hope they paid her a nice fat fee."

"I don't know about that, but there's no doubt she was there all right. Arrived at the time she said she did, spent the night with her sister, caught the workmen's bus back early the next morning—according to the sister, anyway."

"And you believed her."

"Yes, I did. In any case, the WI meeting didn't break up until ten-fifteen and then Mrs Price's sister asked some friends back to have coffee with them. That took another hour or so. So unless Mrs Price had a magic carpet..."

"Did you check up with the friends?"

"One of the women concerned happened to come in while I was talking to Mrs Price's sister. And yes, she confirmed it all—I did it as tactfully as I could. I didn't want to cause a lot of gossip unnecessarily."

"Fair enough. Interesting, though, isn't it? That's why she asked Pettifer for the evening off so far ahead. Three months ago, didn't she say?"

"That's right. I remember."

"He knew as long ago as that," murmured Thanet. Somehow, the thought now seemed significant, though he couldn't see why it should be.

"On the way back I called in at the Sitting Duck," said Lineham. "It's owned by a chap called Frith. He and his wife wait at table when they're very busy and they both helped serve the Pettifers on the night of the anniversary dinner. They remember the occasion well because Pettifer made such a production of it—a special meal, ordered in advance, all his wife's favourites... champagne and roses waiting on the table when they arrived..."

"She certainly brought out the romantic in him, didn't she? How did they seem together that evening?"

"All lovey-dovey. Long looks, holding hands, that sort of thing . . ."

The telephone rang. It was the lab. They'd run the tests for paracetamol first, at Thanet's request, with negative results. With the field now wide open for the drug that killed Pettifer, it might be days before they came up with an answer. They did, however, confirm that Pettifer had taken a milky drink some hours before he died.

"So she was lying about the paracetamol," Lineham said with satisfaction.

"Presumably. Though I don't see why she should have. And I can't really see that it gets us much further."

The telephone rang again. And this time it was important. Lineham could tell by the narrowing of Thanet's eyes, that alert, focusing look. He waited, eagerly.

"Lee does own an old Morgan," Thanet said, putting the phone down. "And it really would be too much of a coincidence if there were two of them in this case. I think we're temporarily entitled to assume that the one parked near Pettifer's house that night was Lee's, don't you? Come on, I think it's time we paid another visit to Mrs Pettifer. She really has got some explaining to do now."

She might be a good actress, he thought as he and Lineham hurried down the stairs, but he didn't see how she was going to talk herself out of this one.

15

It was dark by now and, illuminated from within, the stained-glass panels on either side of the front door of

Pine Lodge glowed sapphire and emerald, ruby and gold as Lineham brought the car to a halt on the gravelled drive.

It was some minutes before Mrs Price answered the door. She had evidently been upstairs, for they glimpsed a descending blur of movement before she called out nervously, "Who is it?"

"Inspector Thanet, Mrs Price."

Bolts were drawn, a chain rattled and the key turned in the lock before the door swung open. "I'm sorry," she said. "I seem to be a bundle of nerves these days. I am glad you've come, Inspector," she added as the two men stepped past her into the hall. "It's Mrs Pettifer." And her eyes darted sideways and upwards at the stairs.

Thanet noticed that she was wearing her wrap-over flowered apron inside out.

"What's the matter with Mrs Pettifer?" he said.

"I don't know." Mrs Price clasped her hands together and began to massage the back of one hand with the fingers of the other, as if trying to erase her anxiety. "She's been up there for hours, ever since lunch in fact. She said she felt tired, she was going to lie down for a bit. And now, well, she's locked the door and she won't answer."

Thanet and Lineham exchanged a glance, the same thought in both their minds.

"We'll go up and take a look, shall we?" Thanet set off up the stairs without waiting for an answer. Lineham followed and Mrs Price came behind, more slowly.

No light showed beneath Gemma Pettifer's door. Thanet knocked gently. "Mrs Pettifer," he called in a low voice, trying to betray none of the urgency he felt. "It's Inspector Thanet. I'd like a word, if I may."

No answer.

Thanet called again, a little more loudly, but still there was no sound from within. Finally, "Mrs Pettifer," he said, very distinctly, "you must realise we're getting worried about you. Please, open the door, or I'm afraid we'll have to force it."

Was that a sound? He strained to listen more intently. Then light spilled across the toes of his shoes. He felt taut nerves relax and, glancing over his shoulder at the others, saw his own relief mirrored in their faces.

The sounds within were more distinct now and he waited without urgency, content to be patient. Finally, the door opened.

"Are you all right, Mrs Pettifer?" he said.

A fatuous question. Patently, she wasn't. She looked dazed, drugged—sleeping pills, perhaps?—and her long hair was tangled, matted almost, as if it hadn't been combed for a very long time. Her robe, hastily dragged on, imperfectly concealed her swollen belly and with one hand she clutched it together across her breasts. With the other she supported herself against the door jamb, swaying a little and sagging as if she were on the verge of collapse.

"Perhaps you ought to lie down again," he murmured, acting swiftly. Deftly he stepped around her, began to persuade her back towards the bed, half supporting her. They were almost there when he sensed the beginnings of resistance, a stiffening of her body, and he could almost feel the effort with which she stopped, set her shoulders back and stepped away from his arm.

"It's all right, Inspector, thank you. I . . . it's just that I was still half asleep."

It was an admirable effort, but the flatness of her tone betrayed her. It had been far more than that, he could tell. He studied her face closely, shocked by her bleached pallor, the bruised hollows beneath her eyes and the dullness of the eyes themselves. Delayed shock, he judged. It would be inhuman to question her in this state. She needed a doctor, not a policeman.

She was asking him what he wanted to see her about, seating herself on the chaise-longue near the window.

"It doesn't matter," Thanet said. "It can wait until

tomorrow. I can see you're not well. I apologise for disturbing you."

Some of his colleagues, he knew, would find his attitude laughable. The weaker your adversary the better, they would say. And on occasion, with case-hardened villains, he would agree with them. But in a case like this, when even now there was no certainty of murder, only a suspicion of it, the idea of taking advantage of Gemma Pettifer's condition sickened him. He began to move towards the door.

"No, wait!" She lifted her hand imperiously. "I really would rather hear it now," she said. "Otherwise"—and she gave a travesty of a smile—"I shall lie awake all night worrying about it."

She might have wanted it to appear a joke, but Thanet could see that she meant it. He hesitated.

"I don't think you're really up to it."

"Nonsense. I'm fine, really. I told you. I was very soundly asleep, that's all, when you knocked. And don't apologise again, it's not necessary. Now, please, do sit down, Inspector. It's all right, Mrs Price. Don't look so worried. Give me a few minutes after the Inspector has gone and I'll be down for supper. Something light. A little cold chicken and some salad, I think."

It was a brave attempt and Thanet saluted it by giving in, seating himself on the chair towards which she had waved him. Lineham sat down gingerly on the edge of the bed.

"Now then, Inspector," she said. She folded her hands in her lap and looked at him expectantly.

"Would it surprise you, Mrs Pettifer, to learn that whatever it was that killed your husband, it wasn't paracetamol?"

"Not really. Because I still can't, and won't, believe he committed suicide. In which case I wouldn't expect him to have been given what we normally use."

"But you're still certain that it was paracetamol you gave him earlier in the evening?"

"Oh, yes, absolutely. I told you, we never kept anything else in the house—apart from the drugs my husband would carry in his bag, of course. But I would never have dreamt of touching those."

"Did you actually see your husband take the tablets?"

She frowned, thinking back. "I don't think so . . . No, I remember now, I went back into my room. I was more or less ready to leave by then and I realised I'd forgotten to put out the typescript I wanted to take with me—the play I wanted to discuss with my agent."

"Could you tell us exactly what you did do, from the time you came upstairs?"

"I'll try. Let me see . . . I got changed while my husband was having a bath. I'd made up earlier, before he got home. When I heard him come out of the bathroom I went downstairs, made the cocoa and took it up to his room. He was in bed by then. I put the mug down on his bedside table and went into the bathroom for the paracetamol. I returned to his room, handed him the tablets, then went back into my room. I took the typescript from the drawer in my bedside table and laid it beside my handbag on the bed. Then I went back into my husband's room, to say goodbye to him."

"Had he taken the tablets?"

"Well, I assumed he had, naturally. After all, he wasn't a child, Inspector. I didn't feel I had to stand over him and watch while he took them."

"No, I can see that. What was he doing?"

"Sitting up in bed, holding the mug of cocoa."

"Drinking it?"

"He had both hands clasped around it, as if he was cold. When I came in, he put it down on his bedside table."

"Was there anything else on the table?"

She passed her hand over her forehead, as if the strain of recalling all these details was beginning to tell on her. "No, I don't think so. No, I'm sure there wasn't."

"Did he say anything?"

"He said . . . he said . . ." To Thanet's dismay her face

crumpled and her eyes filled with tears. She reached blindly for a box of tissues which stood on a little table beside her.

"Look, I really think we'd better leave this till morning," said Thanet.

She shook her head vehemently. "No. No, it's all right. Really. It's just that . . ." She blew her nose. "It was the last thing he ever said to me, you see, and I didn't know . . . He said, 'Don't kiss me, darling. I don't want you to catch my cold.'" Her lips twisted. "It just seems such a . . . trivial way of ending a life together."

Thanet had heard this many times before. "If only I'd known," people would say. To be deprived of saying goodbye made them feel cheated, as though some premonition should have warned them to invest the occasion with a proper dignity. He sometimes felt that the ideal way to live would be always to treat each day, each encounter with loved ones, as one's last. Only thus could one avoid the endless self-reproach, self-recrimination, with which so many flagellate themselves after a sudden loss. A counsel of perfection, of course, he knew that . . .

"If only I'd insisted on staying . . ." she was saying.

"It's pointless reproaching yourself in that way. Your husband insisted, you said."

"I know. All the same . . . If I'd stayed, he might still be alive now."

"That's really most unlikely. If someone is determined to commit suicide . . ."

"But he didn't!" she flared. "How often do I have to tell you? He couldn't have . . ."

"So you keep on saying. But have you ever given any thoughts to the mechanics of it?"

"What do you mean?"

"Well, we both know that as a doctor he would never have been so stupid as to go to bed with a container of pills and a bottle of alcohol on his bedside table. Agreed?"

She nodded.

"And so, if we rule out both suicide and accident, we are left with only one other alternative."

"Murder," she whispered. "Go on, say it. I've said it over and over again in my mind and now I've just got to say it aloud. Murder, murder, murd..." She was shaking and her mouth was out of control. She pressed the back of one hand against her lips and stared at Thanet, her eyes huge and pleading, begging for understanding.

"Mrs Pettifer," said Thanet. "I really must insist that we continue this conversation tomorrow morning. After a good night's rest..."

"But don't you see, I won't get a good night's rest if we stop now! Look, I'm sorry... It was just such a relief to get it out at last... Just give me a few moments and I'll be all right..." She put her head back and took several deep, rhythmic breaths. Then she ran her hand through her hair, faced him gravely. "You see," she said. "I'm fine now."

Thanet did see. He saw that Gemma Pettifer was able to discipline her physical reactions to a quite remarkable degree, somehow to divorce mind and body so that her outward behaviour gave no indication of her true feelings. It was, he supposed, an essential element of the actor's craft. He had heard of actors who could be in a towering rage behind the scenes and could simply switch that anger off, could walk on stage and take part in the sweetest of love scenes without betraying even a hint of the true state of their emotions. So, how much could he believe of what Gemma allowed him to see? And yet... He studied her near-haggard appearance, the drained pallor of her skin... She had not known that she was going to have an audience tonight. Was he being unjust to her? Or—and he could not dismiss the possibility—was this the face of guilt?

She was waiting, watching him intently. "You were saying that we are left with only one other alternative, Inspector."

Mentally, he shrugged his shoulders. If this was what she wanted...

"Murder, as you so rightly said, Mrs Pettifer. But if someone did kill your husband, how did he manage to do it? There was no sign of a forced entry, so how did he get in? And how did he administer the overdose?"

"Well . . ." She fell silent, her eyes abstracted. "I suppose," she said at last, "if it was some patient of my husband's, someone with a grudge against him . . . One does hear of such things, after all. Someone who felt that he had been badly treated, or who had lost a relation—a wife, or even a child—and felt that my husband had been neglectful or had prescribed the wrong course of treatment . . ."

Or a junior doctor who felt he'd been given a raw deal, thought Thanet. "Do you know of any such person?"

"No. But then, I wouldn't have. My husband never discussed his work with me." She shivered and drew her robe more closely about her.

Thanet remembered her revulsion towards any kind of sickness.

"Go on," he said.

"Well, my husband was a very conscientious man. Even if he hadn't been feeling well himself, if a patient had come knocking at the door Arnold might well have gone down to see what was the matter."

"Would he have let him in?"

"Oh, I should think so. In any case, he would hardly have stayed talking on the doorstep in his dressing gown, would he?"

"And then?"

"Well, if the man had appeared distressed, Arnold could have offered him a drink . . ." She grimaced. "No, to be honest, I can't see Arnold offering a patient a drink . . . Well, then, could this visitor have knocked my husband out, carried him upstairs and then have dissolved the tablets, got him to drink the solution while he was still dazed, before he came around properly?"

"But your husband wasn't knocked out. There was no sign of a blow to the head or indeed of any other sign of violence."

135

"Then it must have been someone he knew socially, someone to whom Arnold would have offered a drink. Then the drug could have been slipped into Arnold's glass . . ." Her eyes flew open wide.

"What is it?"

"I've just thought. How stupid of me not to have seen it before, how incredibly stupid . . ."

"What?"

"Desmond Braintree! There was all that performance about an illegible prescription!" Breathlessly she related once more the facts given to Thanet by Dr Lowrie. "Don't you see?" she finished.

Had she had Braintree in mind right from the beginning of this conversation? Thanet wondered. Had he been watching once more a carefully calculated performance?

"Mrs Pettifer," he said, avoiding a direct answer, "let me just get this clear. You are suggesting that your husband's death was murder, carefully arranged to look like suicide."

"Yes," she said impatiently. "Of course I am, yes. And . . ."

"Please, just a moment. Now, if that is so, perhaps you could help me to understand one or two points which are puzzling me."

"By all means, if I can."

Thanet gave her an assessing look. Was she fit to be challenged? He could scarcely stop now. He seemed to have manoeuvred himself into a position where he had no choice but to go on. And after all, he told himself, she had several times been given the opportunity to call a halt, if she so wished.

"First, then," he said, ticking off his fingers, "you tell us that your husband had a cold. But he didn't. Two, you tell us that you gave him paracetamol, but we know that he didn't take any. Three . . ."

He paused. Gemma Pettifer was sitting quite still on the very edge of the chaise-longue, leaning forward and staring at him as if mesmerised.

"Three. You say that when you left your husband in bed that night there was nothing on his bedside table. But *your* fingerprints as well as his were on the bottle of port which we found on that table after his death and what is more your fingerprints and *yours alone* were found on both the empty glass and on the container which had held the tablets that killed him . . . Mike, quick!"

Gemma Pettifer's eyes had rolled up, her body had begun to sag, to slide. Both men leapt forward.

They just managed to catch her before she hit the floor.

16

"She's guilty, isn't she?" said Lineham. "I mean, the way she reacted . . ."

"I don't know," Thanet snapped. "And that's the truth."

They were driving back to the office. When Gemma Pettifer had collapsed they had carried her across to her bed and summoned first Mrs Price, then Dr Barson, who had come at once. Thanet was still smarting from the memory of Barson's comments when he had seen his patient's condition.

"I should have trusted my own judgement," Thanet growled, "and not gone on when she insisted. I could see she was . . ."

Lineham wasn't listening. "It's obvious she was just trying to put us off the scent by pointing us in the direction of Dr Braintree. We surely don't need much more before we . . ."

"Mike."

". . . charge her. We still haven't questioned her . . ."

"Mike!"

". . . about the car, of course. But if she was here that night . . ."

"MIKE!"

Lineham cast an astonished glance at Thanet, who very rarely raised his voice. "Yes?"

"Just ease your foot off that accelerator, will you? You're making me nervous. And stop letting your imagination run away with you."

"Imagination! Those things you mentioned to her weren't imagination, were they? Nor was her reaction . . ."

"Maybe not. But neither are they conclusive enough to make me want to charge her. Just because she's a liar, it doesn't necessarily mean that she's a murderer."

"I can see that. But the fingerprints . . ."

"Their significance could be demolished by any good defence counsel. The container could well have been used before, handled by her on some previous occasion. Ditto the glass."

"But the fact that his prints weren't on either of them . . . !"

"I agree, that's difficult to explain away. Nevertheless, it's not enough for a conviction and you know it."

"Then there's the note. If Pettifer didn't write it, she'd have had a better opportunity to practise copying his handwriting than anyone."

"Yes, *if*. We still don't know it wasn't genuine. Anyway, you know how easy it is to come unstuck over circumstantial evidence. We need more than that, much more, before she could be charged."

"But there is more! There's motive . . ."

Grudgingly Thanet conceded that he had to agree to that.

"And opportunity, too. Now that we know Lee's car was seen in the vicinity that night."

"We don't *know*," Thanet objected. "We're just assuming."

"Well, yes, I realise that, but you said yourself that it

would be too much of a coincidence if there were two vintage Morgans in this case."

"I'm well aware what I said," snapped Thanet.

Lineham knew when to let something drop. He allowed several minutes to pass before he said diffidently, "As a matter of interest, sir, why didn't you bring the matter of the car up first? I mean, that was why we went to see her, after all."

"Honestly, Mike, I sometimes wonder if you're human! You could see for yourself the state she was in . . ."

"If it was genuine. Well," he said, to Thanet's furious look, "you did say yourself that it was difficult to tell if she was acting or not."

"All right, Mike. Look, I'm sorry. There's no reason why you should be getting the sharp edge of my tongue, just because I'm feeling guilty about her passing out like that. But it was a genuine collapse. Dr Barson was pretty unequivocal about that, wasn't he?"

They exchanged rueful grins.

"Look," Thanet said, "I concede all the points you're making. Dammit, I know that practically everything new we learn seems to point to her, and yet . . . The truth is, Mike, there's something about this case that makes me very uneasy."

"Uneasy?"

"Yes. It's all wrong, somehow. Not just the things which don't add up. It feels wrong. And I just can't see why. What is more, I simply don't understand why, if she did kill him and set it up to look like suicide, she should be handing us the theory on a plate, putting the noose around her own neck, so to speak."

Lineham had no answer to that. They had arrived back now, and they climbed the stairs to the office in silence.

Thanet checked quickly to see if anything interesting had come in, but nothing had. He plumped down into his chair with a sigh. His back gave a protesting twinge. This was an infallible signal that it was time he went home. Ever since he had injured it a few years ago it

had played up when he was tired. He eased himself
into a more comfortable position and glanced at his
watch: half past seven and the day's reports still to do.

"Better get on with it, I suppose," he said.

Lineham nodded, pulled his typewriter towards him
and began to peck at it, two-fingered.

But Thanet remained quite still, gazing into space.
Gemma Pettifer bothered him. His feeling of guilt had
ebbed and he was angry with himself for having over-
reacted. After all, he told himself irritably, if she were
guilty, he simply could not allow diffidence to put a
straitjacket on him. Sooner or later she would have to
be tackled and that was that. But next time he would
consult Dr Barson first, insist that Barson accompany
him, if possible. He made a mental note to ring Barson
first thing in the morning.

Meanwhile, there was another possible approach to
the problem.

"Fancy a trip to London tomorrow, Mike?"

Lineham raised an abstracted face. "Sir?"

Thanet explained. It was time to tackle Gemma's
lover, Rowan Lee. Also, the night porter at the Lombard
should be questioned, to see if he had noticed the pair
return to the hotel in the early hours of Tuesday
morning. Lineham would have to go to London alone.
If Barson agreed, Thanet wanted to see Gemma Pettifer
again in the morning. Afterwards, he would interview
Dr Braintree and then, if he could trace her . . . Here
he grew vague, despite Lineham's evident curiosity.

Thanet returned to his musing. Gemma Pettifer. She
really was an enigma. If only he could make up his
mind whether her distress was genuine . . . Thinking
back, he was becoming more and more convinced that
it was. In anyone else he would unhesitatingly have
diagnosed delayed shock, perhaps even the first stages
of a plunge into clinical depression. And if that were
true . . . well, he didn't understand it. By all accounts
she was hard, self-seeking, had married her husband for

security rather than love. He would have expected a
show of grief, yes, but this...

With a sigh, he settled down to his reports.

17

Thanet rang Dr Barson at a quarter to nine next morning, as early as he felt he decently could. Barson was
testy. It was his morning off surgery but he had a
number of visits to make. And he wasn't happy about
Gemma Pettifer being questioned until he had seen her
again. She was one of the first people on his list this
morning.

"In that case," said Thanet eagerly, "suppose I meet
you there, wait until you've seen her. If you think she's
fit, I'll talk to her, if not, I'll leave it for today. But
frankly, I really do need to see her if it's at all possible.
If you like, you could stay with her while I talk to her,
and if you think it's too much for her, I'll stop." He
couldn't, he felt, be much more cooperative or considerate than that.

Barson grudgingly agreed, muttering that he had better things to do with his time but that, if it was
that urgent...

It was, Thanet assured him, and the matter was
settled; they would meet at Pine Lodge in half an hour.

When Thanet turned in between the white-painted
pillars, Barson's car was already parked in the drive.
The doctor had been with Mrs Pettifer for a quarter of
an hour or so, Mrs Price said.

"How is she this morning?"

Mrs Price grimaced. "Quiet. Wouldn't eat any
breakfast."

It was interesting, Thanet thought as he waited in the

drawing room for Barson to come down and give his
verdict, that Mrs Price was showing this degree of
concern. Initially he had been certain that she didn't
like Gemma, was covertly hostile to her. Perhaps Gemma's rapidly advancing pregnancy was arousing Mrs
Price's protective instincts. But Thanet suspected that
it was more than that. If, at some point over the last
few days, Mrs Price had had a belated change of heart
towards her late employer's wife, it could only be
because she believed her to be genuinely grief-stricken
by Pettifer's death. And if Gemma had convinced a
hostile Mrs Price of her sincerity . . .

Barson entered the room. "I should think you could
see her briefly now, if you must." Barson was both
grudging and disapproving. "She insists she wants to
see you anyway."

"How is she this morning?" Thanet asked, for the
second time.

"I suppose one could say, as well as might be expected,"
Barson said sardonically. "After all, she has just had a
severe shock in her husband's death, and she is pregnant, we must remember that. We don't want to put
the child at risk too."

"Believe it or not, doctor, I agree, wholeheartedly.
Which is why I rang you this morning. You may think
me inhuman, but I am only doing my job, after all. I'm
sure that your work too has distasteful aspects, that you
sometimes have to do things that you really would
prefer to avoid but can't . . ."

Barson looked a little shamefaced. "You're right, and
I'm sorry, Inspector. I know I must have come over hot
and strong last night. But you in turn must appreciate
that my first concern has to be for my patient."

"I do," Thanet said. "Naturally. And now, having
reached some measure of agreement, perhaps we could
go up. And I meant it when I said stop me if you think
she's not up to it. She wants to see me, you said . . . ?"

Gemma was still in bed, leaning back against the
piled-up pillows as if exhausted. Her hair had been

brushed back and tied loosely at the nape of her neck, accentuating the pallor of her skin and that taut, stretched look about the eyes which Thanet didn't like one little bit. Privately, he thought she looked worse than last night and was glad that Barson was there. Even now he hesitated. He really did not want a miscarriage on his conscience. But the decision was quickly taken out of his hands. As soon as she saw him, urgency flared in Gemma's eyes, dispelling that frightening blankness.

"Inspector," she said. "I'm so glad you came. There's something I must tell you. Please . . ." and she indicated the chair beside the bed.

Thanet sat down and then watched with amused admiration as she skilfully persuaded Dr Barson that his presence was unnecessary but that she would be grateful if he could wait downstairs for a little while longer in case she needed him. Thanet reminded himself not to underestimate her in the coming interview.

When Barson had reluctantly left the room she said, "I really am glad you came, Inspector. It's been worrying me . . . You see, I haven't been quite frank with you."

So, confession time, thought Thanet, wondering what was coming. He settled down to listen.

She was frowning, her fingers plucking nervously at the bedspread. "You remember I told you that, when I realised my husband wasn't well that night, I suggested that I cancel my trip to London, but that he insisted I still go?"

She waited for Thanet's nod before continuing.

"Well, I wasn't very happy about it, as you can imagine, especially as Mrs Price was away for the night, but I had been so looking forward to discussing this new part with my agent—I hardly ever seem to go out, these days—so I said that I would compromise, come straight home after dinner instead of spending the night in town as I'd intended. But he said no, there was no need, a cold was nothing to fuss about and he'd be perfectly all right. Then he suggested that, if it would make me any happier, I could give him a ring about ten o'clock, before he settled down for the night. It wouldn't disturb him, he said, he had no intention of going to sleep during the evening in case he then wouldn't be able to sleep through the night.

"Well, it seemed a good idea, so that's what I did. I had dinner, got back to the hotel about ten with . . . with Mr Lee. We . . . we didn't want to be seen going up to my room together, so he went into the bar for a drink and followed me up ten minutes later. Meanwhile I rang Arnold . . ."

Her fingers had increased their nervous activity and now she plucked at a thread which had worked loose. "He sounded very strange . . ."

"Strange?"

"Well, urgent. In a state. Most uncharacteristic, I assure you. Arnold was the last man in the world to flap about anything."

"What did he say, exactly?"

"He said, 'Gemma, for God's sake get down here as fast as you can.'"

"Go on."

"I asked him what was the matter, but he wouldn't tell me, said he'd give me the details when I got here. Then he said, 'You will come, won't you?' So I promised I'd leave immediately and he rang off."

"Was he speaking clearly?"

She frowned. "What do you . . . Oh, you mean, was he already drugged, by then? No, he sounded perfectly coherent."

"So what did you do?" Thanet knew, of course, but he wanted to hear the story from Gemma herself.

"Well, I was frightened, naturally. It was so unlike Arnold to be alarmist. I really thought it must be something serious. But it was too late to catch the ten-twenty from Victoria and I knew the next train wasn't until twelve-fifteen. If I waited for that, I wouldn't get home until after two—and if it was that urgent . . . So I asked Rowan if he would drive me down." She grimaced. "I know it doesn't sound very good, getting my lover to answer my husband's SOS, but I really couldn't think what else to do. I could have taken a taxi, I suppose, but Rowan was there, on the spot, and his car was parked near by and it seemed the obvious solution. He wasn't very pleased, of course, but he agreed and we left at once."

"You checked out of the hotel?"

"I didn't bother. I didn't want to be held up. They know me there, I always use the same hotel when I stay in town, so I knew it wouldn't matter about the bill, I could always settle up later. So I just stuffed my nightdress and my toilet stuff into my shoulder bag and left. That's all I ever bother to take when I'm only away for one night. Anyway, we got to Sturrenden about a quarter to twelve. Rowan's car practically came out of the Ark, so it took longer than I'd hoped. I was on tenterhooks all the way, and when I got here and found that Arnold was out, I was furious, I can tell you."

Thanet was astounded. "Out?"

"Well, that's what I thought at the time. Now, of course, looking back..." She bit her lip. "He must already have been..." Tears filled her eyes and she dashed them away impatiently. "If only I'd *known*..."

Thanet waited for a few moments until she had regained her composure and then said, "Look, if you want to stop there for the moment..."

"No! I'd rather finish, get it over with. You can't imagine how I've dreaded telling you."

Thanet could. And if her story was true... Suspend judgement, he told himself. Let's hear the rest of it. "If you're sure, then..."

"I am."

"Well, then, let's go back a little. When you arrived, what did you do, exactly?"

"Well, when we got here the house was in darkness and I was surprised. I suppose I'd expected lights to be blazing everywhere, a sort of signal of a state of emergency. So I was a bit nonplussed. Rowan said he'd hang around for a little while until he was sure everything was all right, and we arranged a signal, switching the bedroom light on and off twice, if I didn't need him. He was to wait a quarter of an hour . . . Anyway, when I got to the front door I found I couldn't get in. It was locked and bolted on the inside. I tried throwing gravel up at our bedroom window, but nothing happened. So then I went around to the back. I knew I wouldn't be able to get in that way because I didn't have a key, but I did think that there might possibly be a window open or something . . . not that I particularly wanted to go crawling through windows in the middle of the night like this"—and she indicated the mound of her belly beneath the bedclothes—"but I wasn't thinking very coherently . . . And then I saw that Arnold's car had gone from the garage. And, as I said, I was *furious*."

"Furious?"

"Well, I immediately thought that he'd gone out on a night call. At that point, you see, I had no idea that he hadn't come home in the car that afternoon as usual, that he'd left it at the Centre. So I assumed that he'd done what he always did when he had to go out at night, left the front door locked and bolted and let himself out the back way—it's much closer to the garage."

"But he wasn't on duty that night."

"No, I know. But if there'd been some emergency, if the doctor on duty had already been called out and someone urgently needed treatment . . . It's happened before. My husband was a very conscientious doctor, Inspector. He wouldn't have allowed the fact that he was theoretically off duty to stop him answering a call—or the fact that he was feeling under the weather himself, either. So, as I say, I was livid. To think that he'd dragged me all the way down from London worrying myself sick and then had the nerve to go out knowing I wouldn't even be able to get into the house . . ."

"But didn't you wonder why he should have done such

a thing? I mean, by all accounts your husband was most solicitous for your welfare..."

"Of course I wondered! I went back and told Rowan what had happened and we... well, we decided there was only one conclusion we could draw..." She broke off, lips trembling.

Thanet could see what was coming but he said nothing, simply waited.

She glanced at him uneasily and then said, "We thought that Arnold must somehow have found out about us and that he'd arranged the whole thing on purpose, to punish me."

"You mean, he knew before you left, and stage-managed the whole performance—the cold, the phone call...?"

"Oh, no. Absolutely not. I'd swear to that. When I left him that evening, everything was as usual between us, I'm certain of it. No, we assumed that somehow he'd found out during the course of the evening."

"How?"

"I've no idea. A phone call from a so-called well-meaning 'friend,' I suppose... anything... Anyway, that's what we thought. So, as you can imagine, I was dreading getting home next morning. I knew he'd be in, it was his morning off. And then, when I found out what had really happened... I was *there*, don't you see, at the crucial time. If I'd somehow got in, found him then, it might not have been too late to save him..." She buried her face in her hands, began to weep.

"I'll call Dr Barson."

"Just a moment..." She lifted a streaming face, put out a hand to restrain him.

Thanet waited while she took a tissue from a box on the bedside table, mopped at her eyes and blew her nose.

"I know you don't think much of me," she said at last in a low voice. "And I don't blame you." Her nose wrinkled in self-disgust. "The ungrateful, unfaithful wife... I've played the part so many times on stage it

147

didn't seem wrong, somehow, to play it in real life. I don't know whether you can believe it, but I'll tell you this." She lifted her head with something like pride. "My husband loved me very much, but I never deceived him in *that* way—never pretended to love him in return. He said he didn't mind, he was prepared to wait, that he'd be such a perfect husband that I'd be bound to grow to love him in the end. He made a joke of it. The irony is . . ." and her composure began to slip again, "that it was true. I had grown to love him . . . but I never realised, until it was too late."

18

Predictably, Barson was furious to find Gemma in tears.

"I thought you promised not to upset her," he muttered angrily.

"She insisted . . ."

"Then you should have over-ruled her," Barson snapped.

Gemma lifted a drowned face. "Please don't blame Inspector Thanet, Charles," she said. "He wanted to stop, several times, but I just wouldn't let him. Anyway," she said, pausing to blow her nose, "it may not look like it at the moment but it's an enormous relief to have got all that off my chest. I'll be much better now, you'll see."

If Barson was curious he did not show it, simply said a dismissive goodbye to Thanet, who obediently left the room.

Downstairs, Thanet hesitated. There was something he would like to ask Barson. He decided to wait.

Barson came down about ten minutes later. "I thought you'd gone," he said curtly.

"No. There's something I wanted to . . ."

"You're not seeing her again today and that's that. I refuse to risk it. There's a limit to what someone in her condition can take."

"No, no. It's you I wanted to see."

Barson's anger had carried them through the hall and across the drive. Now he paused in the act of getting into his car. "Me?"

"Yes. It occurred to me . . . You told me you'd known Dr Pettifer a long time. That you were medical students together."

"That's right."

"I wonder if you could tell me . . . Would you say that he was a vindictive man?"

The question took Barson by surprise. Slowly he straightened up and stood with one hand on the car door, the other on the roof. "Vindictive . . . ?"

Thanet waited.

"I wouldn't have said so," Barson said slowly. "But then, we've always been on good terms even if we haven't been what I'd call close friends."

"I know. That's why I was wondering about your student days. You must have seen quite a lot of each other then . . ."

"There was one incident," Barson said slowly, with that look of surprise which Thanet had often seen on the face of a witness recalling an incident long buried in the past. "I'd forgotten all about it. There was a character called Taylor, who was a bit of a practical joker— well, I suppose there usually is, in any fair-sized group of students. Arnold of course was totally lacking in any sense of humour. He was very serious-minded, dedicated to his work even then . . . Look, I'm not sure that I want to go on talking about this."

"Dr Barson," Thanet said softly, "you are an intelligent man. I find myself wondering why you have never questioned the necessity of our repeated visits to Mrs Pettifer."

Barson's eyes slid away from Thanet's. Then he lifted

149

his hands in a little gesture of defeat. "All right, I'll confess. I rang Dr Lowrie, to commiserate, that first day. You'd just been to see him and he was still rather shaken. He told me that you weren't satisfied, that there might even be a possibility of its having been murder. He told me in confidence and I have spoken about it to no one, I assure you."

"I see. In that case you must surely understand that I really do have to try to find out all I can about Dr Pettifer. I don't ask questions just to satisfy idle curiosity, I promise you."

Barson studied Thanet's face for a moment before saying, "I believe you."

"In that case, could you go on with what you were telling me just now?"

Barson sighed. "I suppose so. It just smacks of disloyalty, that's all. Though why it should feel worse to speak ill of the dead than of the living I can't imagine."

"Perhaps it's because they can't strike back."

Barson gave a rueful smile. "You're probably right. So . . . where was I?"

"You were saying how serious-minded Pettifer was."

"That's right. Well, he was. So I suppose it was inevitable that sooner or later he should have become Taylor's target."

"What happened?"

"Well, it was a bit much really. One day Taylor slipped a diuretic into Pettifer's coffee."

"What's a diuretic?"

"Makes you want to pass water all the time. Anyway, Taylor stupidly mistimed the thing. Instead of giving Pettifer the stuff at a time when Pettifer would at least have the opportunity to go and pee when he wanted to, he gave it to him when there was to be an important lecture later on that morning. God, I can't think how the incident could have slipped my mind. It was hideously embarrassing . . . Fortunately Pettifer was sitting near the back, but he didn't make it to the door. You can imagine how he felt . . ."

"I can imagine how anyone would have felt, in circumstances like that." But Pettifer especially, Thanet thought. Stern, proud, this would have been precisely the sort of humiliation he was least equipped to bear. "So, what happened?"

"For a long time, nothing. Everyone knew who was responsible, of course, but nothing overt was said, either to or by Pettifer. We felt sorry for him, felt Taylor'd gone a bit far and the whole thing had turned sour. Pettifer had never been on particularly friendly terms with Taylor and now he more or less ignored him. And he made no move to retaliate until the following June."

"What did he do?"

"It was simple but lethal. Devilishly clever, too. We were taking our finals, you see, and on the first day Pettifer slipped lactulose into Taylor's breakfast cornflakes. It was easy enough to do, the plates of cereal were all set out and we used to take it in turns to distribute a trayful. And lactulose is near enough tasteless and colourless . . . It's an aperient," he explained to Thanet's blank look, "produces the same effect as a diuretic, but on the bowels instead of the bladder."

"Diarrhoea . . ."

"Galloping diarrhoea in this case."

"God, what a revenge! What happened to Taylor?"

"He managed to scrape through his exams, just. But he had been one of the most promising students of the year . . ."

So, Thanet thought, watching Barson drive away, here was a side of Pettifer's character hitherto unsuspected. He wanted to think over the interview with Gemma Pettifer, but he didn't want to sit here in the car in full view of her windows. He drove out of Brompton Lane and parked around the corner.

This was a pleasant residential street with wide pavements punctuated by ornamental cherry trees. The leaden skies of yesterday had disappeared overnight, blown away by the frisky wind which was plucking at the dying leaves, tossing them in the air and then cradling them as they floated to the ground. At the far end of the road an old man was moving methodically along the pavement, brushing the leaves first into long crimson ribbons snaking along the gutters, then into piles which he finally shovelled into a metal container on wheels.

Thanet watched him absentmindedly, his thoughts far away. He still couldn't make up his mind about Gemma Pettifer. She was convincing, yes, but then she had spent many years perfecting the art of being so. Suppose that she was lying, that the whole thing was a very clever scheme to kill her husband and deflect attention from herself by playing the unfaithful wife who realises too late the depth of her devotion to her husband . . . Suppose that the stories of the cold, the paracetamol, the promised phone call, Pettifer's cry for help were an ingenious tissue of lies devised to explain away her presence on the spot at the crucial time . . .

Or . . . Thanet's pulse beat faster as a completely new idea came into his head. Suppose that Gemma's story was true, that the deception was not hers but Pettifer's. Suppose that, contrary to her belief, he had indeed found out about her lover, had stage-managed the performance of illness and phone call, but that, contrary to appearances, Pettifer had intended the suicide to be an *attempt only*. Suppose that Gemma had been meant to arrive in time, rush him to hospital and, filled with guilt, be forever afterwards a loving, faithful wife? Such a plan would neatly have served the dual purpose of revealing to Gemma the depth of his despair and bringing her smartly to heel. And it would explain so much—why Pettifer had arranged to have his car repaired, for example, why he had obviously envisaged a future in which he and Gemma would be able to enjoy a luxury cruise together. Or perhaps the cruise had been intended to prick Gemma's conscience—even to underline the generosity of the love she was rejecting . . .

So, what had gone wrong?

She hadn't been able to get into the house.

And there was the rock upon which this ingenious theory foundered. Surely, if Pettifer's life had depended on it, he wouldn't have made the mistake of bolting the door against his only hope of rescue?

For that matter, why had he bolted the door at all, if he was expecting her home?

Perhaps he had counted on the fact that Gemma, disturbed by his appeal, would be determined to get into the house somehow. But she hadn't because, when she had gone around to try the back door, she had seen . . .

Thanet jerked bolt upright in his seat. That was it! *She had seen that the car was missing.* And that had made her angry, had made her feel that she had been dragged down from London in the middle of the night on false pretences. She had gone back to London, leaving Pettifer to die, his plan ruined by the simple fact that he had forgotten the significance that missing car would have for her.

"You all right, Guv?"

The street sweeper was knocking on the car window, his face creased with concern.

Thanet wound down the window. "Oh, yes, fine, thanks. I was just thinking."

The man grinned. "You want to be careful. All them faces you was making . . . If that's what thinking does for you . . ."

Thanet grinned back. "You've got a bit of a job on there, haven't you?" he said, nodding at the leaf-strewn pavements, the metal container. "I thought they had special lorries to do that these days."

"They have. In theory, like. But one of them's broke down, so they gives me a ring . . . I'm retired, see. 'Want your old job back for a coupla days, Ern?' they says. 'Why not?' says I. 'Earn a bit of extra towards Christmas.' And it makes a change, working again."

It was so easy for plans to go awry, Thanet thought as

he drove away. Something unexpected turned up and that was that.

But, leaving aside the possibility that Pettifer's plan had misfired, there was to Thanet's mind one serious objection to this new theory of his: he couldn't really see Pettifer as a man who would resort to suicide as emotional blackmail. The explanation might be neat, logical, feasible even, but was it psychologically sound?

Thanet burned to discuss it all with Lineham, but Lineham was in London, unavailable until late afternoon. Thanet decided that meanwhile he would stick to his original plans for the day. He stopped at a phone box, asked Bentley to try and trace Mrs Blaidon, Pettifer's mother-in-law by his first marriage, and to arrange if possible for Thanet to go and see her this afternoon. Then he drove to the Medical Centre. Braintree was next on the list.

The receptionist was apologetic. "I'm afraid you've just missed him."

"Do you happen to know where he'll be going first?"

"I'm sorry. I know the names of all the people doctor'll be visiting, of course, but I've no idea in what order. He arranged that to suit himself."

"Have you any bright ideas how I can contact him?"

"Good morning, Inspector." It was Lowrie, on his way out. "How's it going?"

"I was hoping to have a word with Dr Braintree this morning, but I've just missed him, apparently."

"Inspector?" Mrs Barnet had come out of her little office, had obviously heard this brief exchange. "Did you say you wanted to see Dr Braintree? Only I was talking to him just before he left, and he said that he had to call in at home before starting his visits. If you hurry, you might catch him there."

"Thank you." Hurriedly, Thanet scrawled down the address.

As he turned to leave, Lowrie said sharply, "Just one point, Inspector." Taking Thanet by the arm he drew him aside, spoke softly. "Braintree . . . I know you've got to do your job, but go easy on him, will you? As I told you, he's had a rough time lately, one way and the other. He shouldn't really be back at work yet, but with so much to do... And now, of course, with Fir on holiday and Pettifer gone... I've managed to persuade a colleague of mine who's retired to help out until Fir comes back, but if Braintree were to crack up again we'd really be in the soup."

"Don't worry, I'll be careful," Thanet said.

Braintree lived in a peaceful little cul-de-sac of new neo-Georgian houses in one of the better suburbs of Sturrenden. Thanet rang the bell beside a purple front door which looked like an advertisement for high-gloss paint, winced at the musical chimes and waited, studying the house. Being new, it was to be expected that it should be in good condition, but it positively sparkled with the effort and energy that had been lavished on it. The windows shone, the small square panes were row upon row of little mirrors, and the paintwork was gleaming, spotless.

The woman who opened the door was equally trim in a neat cotton shirtwaister and frilly apron. Her face was scrubbed and shiny, her hair cut in an uncompromising bob.

"Yes?" she said, with a smile which did not reach her eyes.

Thanet explained.

"You'd better come in," she said, with a quick, darting glance to left and right, up and down the road.

The hall was close-carpeted and, just inside the front door, on a little rubber mat obviously placed there for the purpose, stood a pair of man's shoes. Mrs Braintree herself was wearing slippers and to his astonishment Thanet caught a brief, assessing glance at his own inoffensive suede Hush Puppies. He waited incredulously for her to ask him to remove them.

But she didn't. She pushed open a door on their right and said, "If you wait in here, I'll fetch him."

The room was expensively furnished and totally devoid of character—magnolia emulsion paint on the walls, mushroom velvet curtains and three-piece suite. There was a sheepskin rug in front of the imitation-log gas fire, an island of luxury on the broad expanse of highly-polished parquet floor, but Thanet couldn't imagine that Mrs Braintree would ever contemplate using it for anything as untidy as making love. There was a television set, but no stereo system, no radio, no books, nor any magazines or newspapers to lend the room a human face. It was as bleak and impersonal as a room setting in a furnishing store.

Thanet began to feel sorry for Braintree. How could the spirit flourish in an atmosphere as sterile as this? I bet she was a nurse before she married him, he thought, and if she was I'm glad she never had to look after me. Yes, he thought as she came back into the room with her husband, she would have lacked that inner warmth which somehow survives despite the relentless drudgery and constant proximity to human suffering. Mrs Braintree wouldn't ever have had to hold back from becoming emotionally involved. Her patients to her would have been flesh, bones, blood, not people.

"You wanted to see me, Inspector?"

"Just briefly, if you can spare the time. It's about Dr Pettifer, of course." Thanet studied with interest the youngest of the partners in Pettifer's practice.

Dr Braintree was in his early thirties. Tall, thin and slightly hunched, with black hair which flopped over his forehead, he looked like a dejected crow.

"Do sit down."

"Thank you." Thanet glanced meaningfully at Mrs Braintree, hoping that she would take the hint and go, but she either didn't notice or chose to ignore it, plumping herself squarely down beside her husband on the settee.

Thanet seated himself opposite them.

"This won't take too long I hope, Inspector. I have a number of visits to make before lunch." Braintree caught

Thanet's involuntary glance at his slippers and looked uncomfortable.

"I hope not too, doctor. I'm making routine enquiries and naturally I'm asking the same questions of everyone connected with Dr Pettifer. First of all, could you tell me if you thought him to be unusually depressed at the time of his death."

"No, not at all."

"Or if you know of any possible reason for his suicide?"

"No, none."

"But he must have had one, mustn't he?" cut in Mrs Braintree. "Or he wouldn't have done it. Stands to reason."

Thanet ignored the interruption, preoccupied with how to put the next question. Remembering Dr Lowrie's plea he decided on an oblique approach.

"How did you and he get on together?"

But his delicacy was wasted.

"You've been listening to gossip!" burst out Mrs Braintree. "You have, haven't you? And it's not true, is it, Des? You shouldn't believe all you hear, Inspector. There's a lot of people about always willing to shoot down other people's reputations."

"I can assure you that I don't believe all I hear, Mrs Braintree. But I do have to listen, and check. Which is what I am doing now."

"But why? How could it matter whether him and Des got on or not? Which they did, anyway, but . . ."

"You must see that Dr Pettifer's state of mind at the time of his death is highly relevant . . ."

"So that's it! You're looking for a scapegoat. And you've decided my husband's it. That is it, isn't it!" Her face was pink, her eyes bulged and she seemed unaccountably to have grown bigger as she sat there.

Braintree, by contrast, seemed to have shrunk.

"Betty," he said, in a feeble attempt at admonition.

"But that *is* what he's trying to do, can't you see?" she said, turning to him. "And you're not going to get away with it," she flung at Thanet.

"Mrs Braintree!" he said. "I'm not trying to get away with anything. I just want to . . ."

"My husband's done nothing to be ashamed of and . . ."

"Please. Would you mind . . ."

"I'm not going to sit here and . . ."

"Mrs Braintree! WILL YOU BE QUIET!"

There was a second's astounded silence and then she shot up, like a jack-in-the-box. "I'm not going to sit here and be insulted in my own home. Des, it's time you were getting on with your rounds."

"Doctor Braintree," Thanet said in a quiet, deadly tone, "is going to stay where he is until he has answered the questions I wish to put to him. Alternatively," he went on, raising his voice as she opened her mouth to protest, "he can accompany me to the police station where we should be able to talk IN PEACE."

She stared at him for a moment longer and then, turning on her heel, flounced out of the room. Thanet could have sworn he heard the ghostly rustle of starched skirts. He expected her to slam the door and was interested to see that she carefully left it a little ajar.

"I'm sorry, Inspector." Braintree made a hopeless gesture. "My wife means well. She just tends to get a little worked up, that's all. Since my . . . illness, she has tended to be somewhat overprotective."

"Perfectly understandable." Thanet thought briefly and with gratitude of Joan's loving and equable temperament. "And I expect she's rather upset about Dr Pettifer's death. Everyone is, naturally."

"Quite. And of course, with Dr Fir still away, the work load is a bit much at present. So if we could be fairly brief . . ."

Thanet lowered his voice. "I'll be honest with you, doctor, and ask you to . . ." He remembered the door. He rose, shut it and returned to his chair before continuing. Braintree had got the message, he could see. " . . . to keep what I say in strictest confidence. You'll have gathered we're not very happy about this business. There seems to have been no reason whatsoever for Dr Pettifer to commit suicide—which means, of course, that we really have to satisfy ourselves that there was nothing . . . well . . . sinister about his death."

Braintree had turned the colour of grubby linen. He glanced at the door, edged forward on his seat. "You mean, he might have been *murdered*?" His voice was no more than a horrified whisper.

Thanet found that he, too, was sitting on the edge of his chair. We must look like a pair of conspirators, he thought. "It's no more than the remotest of possibilities," he said, wishing that this were true. "But you must see that, all the while it's on the cards, we can't sit around doing nothing."

"Of course. So, how can I help, Inspector?" His tone was fearful.

Thanet could see that Lowrie was right. He would have to be careful. Briefly, resentment flared in him. He was sick and tired of handling people with kid gloves. This was, potentially at least, a murder enquiry, he reminded himself, and if Braintree couldn't be asked a simple, straightforward question, then he wasn't fit to be back at work.

"If you could just tell me where you were on Monday evening?"

"Oh, my God!" Braintree buried his face in his hands. "I just can't *think*," he moaned. He raked his hair with his fingers.

Thanet waited.

"Monday evening . . . ?" Braintree said, speaking through clenched teeth.

"Dr Lowrie was at a meeting with Mrs Barnet," prompted Thanet. "Perhaps you were on call?"

Braintree's face was suddenly luminous with relief. "I remember now! Betty and I were at the Tennis Club end-of-season dinner dance, at the Wayfarers."

"You weren't on call, then?"

"No, Lowrie was. If we're on duty and we have to go out, we just leave phone numbers so that we can quickly be contacted. Originally, I was supposed to be on duty on Monday, but I swapped with Lowrie, because of the dinner dance—I don't like drinking alcohol if I'm on call," he explained. "Lowrie was only attending a meeting and Mrs Lowrie is away at the moment, he was quite happy to exchange."

"I see." Quickly, Thanet took the details. Braintree had taken evening surgery. The last patient had not left until six-thirty. Braintree had had a scramble to get home, change and be ready by seven; then the two other couples in their party had arrived for a drink before they all left for the dinner dance, which had ended at 1 a.m.

It could easily be checked, verified by people who could have no possible reason for lying, Thanet thought as he took names and addresses. He was therefore inclined to believe it. He thanked Braintree and managed to get away without a further encounter with Mrs Braintree, whom he glimpsed hovering in the kitchen doorway as he hurried through the hall. No doubt she would pounce upon her husband the moment the front door closed.

So that promising avenue had turned out to be a dead end, Thanet thought as he climbed into his car. And he was back to the old dilemma: suicide, or murder?

The pendulum began to tick away in his brain again as he headed back towards the centre of town.

It was, it wasn't. It was, it wasn't.

And—she did, she didn't. She did, she didn't.

19

Wondering if he was wasting his time, Thanet set off after lunch to keep the appointment which Bentley had managed to arrange with Mrs Blaidon. It was a glorious autumn afternoon and before long he began to feel as though he had been let out on holiday. He hadn't been in what he thought of as "proper country" for some time and now he wound down the car window to breathe in great draughts of sweet, clean air. All about him the rich landscape of Kent slumbered in the mellow warmth, satisfied that once again it had yielded up its abundance and could now lie dormant, replenishing itself with the strength necessary to bring forth next year's harvest.

At one point Thanet stopped the car and pulled into the side of the road, drawn by the beauty of the view. Leaning on a five-barred gate he gazed with profound satisfaction at the multi-coloured patchwork spread out before him. Fields of stubble, scorched black by the ritual purification of post-harvest fires, and meadows dotted with grazing sheep and cattle intermingled with orchards and woodlands in a satisfying natural harmony made breathtaking by the glowing colours of the autumn foliage. Along the hedgerows ripening blackberries hung in clusters and the glowing berries of hawthorn and wild rose were festooned with the fluffy white trails of the wild clematis, so aptly called Old Man's Beard.

Thanet plucked a handful of blackberries and ate them, their sun-ripened warmth seeming to encapsulate for him the essence of the richness about him. He had lived in Kent all his life and, although he never thought of himself as a country-man, knew that if he were ever to be uprooted from all this something in him would wither and die.

The village of Borden was tucked away at the heart of a complex, twisting network of narrow country lanes. Thanet twice lost his way and it was with relief that he at last found it and stopped to ask for directions from an old man leaning on the tiny wicket gate of his front garden and puffing peacefully at his pipe.

The man considered Thanet's question, then removed his pipe in a leisurely manner. "Catchpenny Oast?" he repeated. "That'll be Mrs Blaidon's place."

"That's right."

"You goes up there about half a mile," the old man said, pointing with the stem of his pipe, "then just past the King's Arms you turns left, and a bit further on you'll see her sticking up above the yew hedge."

Presumably he was referring to the Oast house and not to its owner, thought Thanet with an inward smile as he thanked him. The tall, conical roofs of the oast houses, topped with their white cowls, are one of the most distinctive features of the Kentish landscape. Now that relatively few of them still perform their original function of drying the famous Kentish hops, many have been converted into delightful homes.

The yew hedge surrounding Mrs Blaidon's garden was tall and thick, immaculately clipped. Thanet parked his car at the side of the road and approached the white five-barred gate. As he unlatched it a large black-and-white cat sitting on one of the gateposts jumped down and stalked off sedately around the corner of the house, disappearing from view with a contemptuous flick of the tail.

Catchpenny Oast was a most attractive conversion. Efforts had clearly been made to retain as far as possible the original features of the building and to ensure that any new materials were carefully matched with the old. Thanet approved of the casement windows with the traditional small square panes and the heavy old wrought-iron fittings on the bleached, weathered wood of the massive front door.

Before he could knock, however, the cat reappeared and without a glance at Thanet returned to its perch on the gatepost.

"Ah, there you are. Thought you'd got lost." A woman had appeared at the corner of the house and now advanced towards him, peeling off her gardening gloves and stuffing them into the capacious pockets of her canvas apron. She put out her hand. "Inspector Thanet, I presume."

Dismissing the fanciful notion that the cat had informed her of his arrival Thanet shook hands, studying her with interest. Not exactly a face to launch a thousand ships, he thought, but certainly one to catch and hold the interest; long and narrow, with slightly protruding teeth and unusually penetrating brown eyes. Her greying brown hair was caught up in an undisciplined bun.

She led him around the side of the house, removing her apron as she went. Underneath she was wearing a baggy tweed skirt, a woollen blouse and a shapeless brown cardigan held together at the front with a big safety pin.

"We're outside," she said. "Lovely day, brought Mother out."

At the back of the house, tucked into the angle between the roundel and the rest of the house, was a little paved terrace furnished with comfortable cane chairs and a bamboo table. In the most sheltered corner, so swathed in shawls and rugs as to be almost invisible, sat an old, old lady. Two rheumy eyes gazed vacantly out across the garden. Beside her, curled up on the trailing corner of one of the rugs, slept a tabby cat and a third cat, ginger this time, raised its head lazily to survey Thanet from the cushioned comfort of one of the chairs.

Mrs Blaidon dropped her apron on to the table and crossed to bend over her mother.

"We've a visitor, Mother," she said loudly.

Slowly the old lady's eyes focused on her daughter's face.

"A visitor!" Mrs Blaidon repeated, even more loudly, pointing with vigorous stabs of her finger at Thanet.

The eyes swivelled slowly to Thanet and then, in mild bewilderment, back to Mrs Blaidon, who patted her mother's lap reassuringly before straightening up.

"Deaf as a post," she explained unnecessarily, mouth

tucked down ruefully at the corners. "And stubborn, with it. Won't wear a hearing aid for love nor money. Sit down," she added abruptly.

He did so, wondering if her curiously staccato mode of speech had come about through years of living with someone who was deaf.

Mrs Blaidon scooped up the ginger cat and sat down on the chair it had occupied, settling it absentmindedly on her lap. It was such an habitual gesture that Thanet wondered if she was even aware that it was there.

"Right," she said, eyes bright with interest. "I'm bursting with curiosity. About Arnold, is it?"

"You've heard about his death, then?"

"Andy rang up. Hadn't heard from him since Christmas. In a state. Won't be hypocritical, pretend I'm sorry Arnold's dead."

"You didn't like him?"

She pulled a face. "Cold fish. Did you know him?"

"Only by sight."

"If you had, you'd know what I mean. Ghastly man. Andy right, then?"

No point in beating about the bush with this one, Thanet thought. Polite formalities would be brushed aside like so many flies. Straight to the point in as few words as possible would be the approach that Mrs Blaidon would appreciate.

"Well?" she said impatiently. "Was he murdered or wasn't he?"

"We don't know yet."

"Taking your time, aren't you?"

"Complications," Thanet said, equally terse. He was disconcerted to see a gleam of amusement in her eye.

"Don't huff."

Thanet opened his mouth to deny the allegation, realised that he would be wasting his time. Instead, he grinned. "It doesn't sound as though you'd be surprised if he had been."

"Not really."

"Why?"

"Told you. Awful man. Never understood why Diana married him. No, not true. Desperate for a husband. Simple as that."

"He was the sort of man who made enemies?"

She frowned. "Bit strong, that. Not the sort to make friends, that's all. No warmth in him. Good doctor, though. Loved his work, grant you that. Nothing else, though."

"Not even your daughter?"

She gave a bark of laughter. "Loved her money, more likely."

"And Andrew?"

Her expression softened. "Fond of him in the end. But never should have adopted, not cut out to be parents, those two."

"You mean, your daughter wasn't keen on children either? Then why on earth . . . ?"

"Fifteen years ago things were different. If you didn't have children . . . Pariahs, almost. More enlightened nowadays. Diana felt some kind of freak. Damned unfair, the woman always blamed. She really resented that, I can tell you. Adopted in self-defence, really."

Thanet stared at her, wondering if he had heard aright. Could he have misinterpreted that peculiar shorthand speech of hers?

"What do you mean, that it's unfair that the woman should always be blamed?"

"Not her fault they couldn't have children. His."

His fault. So *Pettifer had been sterile*. And if that were so . . .

As his entire thinking about the case began to somersault Thanet pulled himself up short. This was so important he couldn't risk misinterpretation, dared not accept as fact something which might be only a biased guess.

"Who told you that?"

"Diana, of course."

"She could have been trying to put the blame on him

because she couldn't face the fact that the fault was hers."

Mrs Blaidon waved her hand dismissively. "Psychological clap-trap."

"But I understood that she even had an operation..."

"Blocked tubes. Soon put right. That's when she found out. Until then, Arnold never had any tests. But when her tubes were cleared and still no patter of tiny feet... Saw the written report from the hospital myself. Sperm count non-existent, it said. Nothing you can do about that. But look here, aren't we straying a bit? What the devil has Arnold's sperm count got to do with his death?"

Didn't you know that his second wife is having a baby? Thanet wanted to say. But he didn't. She would find out soon enough and put two and two together. As soon as he decently could he brought the conversation to a close and left.

Pettifer had been sterile.

Therefore he must have known that Gemma had a lover right from the very first moment she told him that she was pregnant, several months ago. And if that was so...

Thanet felt that he was on the very brink of a completely new understanding of the case. It was as though he was looking at it through a kaleidoscope. The pattern he had seen until a few minutes ago had suddenly fragmented and now all the pieces were whirling around in meaningless gyrations. Perhaps in a little while they would begin to float down, to settle and he would see the true picture beginning to take shape.

Meanwhile... The questions came thick and fast.

Why, for months, had Pettifer played the role of delighted expectant father, knowing that the child could not be his?

If he had loved Gemma as passionately as everyone seemed to think, how had he managed to conceal so effectively the jealousy he must have felt?

And, above all, why? Why had he never, by word or implication, indicated that he knew of her infidelity?

Thanet felt convinced that if he could only find the answer to this last question, the case would be solved.

20

"Where the hell have you been?"

For the last hour Thanet had been pacing about his office like a caged bear, burning with impatience for Lineham's return.

Lineham looked taken aback by this greeting, as well he might.

"In London, sir..."

"I know you've been in London, man. But what took you so long?"

"Well, I had a bit of bother tracking down Mr Lee. First of all I..."

"All right, all right." Thanet waved away the explanations, then sat down heavily behind his desk. He was being unreasonable and he knew it. "Hell, I'm sorry, Mike. I'm sure you haven't been wasting your time. It's just that there have been developments in the Pettifer case and I didn't want to go home until I'd discussed them with you."

"Oh? What?" Lineham said eagerly.

"All in good time. Tell me what you found out in London."

Lineham had gone first to the hotel. The manager had checked his records and had confirmed that, yes, Gemma had made one long-distance phone call at around ten o'clock that night. He had given Lineham the night-porter's address and the poor man had duly been roused from his well-earned slumbers and had

confirmed that although he hadn't seen Gemma and
Lee leave the hotel just after ten, he had seen them
return at around 1.30 a.m. He had not questioned Lee's
presence as he had seen him with Gemma on a number
of previous occasions and assumed he had every right to
be there.

It had then taken Lineham some time to track down
Lee, whom he had finally run to earth at the rehearsals
of a fringe theatre group in Putney.

"And a pretty weird lot they were, too," he said, eyes
rounding reminiscently. "Do you know..."

"Lee, Mike. What about Lee?"

Lineham's top lip curled up contemptuously. "Male-
model type. The sort you see on knitting patterns.
Appeals to women, I suppose. Good-looking, skin-tight
trousers, shirt unbuttoned to the waist, gold medallion
nestling in the hair on his chest, that sort of thing."

Thanet grinned. "Not your idea of masculine charm,
eh, Mike?"

Lineham ignored Thanet's teasing. "He was still hop-
ping mad with Mrs Pettifer."

"What about?"

"Her getting him to drive over a hundred miles at
night to answer a dud SOS from her husband. I gather
the atmosphere on the way back to London was distinctly frosty. In fact, I have a feeling that that affair
won't be going on much longer."

"Gave you that impression, did he?"

Lineham looked disgusted. "It was the way he talked
about her... 'You know what older women are,' wink,
wink. 'They can teach you a thing or two but after that,
well, you've got to admit that their charms are somewhat faded.' Yuk!"

"Delightful. Anyway, I gather he confirmed her story."

"Oh, yes, down to the last detail."

"What do you think, Mike, now you've seen him? Do
you think he and Mrs Pettifer did the foul deed together?"

"Not on your life! Honestly, sir, I don't think that one
would put his neck on the chopping block for anyone.

What a nice girl like Deborah Chivers can see in him really beats me."

"You're sure?"

"As sure as I can be."

"Even taking into account the fact that he's an actor too? And, whatever you think of him as a person, a good one?"

"Believe me, I'd be only too delighted to be giving a different answer. But no, I think his involvement begins and ends with his driving her down to Sturrenden and back that night."

"Hmm. Only, as I said, things have changed a bit since this morning. The last of our suspects, Braintree, is now out of the running—I checked while I was waiting for you to get back and, believe me, his alibi's cast-iron. And I learnt one very interesting fact from Pettifer's mother-in-law by his first marriage." Thanet stopped, took out his pipe and began to fill it.

"Yes?"

Mischievously, Thanet prolonged the suspense for a moment or two longer, waited until his pipe was drawing properly before dropping his bombshell.

"*Sterile?*" Lineham's face was a study. "But that means..."

"Yes?"

"Well, that the baby isn't his, for a start. And that he must have known it wasn't right from the beginning. Which means..." Lineham paused, taking in the implications.

"... that our pillar of respectability and integrity has been lying in his teeth for months. Living a lie, in fact. And damned convincingly, too. He certainly had us fooled," Thanet added, with a degree of bitterness.

"And his wife, too?"

"Ah, now that's what I'd really like to know. Did he tell her he knew, or not?"

"He couldn't have, surely, sir. I can't believe that if he had they would have been able to hide the fact that their relationship had changed from Mrs Price, for example, who was living in the same house with them all the time."

"And why should they bother to keep up a pretence like that, anyway? I mean, I can imagine Pettifer not wanting other people to know he'd been made a fool of—can't you?—carrying on as though nothing had happened because he couldn't bear to lose face. But why should she?"

"Perhaps he threatened to divorce her if she didn't."

Thanet shook his head. "It's no good, Mike, it just doesn't ring true. If there was collusion between them, then she really put her heart and soul into it, didn't she? Think of the anniversary dinner. Why should she bother to put on an act like that in front of a lot of complete strangers? No, the more I think about it, the more inclined I am to believe he didn't tell her."

"But why should he have, for that matter? I mean . . ."

The phone rang. "It's for you," Thanet said, passing it to Lineham.

"Yes? Oh, hullo, Mother. Look, is this important? It really isn't very conven— Oh. Oh, I see. Well, I don't know. Louise'll be expecting me. Yes. Yes, I do see. Yes. Well, I suppose I could. All right, I'll call in on my way home. I'm not sure." He glanced at his watch. "I can't be certain." There was irritation in his voice now. "I really can't be sure . . . Say an hour, then. I'm sorry, Mother, you know how it is, I just can't be more definite than that. No, I'm not cross. Yes. Yes. See you later, then. 'Bye." He shot an apologetic glance at Thanet. "My mother," he said unnecessarily as he put the phone down. "A minor crisis. Do you think . . . Would you mind if I just made a quick call to Louise, sir?"

"Go ahead."

Lineham lifted the receiver, began to dial, stopped. Gently, he put the phone down again. "I'll leave it for the moment," he said sheepishly.

Obviously Lineham was hoping that if he was late getting home Louise would simply assume that he had been delayed at work. That way, a clash over his

170

mother's demands could be avoided. Thanet opened his mouth, clamped it shut again. Lineham's private life was not his concern unless or until Mike brought himself to ask outright for Thanet's advice or opinion, as he had on occasion in the past. But it was hard to stand by and watch this gradual widening of the rift between Mike and Louise. Thanet was fond of them both. Now, he found himself hoping that he wouldn't later on kick himself for not having spoken out in time.

"Of course," said Lineham, "there's always the possibility that he didn't tell her because he just hoped the problem would go away."

Thanet wondered if Lineham realised just how accurately this suggestion mirrored his attitude to his own domestic problems. He shook his head. "I just can't believe that, Mike. From what we've learnt of him, that just wouldn't be in character. Everyone agrees he was the sort of man who tackled problems head on. And he was such a proud man . . ."

"Perhaps he didn't tell her because he didn't want her to know he was sterile."

"I thought of that, but that's no answer either. There was no need for her to know, was there? After all, he could have learnt about the affair in a number of ways, couldn't he?"

"True. Though I suppose that if he didn't want her to know he was sterile, then when she first told him about the baby he'd have had to pretend to be pleased, wouldn't he?"

"Not necessarily. After all, he'd made it clear he didn't particularly want children. I shouldn't have thought she'd have been in the least bit surprised if he hadn't been very happy about it to begin with, especially as he hadn't been consulted. Even so, everyone agrees he was—or appeared—delighted about it in the following months. And that I simply cannot swallow. Pettifer being pleased that his wife was carrying another man's child . . . So we come back to the same question, don't we? Why the elaborate charade?"

171

"You don't think we're trying to make it too complicated, sir? After all, it could simply be that he loved her so much he was prepared to have her on any terms. Then he might have found, as time went on and the affair didn't come to an end, that he just couldn't face the prospect of going on like that indefinitely, and decided to kill himself."

"Or perhaps Doc Mallard was right. You remember what he said, about suicide sometimes being an expression of anger rather than of despair?"

"You mean, he did it to punish her?"

"No, that doesn't feel right either, does it? Though it could have been like that, I suppose. Hell, Mike, we're just not getting anywhere, are we? I think it's time we called it a day."

He was sick and tired of going around in circles, he thought as he drove home. His earlier elation had vanished and he felt no nearer now to solving the thing than he had when they first started working on it. His head felt thick, his temples throbbed and he told himself that the best thing now would be to put the case right out of his mind for the evening. He had learnt from past experience that this could be a most fruitful exercise. Superficially at least he had a respite while underneath his subconscious continued to work away at the problem.

As it happened, circumstances conspired to help him carry out this decision, though not in a manner he would have chosen. When he arrived home he found Joan in the sitting room with Ben, wrapped in a blanket, on her lap.

Concern twisted Thanet's stomach. "What's the matter?" he said. He glanced at the clock. Half past eight. Ben should have been asleep over an hour ago.

"Ben can't get to sleep," Joan said, smoothing the child's hair gently back on his forehead. "He's got pains in his tum, haven't you, darling? And a temperature." Her eyes met Thanet's, dark with anxiety, and he knew at once what she was thinking.

Appendicitis?

Apparently not. The doctor had been, diagnosed nothing more serious than a chill in the stomach. "He said Ben'll be better by morning. And we'll have to watch what he eats for a few days."

"I'll take over now," said Thanet. "I'll have supper later. We'll pop you into bed, shall we, Ben, where you'll be more comfortable—and then I'll read you a story, shall I?"

Ben nodded, his eyes overbright, cheeks flushed.

Thanet carried him upstairs and settled down to entertain him, consumed with anxiety. He read three *Paddington* stories, played one game of ludo and then, at Ben's request, "tried" to solve some of the puzzles in Ben's comic with him. Ben was growing sleepy now but he was clearly determined not to relinquish the unusual pleasure of having his father's exclusive attention. Eventually Thanet said, "Just one more then, Ben, and that's it."

But the concession proved unnecessary. Ben's eyes were closing and in a few minutes he was asleep. Thanet gently tucked him in and switched off the light, leaving the bedroom door ajar so that they would be able to hear if he called out in the night.

"Asleep?" Joan asked.

"At last." Thanet sat down with a sigh of relief.

"I'll get your supper."

While Thanet was eating they discussed Ben's indisposition for a little while and then Joan said, "I've got something to tell you. And I'm warning you, you won't like it."

Thanet looked at her warily. "Oh?" And then, as she still hesitated, "Go on, then."

"You won't bite my head off?" But she was smiling.

"Don't I always?" He smiled back. "All the same, you can't expect me to give hostages to fortune. Tell me what it is."

"Mrs Markham wants me to drive her down to

Bexhill on Sunday. Her son has asked her down for a couple of weeks."

"Then why can't he come and fetch her?" Thanet exploded. "He's got a car, hasn't he? Why should you go flogging all the way down to Bexhill? Joan, you did promise . . ."

"I know, I know, but . . ."

"And what about the children? I know it's supposed to be my weekend off, but the way things are going it doesn't look as if I'm going to get it, so I won't be here to babysit." Not to mention the fact that if, by any remote chance, he was free on Sunday, he didn't see why he and the children should be deprived of Joan's company . . .

"Mary said she'd have them. Or they could come with me, of course. For the ride."

"But why can't her son fetch her?"

"He's away on a course this weekend."

"Then why can't she go next weekend? Or travel by public transport? Thousands of people do."

Joan shook her head stubbornly. "There are reasons why it has to be this weekend. If they leave it, her grandson will be home—he's been away in the States for a year—then they won't have the room to put her up."

"Then why couldn't they have invited her before? I'm sorry, darling, I don't want to be unreasonable, but . . ."

Joan laid two fingers gently against his lips. "Just listen for a moment, will you, darling? I know I've been manoeuvred into it again, and frankly, I'm rather cross about it. You're right, I can see that now, she really is expert at it and I've made up my mind that this is the last time I allow myself to be manipulated like this." She took her fingers away, then said complacently, "In fact, you'll be pleased to hear I've already told her so—not in quite those terms, of course. I tried to break it gently, but I made it clear that when she comes back from her holiday I won't be able to continue popping in night and morning and running all her errands for her, as I have been doing. She wasn't very pleased, of course, but I stuck to my guns . . . So there you are. This is my last grand gesture. Truly."

Thanet raised both hands in mock surrender. "All right, all right, I give in." He reached out for her. "It'll be good to have you back," he murmured into her hair.

She pulled a little away from him to look into his face. "The trouble with you," she said, "is that you'd really like me to channel all my energies in your direction." Her kiss softened the impact of this undeniable truth.

"Especially a certain kind of energy," he agreed with a grin, tugging her to her feet. "An early night, don't you think?"

Much later, lying back relaxed and content, Thanet felt curiously wide awake. Usually, after making love, it was he who drifted quickly into sleep and Joan who tended to lie awake, but tonight it was the other way around. Her soft, deep breathing told him that she was already sound asleep and he turned on to his right side, in his favourite sleeping position, and determined to follow her example as quickly as possible.

Half an hour later he was telling himself that he really ought to have known that this was the one way to ensure that he stayed wide awake.

Turning on to his back he folded his arms behind his head and resigned himself to a long bout of insomnia. It was the Pettifer case, of course. Usually he slept like a log, but in each major enquiry there came a point where a sleepless night or two seemed inevitable.

What was so frustrating about this one, of course, was that after four days' work they still weren't even sure whether it had been suicide or murder. Each new bit of evidence that came along seemed to point to Gemma Pettifer's guilt, and yet . . . For some reason he was still unconvinced.

Why?

Deliberately now he made himself go back once more to the beginning and gradually trace the logical

175

progression of the case against her. This got him nowhere, so he started again, this time trying to pinpoint
those elusive moments when he had felt himself close
to understanding the truth of what had happened.

It made no difference. At the end of it he was still as
undecided as ever. He peered at the bedside clock,
groaned inwardly. Half past two. He would feel like a
limp rag in the morning. Yet again he composed himself
for sleep, forcing his mind into other channels. He
thought of Lineham and his mother, of Louise, of Joan
and Mrs Markham, of Ben...

He stiffened. Had Ben cried out? Carefully, so as not
to wake Joan, Thanet got out of bed, threw on his
dressing gown and, shivering a little, went to check.
Ben wanted to go to the lavatory. Thanet carried him to
the bathroom and back and tucked him into bed with a
smile, hiding his anxiety. Ben's forehead was still hot.

"Still got a pain in your tum?"

Ben shook his head. "Can we play another game,
Daddy?" he said.

At half past two in the morning? Thanet opened his
mouth to refuse, then closed it again. Why not? he
thought. He wasn't in the least sleepy and if it would
settle Ben down again...

"Please?"

"All right then." Thanet sat down on the bed, cuddled
Ben to his side. "What shall we play?"

Ben selected "Spot the Ten Deliberate Mistakes."
They took it in turns. By the eighth mistake Ben's
eyelids were drooping, by the tenth he had dozed off.
Thanet sat very still for a while, wanting to be certain
that Ben was sound asleep before risking any movement. Idly, he studied the puzzle picture, looking for
the tenth deliberate mistake. Ah, yes, there it was...

Suddenly it was as though a window blind had snapped
up in his mind, allowing enlightenment to come flooding
in. His brain began to race, to check and cross-check,
to test the bizarre explanation of Pettifer's death which
had so unexpectedly presented itself to him.

Was it possible?

With absentminded gentleness he made sure that Ben was comfortable and returned to his own bed, snuggling up gratefully to the warmth radiating from Joan as she slept.

Was it?

Certainly it explained away so much—everything, in fact, that had so puzzled them. But there was one major snag. His mind twisted and turned, seeking a way around it.

But it was still there when he at last fell asleep.

21

While he shaved next morning Thanet reviewed his solution and found that he still felt the same way about it. It was correct, he was convinced of it, he felt its essential rightness deep down inside him . . . And yet, there was that one great stumbling block—no, not just a stumbling block but an insurmountable wall of illogicality which would have to be scaled before he could truly be satisfied. He couldn't wait to discuss the whole thing with Lineham.

But he had to curb his impatience. When he arrived at the office he found Lineham already at work. Thanet took in the mounded litter of reports on Lineham's desk, the sergeant's bleary eyes and day-old stubble and said, "What the hell have you been playing at, Mike? You look as though you haven't been to bed all night."

"Well, as a matter of fact . . ."

". . . you haven't. Well, for God's sake go and get yourself freshened up. We'll leave explanations until you're looking a bit less like the morning after the night before. And get a move on. We have to talk."

Lineham's red-rimmed eyes travelled slowly over Thanet's face and then he groaned, said, "I knew it," and put his head in his hands.

"What's the matter?" Thanet said, beginning now to be concerned. "Are you ill or something?" He devoutly hoped the "or something" was not a serious rift with Louise. If Lineham had been here all night...

"No. It's not that. It's just... Oh, never mind." Lineham began to close files and shuffle them into neat stacks.

"What do you mean? You can't act as though the world's come to an end and then say, 'never mind.'"

Lineham sat back in his chair and looked at Thanet. "Well, just tell me this, sir... That look on your face... You've cracked it, haven't you?"

"The Pettifer case, you mean? I think so, yes, but..."

The look of despair on Lineham's face was so exaggerated as to have been comic, Thanet felt, had it not so patently been genuine. "What is the matter, Mike?" he said, gently.

"It's just that... Oh, you'll just think I'm a fool. Or presumptuous. One or the other, for sure."

"How do you know, until you've tried me?"

Something in Thanet's voice must have given Lineham reassurance because he studied the older man's face for a moment and then said, "Well, there's no reason why I shouldn't, I suppose. It's just that, for once," he burst out, "just for once, I'd hoped I'd get there first." He shrugged. "I've spent the whole night working through the files. I've so often seen you do it, when you feel we're getting close to a solution, and I thought... Oh, I'm a damned fool, that's all."

"Go and freshen up, Mike, then come back and we'll talk about it. But just get this into your head, will you? At your age, *I* would have felt—in fact, I often did feel—precisely as you are feeling now. Now go. And get yourself some breakfast while you're about it. No one can work efficiently on an empty stomach and I need your help."

Lineham went. While he was gone, Thanet turned the situation over in his mind. It was true that at Mike's age he had frequently felt as Mike did now—but with a difference. Thanet wasn't certain but he sensed in the sergeant some deeper need this time to have solved the case first, a compensatory need perhaps. But to compensate for what? A sense of failure in some area of his life? Of course—his relationship with Louise. That must be it. The trouble between them must be even more serious than Thanet had thought. Or had he just been choosing to ignore what he didn't want to see? He remembered the conversation with Joan the other day, how she had urged him to speak to Lineham, and he frowned. Had he been shirking his responsibilities simply because they were unpalatable? No, dammit, he had given Lineham enough openings to talk, if the sergeant chose to do so. Besides, if Lineham's marriage really was on the rocks, then he needed expert help, not the well-intentioned fumblings of the amateur Thanet felt himself to be. But Lineham's work... well, that was a different matter. Lineham's state of mind in that area was fairly and squarely Thanet's responsibility and he would have to think of some way in which the sergeant could receive that boost to his morale which he so clearly needed.

By the time Lineham returned, looking relatively fresh and alert, Thanet thought he saw how this could be done.

"Now, then, Mike," he said, "sit down and let's see if we can get this straight. It's true that I think I can now see exactly what happened in the Pettifer case—though there is one big snag I'm hoping you'll be able to help me with—so there's no point in pretending you're going to get there first. But I don't see why it still shouldn't be perfectly possible for you to work it out for yourself if you want to."

"What do you mean?" There was a wary gleam of

anticipation in Lineham's eyes, as if he'd like to believe Thanet but couldn't quite bring himself to do so.

"Put it this way. Why not look on this case as a learning exercise? Then, if you do manage to work it out for yourself, next time you'll find it that much easier. Practice and experience really do count, you know."

"I don't see how I could. I've been thinking all night"—Lineham gestured at the files—"and I've got precisely nowhere."

"Look, Mike," said Thanet, leaning sideways to take his pipe from his pocket, "a good detective not only has to be intelligent, persevering and prepared to do endless boring, routine work, he also needs one other quality." Thanet took his pipe apart, blew through the stem and, satisfied, reassembled it. "Some people call it intuition and talk about it as if it were magic. Some consider it unreliable—and, admittedly, the dictionary definition of intuition is 'immediate apprehension by the mind without reasoning.' I don't quite see it like that. I see it, rather, as the ability to make connections which are there but are not immediately apparent. Subterranean connections, I suppose you could call them."

"I don't follow you." Lineham was sitting back in his chair, arms folded, listening intently. Clearly the therapy was working and Thanet tried not to feel too smug.

"Well, say a man has a motor-bike accident. The *apparent* cause of the accident is that someone stepped off the kerb without looking and caused the driver to swerve, skid and crash. But the *real* reason was that, the night before, the man who stepped off the kerb had had a row with his girlfriend and he was thinking so hard about that that he wasn't looking where he was going. The connection between this girl and the man on the motor-bike is not immediately apparent, but it's there all right. Life's made up of subterranean connections like that and part of our job is to try to work out what they are. Now when you apply this to the Pettifer case . . ."

"Yes?" Lineham was engrossed now, eager.

Thanet took out his pouch and began to fill his pipe, pressing the tobacco carefully down in the bowl with his forefinger as he talked. "Well, when I was thinking about it last night I began in the usual way, looking back and reassessing, the sort of thing we do all the time. Now this case was unusual in that, whereas we normally know from the start whether a murder has been committed or not, this time we were not sure. So I took that as my starting point."

"You mean, you began by looking at the reasons why we suspected that it might not have been suicide."

"Yes. Now, you go on from there."

Lineham's eyes narrowed in concentration. "Well, first of all, there was general agreement that Pettifer had no reason to kill himself. His housekeeper, his wife, his secretary, his partner, all said the same thing, that he had no financial worries, he was in good health and he had no marital problems either." Lineham's eyes darkened and Thanet said quickly, "That's right. That's important. No one around him at any time suspected that there was anything wrong between them. Of course, we soon found out that Mrs Pettifer had a lover; but we still believed her husband had been unaware of this until, quite by chance, we discovered from his previous mother-in-law that Pettifer was sterile and must therefore have known about his wife's infidelity for months, right from the time she first told him she was pregnant."

"Not by chance, sir." Lineham was looking discouraged again. "I'd never have thought of going to see her. Why *did* you?"

"A general uneasiness, I suppose, revolving around the question of children. Things just didn't add up. The inconsistencies in Pettifer's attitude were too great. He apparently took pains to make sure his second wife wouldn't want children before he even asked her to marry him, yet everyone agreed he was over the moon when she became pregnant. Then Dr Lowrie told me that Pettifer didn't really like children—that, although Pettifer became fond of his adopted son, initially he had agreed to the adoption chiefly to please his first wife. Anyway, let's leave that for the moment, go back to the reasons why we suspected it might not have been suicide."

Lineham considered. "Well, I suppose the first specific indication was that holiday booking. You don't pay a couple of thousand quid for a holiday just a few hours before you intend to kill yourself."

Thanet was lighting up now and he waited until the match had burned down to the end before extinguishing it with a quick flick of the wrist and saying, "Quite. Go on."

"Then there was the car. Why bother to arrange for your car to be repaired if you know you'll never need it again? And the next thing was the note." Lineham was getting into his stride now. "The mis-spelling of Andrew's nickname, I mean. That really did seem suspicious, because if Pettifer had always spelt it one way he was hardly likely to alter it, even under stress—and of course that rather peculiar spelling was the sort of thing that no one but Andrew would know about unless they had actually seen Pettifer's letters to Andrew. And then we found out about the fingerprints. Why should Mrs Pettifer's prints be on not only the port bottle but the tablet container and glass too, when according to her she hadn't handled any of them? Later we found she'd given Pettifer the port for his birthday, but that didn't explain the other prints away. Even more interesting, of course, was the fact that, although Pettifer's prints were also on the bottle, they weren't on either container or glass . . ."

"Exactly. So by this point we had moved on from a general suspicion of murder to having a specific suspect."

"Mrs Pettifer. Yes." Lineham was frowning in concentration. "Then came the discovery that she had a lover, which meant that she also had a possible motive for wanting her husband out of the way."

"Go on."

"Well, next we got the PM results, which showed that Pettifer had been in perfect health, so that our last hope of finding a possible reason for suicide was gone . . ."

". . . unless, of course, he had killed himself through grief because he had found out that his wife had a lover."

"Yes, but at the time we still didn't think he had found out. There was absolutely nothing in his behaviour to indicate that he had. On the contrary, everyone agreed that he was in the best of spirits . . ." Lineham stopped, his forehead creased. "Though it really is beyond me to understand why he should have chosen to carry on all those months as though nothing had happened . . ."

Thanet waited. Would Lineham at last see the crucial significance of this aspect of Pettifer's behaviour?

Apparently not. Lineham shook his head sharply, as if to clear it of confusion. "I just can't see . . ."

"Leave it for the moment. You will, shortly, if I'm not mistaken. Get back to the post mortem."

"Yes, well, the other interesting thing about that was that there were no signs of the cold which Mrs Pettifer claimed was the reason why her husband had gone to bed early and she'd had to dose him with paracetamol. And, when we asked around, we discovered that no one else had noticed any cold symptoms. For that matter, we later heard that there were no traces of paracetamol in his stomach . . ."

"In short, her story was riddled with discrepancies."

"Exactly. And then," Lineham went on eagerly, "to cap it all, we discover that the night Pettifer died Mrs Pettifer got her lover to drive her down to Pine Lodge from London in the middle of the night. She claims she did this in response to her husband's request during a phone call which she says he *asked* her to make, and also says that when she did get here she couldn't get into the house and drove straight back to London in a huff. Lee confirms that they drove back almost at once, but he didn't go up to the house with her and the point is that she was there at Pine Lodge alone for ten minutes or so round about the time Pettifer took the overdose. So, not only did she have motive, she could well also have had opportunity. *But . . .*" Lineham paused.

"Yes, this is where it becomes interesting, isn't it? But . . ."

"But," Lineham went on slowly, picking his words now as he thought aloud, "so much of what she said or did seemed incomprehensible. Why, if she had killed him and arranged it to look like suicide, did she keep insisting it couldn't have been? Why produce the holiday booking, to back up what she was saying—why not just keep quiet about it? Why say he had a cold if he hadn't? Or claim to have given him paracetamol if she didn't? Why, above all, if she did murder him, didn't she give herself a decent alibi, rather than go off to spend the night in a London hotel with her lover? And why *volunteer* the information that she and Lee had made that suspicious dash down to Sturrenden in the middle of the night when she had no idea that we were already on to it? There's the possibility, of course, that she was trying to deflect suspicion by appearing to be ultra-helpful, a bewildered innocent, so to speak, but that still didn't explain why her story was riddled with discrepancies. Unless . . ." he said hesitantly.

Lineham was almost there. Thanet found that he was holding his breath. He was aware, too, of an uncomfortable emotion which was rather difficult to identify. What was it? he asked himself while he waited. Chagrin, perhaps, that by simple logic Lineham was apparently about to arrive at the solution which Thanet had thought attainable only by his own more intuitive approach?

"Unless she said and did all those things in good faith," Lineham concluded.

He sounded bewildered, disorientated, as though he had scaled what he thought was the mountain peak only to find further heights stretching away ahead of him.

"Go on. Go on, dammit. Don't stop. Follow it through."

"But how, sir? I just don't see where all this is leading."

"You will. You will. Just go on. If she said and did all those things in good faith . . ."

"Then," said Lineham slowly, "I suppose someone must have convinced her that they were true."

"Who?" said Thanet softly.

"It could only have been . . ." Lineham stopped. "No, it couldn't have been."

"Who? Dammit, say it, man."

"*Pettifer?*" Lineham's face was a study in bewilderment.

Thanet gave a slow, satisfied nod. "Pettifer."

"But that's crazy!" Lineham burst out.

"Is it? Just think about it, Mike. Why, for instance, should he say he had a cold, if he hadn't?"

"To make her feel sorry for him? So that she wouldn't go to London? No, it couldn't have been that. She said he insisted she went. And, if we're working on the premise that she's been acting in good faith, telling the truth all along . . . It's no good. I just can't see why the hell he should lie about a thing like that."

"Oh, come on, Mike. Don't give in!" Thanet puffed over-vigorously at his pipe in his urgency and a shower of sparks cascaded over his lap. He jumped up, flapping his hand at them. "And stop grinning, will you?"

"Shall I dial 999?"

"Just keep your mind on the job," growled Thanet, sitting down again. If he heard another joke about the Fire Service . . . He had never lived down the day when he had unwittingly set his wastepaper basket alight with an imperfectly extinguished match, just before leaving the office. It had been several years before the burnt carpet had finally been renewed amidst much grumbling from above about waste of tax-payers' money, rank

185

carelessness and the dangers and undesirability of smok-
ing (the Chief himself being a non-smoker, of course).

"Come on, now. Why should he have deliberately
misled her?" Thanet persisted.

Lineham gritted his teeth in frustration, thumped his
fist on his desk. "It's no good. I just can't see it."

"All right, calm down. Let's try another tack. Go back
to what you were saying a moment ago, that he must
have known about his wife's unfaithfulness for months,
right from the moment he first learnt she was pregnant,
but that he apparently did nothing about it. Thinking
about him, about the sort of man he was, how would
you have expected him to react when she told him?"

Lineham considered. "I was thinking about this, last
night. I'd guess he would have been very upset, of
course, but he wouldn't have shown it at the time... Partly
because he was a very controlled sort of person and
partly because he couldn't have let her know that her
news had immediately told him that she was being
unfaithful to him, without giving his secret away."

"That he was sterile. Yes. So, to cover up his real
feeling, he pretends to be pleased. Then what?"

"I'm not sure. When he'd had time to think about it,
I imagine he'd have been very angry. I certainly don't
think he could have dismissed it from his mind. We
know from what Dr Barson told you that he was the
type to bear a grudge and if he was feeling thoroughly
disillusioned... I think he'd have wanted to punish
her."

"Yes, but how?"

"Well, there was no point in confronting her with it.
She might simply have left him to go to her lover. And
even if she didn't, things would never have been the
same between them again. Anyway, that wouldn't exactly have been punishing her, would it? And we know he
didn't disinherit her."

"Which in itself is interesting, isn't it?"

"So what was the point of killing himself! It just
leaves her free to go to Lee as a rich woman."

"Slow down, Mike. You're in too much of a hurry. Try to think yourself back into his mind. He wants to punish her. And the problem is, how? Now, look at that thought in the light of what he actually did. What *did* he do?"

"Well... nothing, so far as I can see."

"I don't think that's quite true. Think back to what everyone said about him, about their marriage."

"That everything in the garden seemed to be rosy, you mean?"

"Too rosy?"

Lineham's eyes narrowed. "You mean, that it was deliberate policy, on his part, to give that impression?"

"Think of the day he died. They all agreed that he was in unusually high spirits, didn't they?"

"You mean, that was all a sham? A calculated attempt to mislead them?"

"Them, yes. And, perhaps... us?"

"*Us*? But..."

"So think, Mike. What have we got now? A desire for revenge, on his wife. A deliberate effort to mislead everyone who knew him and, as a consequence, anyone who might investigate his death. So that everyone would say that he had no possible reason for suicide..."

Thanet stopped. Lineham's eyes had gone blank, his mouth had dropped open. He looked, quite literally, stunned.

"You see?" Thanet said, on a long exhalation of satisfaction.

Lineham's lips moved, but no sound emerged. Finally, "*He set her up*..." he croaked. "That's what you mean, isn't it?" He was silent for a moment or two, then he burst out, "But that really is crazy! Absolutely stark staring bonkers! Sorry, sir, but you can't seriously expect me to believe that in order to punish his wife he decided to kill himself so as to get her convicted of murdering him! Talk about cutting off his nose to spite his face!"

"But why not? Don't you see, it's the perfect solu-

187

tion. In one fell swoop he gets his revenge on his wife *and* makes sure she won't be free to go to her lover or to inherit."

"Perfect solution! Aren't you forgetting one small detail, that he has to kill himself off in the process?"

"Ah, yes. Well, that's the snag I mentioned to you earlier."

"Snag!" Lineham took a deep breath and with a visible attempt at self-control and reasonableness went on, "Look, sir, I don't want to be rude or...insubordinate, and I know you've come up with some pretty weird ideas before and you've been proved right, but..."

"This time, you think I've gone over the top, right? Don't worry, Mike, I can sympathise with how you feel. And, I must admit, I felt exactly the same myself, when I first worked it out—congratulations, by the way. You did it, didn't you?"

"Did what?"

"Worked it out. Yourself."

"Did I, sir?"

"Well, I admit I had to give you a little nudge now and then, but..."

"No, I didn't mean that. I mean, I'm just not convinced we've reached the right conclusion, that's all. Look, sir, Dr Pettifer was an intelligent man. If he really was as vindictive as you seem to think he was, why not work out a way of taking his revenge that would not only leave him alive and kicking but would give him the pleasure of *seeing* his wife suffer? This way he wouldn't even have the satisfaction of knowing if his plan had worked."

"Perhaps he was past caring. Anyway, crazy as it may sound, I'm convinced that that's the way it was." Thanet tapped out his pipe and crossed restlessly to the window. "The trouble is, Mike, there's a piece of the puzzle missing. Somewhere there's a piece of information which would explain everything, something that would make us say, 'Ah, yes, so *that's* why he did it.'"

The telephone rang. Lineham picked it up, listened,

glanced sharply at Thanet. "I'll tell him," he said, a grin
spreading slowly across his face. "I expect he'll come
out right away." He replaced the receiver.

"Well?"

Lineham continued to grin.

"Mike, if you don't take that silly smirk off your face
and tell me... Who was that, anyway?"

"If you'd answered the phone and I'd asked that
question, I think you'd have said it was Fate, sir."

"Mike..." Thanet felt like grinding his teeth.

"It was Mrs Pettifer. Urgent, she said."

"Did she tell you what it was about?"

"She didn't want to discuss it on the telephone. But
apparently she had a letter this morning. Which, she
says, will explain everything."

We must look like two Cheshire cats, thought Thanet,
as he said, "What are we waiting for? Let's go."

22

"I gather she didn't say who it was from," Thanet said.

Lineham shook his head. He was driving fast, but
with concentration. "Said she'd rather not say, until she
sees us."

"I wonder..." Thanet knew that there was really no
point in speculating, but couldn't help himself.

"Her husband?" suggested Lineham, with a mischievous glance at Thanet.

"One of those 'Voice from the Grave' things, you
mean? A bit melodramatic, don't you think? Besides,
he'd hardly have written two letters, surely? If he'd had
anything to say, he'd have said it in the suicide note."

"Except that suicide notes are always made public.

Perhaps he didn't want anyone but his wife to read this one."

"Possible, I suppose. How did she sound? Mrs Pettifer?"

"Relieved, I should say."

"Relieved . . ." mused Thanet. "Anyway," he said as they turned into Brompton Lane, "we'll soon find out now."

Mrs Price answered the door promptly. There was an earthenware jug of chrysanthemums and copper-beech leaves on the oak blanket-chest this morning, their glowing colours reflected in the highly polished surface. "Mrs Pettifer will be down in just a moment." She led them into the drawing room.

"How is she today?" Thanet asked.

Mrs Price gave a slight shrug. "Seems a bit better. More cheerful. I think she had some good news in the post this morning. Didn't touch her breakfast, though."

Footsteps could be heard on the stairs and a moment later Gemma Pettifer entered the room. Traces of yesterday's despair still lingered in the dark smudges beneath her eyes, but the beaten, defeated air had quite vanished away. This morning she had taken trouble with her make-up and her hair was newly washed, floating about her shoulders in a gleaming curtain. She was wearing another filmy Indian cotton dress, this time in a pale, limpid green which emphasised the colour of her eyes. For the first time Thanet recognised that illusion of beauty which she always succeeded in creating upon the stage. This was the Gemma with whom Pettifer had fallen in love. She was carrying an envelope and a heavy book.

"Good morning, Inspector," she said. "Good morning, Sergeant. Do sit down. Mrs Price, what I have to say concerns Dr Pettifer's death and you have been with him so long . . . do stay, if you wish." She sat down in one of the wing chairs beside the fireplace.

Thanet chose the matching armchair on the other side of the hearth. Mrs Price sat down stiffly on the

small upright chair in front of the little writing desk and
Lineham perched on the edge of the settee. He took out
his notebook.

"This came this morning." Gemma handed the envelope to Thanet.

Anticipation fizzed through his veins as he took it,
extracted the single sheet of paper. He glanced at the
signature. Benedict Randall? Thanet had never heard of
him. Quickly, he skimmed the brief note.

Dear Mrs Pettifer,
    I did not return from holiday until yesterday and
have only just learned of your husband's death. He
was a fine doctor and a friend of many years'
standing and it is a tragedy that he was unable to
come to terms with what was happening to him.
Inevitably, I cannot help feeling a measure of guilt
in not having recognised the depth and degree of
his distress.
    If there is, at any time, any way in which I may
be of service to you, please do not hesitate to call
on me.

My most sincere condolences,
Benedict Randall

Thanet's mind raced as he read. Whatever could the
man be referring to? There could be only one possible
explanation. But in that case, why hadn't . . . ?

"He assumes, as you see, that I would know what he
was talking about," Gemma said. Like Lineham and
Mrs Price, she had been watching Thanet eagerly.

"And what *was* he talking about? May I?" Thanet
waited for her nod before handing the letter to Lineham.

"Well, I'd no idea, of course, so I rang him up. We'd
met briefly, once or twice. He's a consultant neurologist
at Sturrenden General. He's very well known in his
field, has a practice in Harley Street."

"What did he say?"

"That my husband was suffering from disseminate
sclerosis—multiple sclerosis, it's often called."

Mrs Price drew in her breath sharply, with a sligh
hissing sound.

"Yes," Gemma said, glancing at her. "You'd well b
able to understand what that would mean to him, M
Price." She turned back to Thanet. "Apparently m
husband asked Mr Randall never to mention this diag
nosis to anyone, not even to me if by any chance w
should meet. Mr Randall assumed that Arnold wante
to tell me in his own good time and also assumed th
Arnold's death had released him from that promise. H
was pretty shattered to find that I still didn't know
anything about it." She shook her head. "My husban
couldn't have borne it, Inspector. He was so proud, s
fiercely independent . . . the prospect would have bee
truly intolerable to him." She shivered and, so fleeting
that Thanet could almost have thought that he ha
imagined it, there was a flicker of repulsion in her eye
Thanet remembered what Deborah Chivers had tol
him of Gemma's loathing of illness.

"I've heard of it, of course, " Thanet said, "but I kno
very little about it."

"Mr Randall explained it to me. And I've just bee
looking it up in a medical dictionary." She opened th
book on her lap at a marked place and handed it t
Thanet.

" '*A disease in which nerve linings around scattere
small areas of the brain and spinal cord are attacked b
some unknown agent,*'" Thanet read aloud. " '*In sever
cases tissue may be destroyed and nerves cease t
function.*'"

"By an unknown agent," Lineham said. "That's pre
ty terrifying."

"I know." Gemma's eyes were dark with imagine
horror. "Mr Randall said that the cause of it is n
known. It doesn't run in families—thank God," and sh
folded her arms protectively across her body. "And it
not contagious. It's a disease, apparently, of temperat

climates, like ours, and my husband was rather older than people normally are when it first attacks. It says in there"—and she nodded at the dictionary—"that the typical victim is a young adult."

"What are the symptoms?" Lineham was staring at Gemma with a kind of fascinated dread.

" *'Weakness, pins and needles,'* " Thanet read aloud, " *'double vision or impaired eyesight, difficulty in walking or in intricate movements such as threading a needle.'* Apparently they last a few days, then they may disappear. But they will recur after widely varying intervals of weeks, months, even years. The pattern is of a series of attacks with these periods of recovery in between. It says here that this is why the disease is frequently not diagnosed in its early stages. Presumably the symptoms disappear, the victim shrugs it off and forgets about it until the next time."

"That's right," Gemma said. "Mr Randall said that this can happen a number of times over a period of years before the patient finally does something about it."

"So your husband suspected that he might have fallen victim to it and consulted Mr Randall."

"That's right. Being a doctor, of course, he was able to refer himself direct to a consultant. People normally have to go through their GPs. And also, he naturally became suspicious far earlier than most people would have."

"Which is why his condition had not yet become obvious and none of the people about him suspected the truth."

"Exactly."

"I remember Dr Lowrie mentioning to me that your husband thought at one time that he might have to have reading glasses, but that it turned out to be unnecessary. That may well have been one of the earlier attacks."

"That's what Mr Randall said. Apparently my husband had his eyes tested, but by then the symptoms had vanished and his eyesight appeared perfect. Then there was the time he pulled a muscle in his leg. Apparently it's very common for people to trip over nothing..."

"I remember that," Mrs Price intervened. "Oh, sorry, Mrs Pettifer, I didn't mean to interrupt."

"That's all right, Mrs Price. Do go on."

"I saw it happen, that's all. I was looking out of the kitchen window. Dr Pettifer was walking down the garden path and he stumbled, tripped and fell over suddenly, just like that. I ran out, but he was already getting up again. But I couldn't understand it at all. There was just nothing he could have tripped over, I looked."

"And how long ago was that, did you say?" asked Thanet.

"About eighteen months ago."

"Just a few months after we were married," Gemma said. "So you see..." She shivered and there, once again, was that flicker of repulsion.

Oh, yes, Thanet saw all right. Here then at last was a believable reason for Pettifer to have committed suicide, Pettifer the "exercise fanatic" as Lowrie had called him... To endure not only increasing immobility, paralysis and dependence but the disgust of the wife he adored... Tragedy indeed. Learning of her unfaithfulness must have been the last straw.

"But the post mortem," Lineham was saying, and Thanet looked at him with approval. It was a point he had been about to raise himself. "Why didn't anything show up in the post mortem?"

"I asked Mr Randall about that," Gemma said. "Apparently it wouldn't show up in a routine post mortem, especially in the early stages of the disease. Even a really good pathologist could miss it. Are you all right, Mrs Price?"

The housekeeper had taken out a handkerchief and was wiping her eyes. Now she shook her head, her face crumpled with grief. "I can't believe it," she said. "To think that the doctor..." She shook her head again, stood up blindly. "If you'd excuse me," she said.

Gemma crossed to put an arm around the housekeeper's shoulders as she blundered to the door. "Why don't you go and lie down for a while? Take the day off, if you like. I can manage perfectly well, I'm sure."

Mrs Price blew her nose, straightened her shoulders. "I'm better off doing things," she said. "But thank you."

It looked as though the two women were beginning to come to terms with each other at last, Thanet thought, watching them.

When the housekeeper had left the room, Gemma came back and stood in front of the fireplace, facing Thanet. "So there we are, Inspector. I must say that, although I feel very sad on my husband's behalf"—and her eyes glistened with unshed tears which she blinked away—"it's a great relief to me to know that there was a reason..."

Thanet was aware that Lineham had made a tiny, restless movement

"...and so glad, for the baby's sake, that the mystery has been cleared up." She laid a protective hand on the mound of her stomach. "It'll be bad enough as it is, knowing that his father committed suicide, but never to have known why..."

Thanet stood up. "Yes. There is just one last question I'd like to ask you, though. Whose suggestion was it that you go to London that night—as opposed to any other night, I mean. Yours or your husband's?"

She considered, head on one side. "His, I think. Yes, it was. I'd been reading a script, considering a part and, as I think I told you before, I simply couldn't make up my mind whether to take it or not, and Arnold said, why didn't I go up to see my agent, discuss it with him."

"When was this?"

"Oh, let me see... Some time early last week."

"And which of you suggested you go on Monday?"

"Arnold did. I remember because I knew that Mrs

Price was going to be away for the night and I suggested I go some other time instead. Arnold said no, that it would give him a chance to get on with something he'd been planning for some time. It was he who suggested I stay the night in London. He said it would be less tiring for me . . ." Her face was beginning to disintegrate. "I'd forgotten that. I suppose he wanted us both out of the house. He probably didn't want to risk one of us finding him before . . . before . . ." She shook her head as the tears brimmed over and began to roll down her cheeks.

Lineham was looking at Thanet with outraged expectancy. Clearly he was waiting for Thanet to disillusion her.

"What I can't bear," she said, "is the thought that he changed his mind at the last minute, that he called me for help and I . . . just went away, left him to die. If only I'd forced my way in, somehow . . ."

"I shouldn't dwell too much on that if I were you. Knowing your husband, what sort of a life do you think it would have been for him, as time went on?"

She compressed her lips, shook her head. "I suppose you're right," she said doubtfully.

Thanet stood up. "Anyway, it does seem as though the mystery is explained at last. I shouldn't think we'll need to trouble you again."

She blew her nose, made an effort to smile, followed them out into the hall. "You know . . ." she said.

With the front door half open Thanet and Lineham paused, turned politely.

"Those cruise tickets," she said. "I'm beginning to think of them as Arnold's last message to me. I think he was saying, Go on living. And enjoy it."

The briefest of glances at Lineham's face was enough. With a hasty goodbye to Gemma Pettifer, Thanet hustled him out to the car. He propelled the sergeant into the passenger seat. Safer, this time, if he took the wheel himself.

"Go on living and enjoy it, indeed!" Lineham exploded as they fastened their seat belts. "Incredible, isn't it? Really incredible!"

"What is, exactly?" Lineham needed to get it off his chest.

"And all that stuff about the baby. Who is she trying to fool?"

"Herself, perhaps?" Thanet said softly. "Or perhaps she really does believe it. After all, Mike, you must remember that as far as she's concerned, her husband could well be the father. She has no idea he was sterile, we can be sure of that."

"But it's all wrong!"

"What is?"

"To let her go on thinking... all those things she is thinking. That he killed himself solely because of his illness, for a start. That he didn't know she was being unfaithful to him... That he thought the baby was his... And all that rubbish about the cruise being a gift for the future and him wanting her to be happy, when we know that he tried to set her up on a murder charge, for God's sake!"

"You're convinced now, then?"

"Oh, yes. No doubt about it. You were right—as usual," he added with a wry grin. "But surely, sir, you're not just going to leave it like that?"

"You mean, you think it's my duty to explain all this to her?"

"Well, yes."

"Why?"

"Well..."

"To punish her for her sins, is that it?"

Lineham had the grace to look abashed.

"No, Mike. My brief is finished and that's that. Our job was to get at the truth of the matter and that we've done. And besides, she may not realise it at the moment, but she's going to pay all right, in her own way."

"What do you mean?"

"Wait until we get back to the office and I'll tell you.

Though that demonstration you gave earlier shows that you're perfectly capable of working it out for yourself."

Lineham did not reply and a glance at his face told Thanet that the challenge had been taken up, the sergeant's righteous indignation diverted.

Thanet swerved to avoid a cyclist who had suddenly wobbled out in front of the car. They were approaching the centre of the town now and the mid-morning traffic was building up.

He settled down to concentrate on his driving.

23

With the Pettifer case closed, Thanet felt free to take Sunday off. Any residual paperwork could be done on Monday. But Joan had promised to drive Mrs Markham to Bexhill . . .

"Why don't I drive you down?" he suggested. "It's a glorious day. We could take a picnic, to the beach."

"Lovely idea, darling." Joan hugged him. "I'll wear my new sweater, to celebrate."

"Smashing, Dad!" (Ben)

"A whole day off, Daddy!" (Bridget)

"Yes, poppet. A whole day." Thanet suppressed a twinge of guilt that this should seem so unusual an occurrence.

The sun shone, the roads were empty, they were all in a holiday mood and the journey was soon over. They delivered Mrs Markham into the arms of her suitably appreciative daughter-in-law, then went down to the beach. They hadn't been here before and were delighted to find that it was sandy.

"I'm glad I packed the buckets and spades," murmured Joan as they settled down.

Bridget and Ben immediately began to discuss and sketch out on the sand ambitious plans for a moated castle complete with drawbridge. Joan and Thanet watched them for a while and then agreed to take it in turns to keep an eye on them while the other relaxed.

Thanet loved the sun and a day as warm as this so late in the year was a bonus indeed. He lay revelling in its mellow warmth, conscious of it soaking into his skin, his flesh, his very bones, it seemed. The plaintive mewing of the gulls, the rhythmic sigh of the sea and the distant cries of children playing receded into a distant music that soothed the spirit. Wonderful to relax like this, he thought. Wonderful not to have to think about work. Glad the Pettifer case is finished . . .

His own voice echoed in his mind. *"You see, Mike, a good detective also needs one other quality: intuition."* Well, Mike had shown him just how essential intuition was.

"What's the matter?" Joan said.

"Nothing. Why?"

"You groaned."

"Did I?"

"Well, sort of. A little groan."

Thanet rolled over, sat up. "I was just thinking what a conceited, condescending, patronising idiot I am."

"Wow! Is that all?"

"That's all."

They grinned at each other.

"And what, exactly, put that ego-boosting thought into your head?"

"I was thinking about Mike." And he told her about Lineham's bitter disappointment that he hadn't beaten Thanet to it, of his own sense of Lineham's need to achieve at that particular moment, of his stratagem to help him do it.

"And did it work?"

"Yes. Only too well."

"So, what are you worrying about?"

199

"The way I lectured him first. Pontificated. Babbled on about intuition, subterranean connections..."

"Subterranean connections?"

Thanet explained, "It makes my toes curl to think about it."

"But why? You did get there before him, after all."

"I know, but... It was the *way* Mike did it. Oh, I know I had to push him a little, to keep him going. If he has a fault in this respect, it's to give up too soon. But he did get there. And by logic."

"So?"

"Well, it shook me. There I was, thinking I had something special, the policeman's nose, some people call it..."

"Well, it is something special. Maybe Mike was able to get there by logic, deduction, whatever you like to call it, this time—but another time it might simply not work."

"That's true, I suppose."

"Anyway, if you didn't get there by logic, how did you get there?"

Thanet had of course told Joan about the outcome of the case, but until now there had been no opportunity to talk at leisure.

Thanet considered. "Well, I suppose the turning point for me was the discovery that Pettifer was sterile."

"Why was that so important?"

"Because it destroyed his credibility. It showed that he'd been acting out a lie to everyone, including his wife, in pretending that there was nothing wrong with their marriage. It made me question everything I had until then accepted. I simply couldn't believe, from what I'd heard about him, that he could just have shrugged his shoulders and ignored his wife's infidelity. And yet he obviously *wanted* everyone to believe he was unaware of it. So I had to ask myself, why?"

"Why do you say you don't feel he could have accepted it? Some men can."

Thanet shook his head. "Not Pettifer. He was a proud

man. Reserved, and devious, too. And vindictive. There's
a story Dr Barson told me about him . . ." Thanet related it to Joan.

She wrinkled her nose. "Nasty."

"Quite. It shows that Pettifer wasn't the type to
forgive and forget. And especially where his wife was
concerned. Everyone agreed, he idolised her. He would
have been shattered. And he'd have wanted revenge, I
was convinced of it. Of course, when we finally heard
about the multiple sclerosis everything became clear at
last."

"Poor man. It's a terrible, terrible disease."

"I know. And for someone like Pettifer . . . He must
have been in despair. As his wife said, it would have been
truly intolerable for him to know that as time went on
he would become increasingly dependent, immobile . . .
To have envisaged progressive paralysis, years spent
in a wheelchair as an invalid . . . And, of course, he would
have been aware of her revulsion from any kind of
sickness. I should imagine that, even before she told
him she was pregnant and he learned she'd been unfaithful to him, he must already have contemplated the
possibility of suicide at some future date, when the
symptoms became more pronounced."

"He'd have been angry, too," said Joan. "People often
are, with a disease like that. They think, naturally, 'Why
me?' "

"I agree. And then she told him about the baby. Now,
looking back, I'd guess that it was at that point that his
anger switched direction and focused on her."

"D'you remember that book I read a year or two
ago?" Joan said suddenly. "By that American woman?
The one about women as murderers."

"Vaguely. I meant to read it, didn't I, and never got
around to it."

"That's right. I told you at the time you'd have found
it interesting. Anyway, the author said that her thinking
on the subject had been shaped by the realisation that
murder could be a psychological alternative to suicide.

She said that, especially in Victorian times, trapped in desperately unhappy marriages by force of circumstance—no money, no chance of supporting themselves by taking a job, no divorce—they often had only two choices, murder or suicide."

"I'm not sure what you're saying. That Pettifer was in that position?"

"To some extent, yes. His hands were tied in so many ways, weren't they? He couldn't make his illness go away, he couldn't try to forget his wife had been unfaithful because the baby would always be there as a reminder..."

"That's true. And, of course, we must remember that at the time she didn't know he was sterile—she still doesn't, for that matter—and she would naturally have expected him to think that he was the father of the child. So he had no freedom of choice there, either: he couldn't say he wasn't without letting her know of his sterility, so he dared not show her what the news really meant to him. I should think he was so afraid of giving his secret away that he covered up his confusion by reacting the opposite way and pretending to be pleased. And then, when he thought about it, he saw how he could use that initial reaction to his own advantage. He saw how he could put an end to his own intolerable situation *and* punish her at the same time. He would kill himself and somehow make sure that she would be blamed for his death. It must have appeared the perfect solution. This way she wouldn't be free to go to her lover or enjoy the wealth she would inherit..."

Joan shuddered. "Really, it makes me shiver to think about it. To be so cold-blooded..."

Thanet squeezed her hand. "I know... Anyway, I'd guess he took his time working out the details of his plan. The most important thing was to make sure that no one would believe he had any reason to commit suicide. This is why it was so vital to convince everyone that he was unaware of his wife's infidelity. I don't suppose it entered his head for a moment that we'd find out that he was sterile. He couldn't have realised that his first wife had told her mother, and even if he had I don't suppose he would have thought we might find out that way. He hadn't seen his mother-in-law for years, they didn't get on, and she must have seemed so remote from his present existence that I don't suppose she even came into his calculations. And he made sure—or so he thought—that we wouldn't find out about his illness, by asking Mr Randall, the neurologist, not to mention it to anyone, even Mrs Pettifer."

"There was a risk there, though, surely. He must have realised that Mr Randall might consider himself absolved from the promise by Dr Pettifer's death."

"True. But it was a risk he had to take. He could hardly go to the length of asking the man to consider his promise binding even after death, without making him suspicious that suicide was on the cards. And in that case Mr Randall might have considered himself justified in breaking that promise and approaching Mrs Pettifer."

"True."

"He had to take some risks, after all. The best he could do was try to foresee as many loopholes as possible, and stop them up. He dared not change his will as insurance against his wife inheriting if his plan went wrong, for example, because that would have told us that he knew about her affair."

"So this was why right up to the end he went on behaving as though he expected to have a future—why he arranged to have his car repaired, for example."

"Yes. And booked that cruise. All designed to make us think it couldn't have been suicide."

"And went on pretending to be delighted about the baby," Joan said with a sigh.

"Exactly. Meanwhile, he made his personal preparations for his death, put his affairs in order and cleared his desk. He was the sort of man who would hate the thought of anyone going through his private correspondence, even after he was dead. That desk of his, together with the method he chose to kill himself, were the only things which made me think he might have killed himself after all. He'd kept the clearance to a minimum, but there was such a vast, obvious absence of personal paraphernalia."

"Yes, I meant to ask you about the method he chose. You said that all the doctors you spoke to agreed that it was the one they would opt for. If he wanted to make sure you thought it was murder, why didn't he choose something less ... oh, dear, what's the right word? Comfortable?"

"I know. That stumped me too. Then I thought, well, yes, he desperately wanted his plan to succeed, but all the other methods would have seemed either so difficult to set up or so messy or painful that in the end he thought, what the hell, you only die once, I'll go out gracefully."

"Yes, I can see that. I suppose that's how it must have been. Just a minute..." Joan scrambled to her feet. The castle was taking shape. Bridget was creating the building itself, Ben digging out the moat. Now they were both claiming the right to construct the most interesting part, the drawbridge with its tunnel beneath. Thanet looked on indulgently as Joan arbitrated. God, what a lucky man he was! He sent up a silent prayer of gratitude as he waited for her to return.

"All settled?"

"More or less. Anyway, what were you saying?"

"Well, having firmly established in everyone's minds the picture of a man with everything to live for, he moved on to planning the details of the suicide/apparent murder. What he had to do was lay a careful trail for the police to follow so that they would be sufficiently suspicious to feel they had to dig a little."

"Which is what happened."

"Yes. The first bit of planted 'evidence' was of course the note, with its mis-spelling of Andrew's nickname."

"Ah, yes, I remember you asking about that right at the beginning."

"I suppose that, knowing Andrew, Pettifer counted on his demanding to see the note and spotting the mistake, as indeed he did."

"That was another risk, surely? What if Andrew had never seen it?"

"Then other things would have made us suspicious anyway. This was just an additional pointer that it hadn't been suicide. For all we know there may yet be other 'clues' we haven't yet discovered. Interestingly enough, though, it was this very bit of 'evidence'—which was supposed to, and did make us suspect that it might have been murder—that in the end put me on to the fact that it had been suicide after all. Together with something else that had absolutely nothing to do with the case. That was where my famous 'intuition' came in."

"What do you mean? No, tell me later, when you've finished explaining what Pettifer planned to do."

"Well, as I said, he wanted first to make us suspect that it was murder and then point us specifically in the direction of his wife. And this was where things began to get complicated. He wanted to ensure that she would appear to have not only motive but means and opportunity as well. In addition, he wanted to discredit her, underline her apparent guilt by making her appear an out-and-out liar."

"A tall order."

"Very. But then, he was a clever man, and, as I said, there was no hurry. Time was on his side. The very nature of his particular disease meant that there was no risk of it being spotted in a routine post mortem in its early stages.

"Anyway, I would think that his decision as to when to stage his 'murder' was made as far back as August, when Mrs Price received an invitation to speak at a Women's Institute meeting in Merrisham last Monday, and asked him if she could spend the night at her sister's. That gave him three clear months in which to work things out. It wouldn't surprise me if, during that time, he employed a private detective to follow Gemma, find out where and when she was meeting her lover. He wanted somehow to manipulate her into spending the night of the 'murder' in London, so that he would have the house to himself. He must have hoped that she would grab the opportunity for a night with Lee so that as soon as we became suspicious of her and checked her alibi we would discover her infidelity."

"And therefore her motive."

"Exactly. In the event, Fate was on his side. Gemma was asked to consider a part in a new play and couldn't make up her mind whether to take it. Pettifer persuaded her into a trip to London on Monday night to discuss the matter with her agent. Meanwhile he had been elaborating his plan. I think, you know, that he probably enjoyed doing that, in a macabre kind of way. It wasn't enough for him that she should simply have appeared to commit the 'murder' before leaving for London. He wanted to enmesh her in a whole web of deceit so that everything she said or did would serve only to incriminate her further."

"You make him sound really diabolical."

"He just wanted to hit back, I think, for what had happened to him. At life, at her . . . at her especially. The higher the pedestal, the more shattering the fall. Anyway, his plan was very neat, very simple, really. He would pretend illness, nothing so serious that it would keep her at home, but sufficient to give her a conscience about going out and make her fall in with his suggestion that she give him a ring around ten o'clock to check that he was all right. Then, when she rang him, he would make a panic-stricken request for her to return home at once. Knowing how uncharacteristic of him such behaviour was, she was sure to do as he asked . . ."

"He must have thought she cared about him to that degree, then."

"I suppose so, yes. But he wasn't taking any chances.

He got her to promise to leave immediately, before he
rang off. The next problem . . ."

"Just a minute. I'm sorry, perhaps I'm being a bit
dim, but I don't quite see the point of all that. You say
he had to get her down to Sturrenden late at night,
presumably so that you—the police—would then find
out that she was on the spot at the time the overdose
was administered."

"That's right. He wanted us to think that she had
slipped him just enough sodium amytal—that was the
drug he used, by the way, we heard yesterday—in the
cocoa she gave him before she left, for him to go off into
really sound sleep so that when she returned later to
finish him off he would still be sufficiently drugged not
to realise what was happening. I bet that if Mrs Price
hadn't washed the mug we'd have found traces of
sodium amytal in it."

"But how would you know she had been there later
that night? I mean, if those two men on patrol hadn't
noticed Lee's rather unusual sports car or if Gemma
hadn't been spending the night with Lee and had come
in a taxi . . . it was taking a chance, surely?"

"Perhaps Dr Pettifer had more faith in the police
than you have, my love," Thanet said with a grin. "No,
sooner or later it would have come out, via the hotel
perhaps. Anyway, as I was saying, the next problem was
to make sure not only that when she got here she
couldn't get in, but that she wouldn't attempt to break
in, either. And this he managed by leaving his car at the
Centre, without her knowledge. It was supposed to
have broken down, but it wouldn't surprise me in the
least if he immobilised it on purpose. He knew enough
about cars to be able to do it, to make sure the fault was
one which could have come about accidentally, so that
the mechanic wouldn't be suspicious. Then, before he
took the overdose, he bolted and barred the front door
so that she wouldn't be able to get in that way and
banked on the fact that, when she went around to the

back and saw his car wasn't there, she'd assume he'
gone out on a night call."

"Another risk."

"Yes, but it worked. You have to hand it to him. Th
risks were all calculated, based on his understanding c
her character, and most of them paid off. She did read
to much of what he planned exactly as he intended sh
should. And he made sure that there were other littl
touches of circumstantial evidence to incriminate her
At some time during those three months he must hav
set aside the drinking glass and the tablet containe
with her prints on them, made sure they were protecte
from dust so that the fingerprints would appear fresh...

"So, what went wrong? Why didn't it work, in th
end?"

"Chiefly, I think, because his understanding of he
didn't go deep enough. He misread the depth of he
feeling for him. He thought that because she had
lover, she didn't care about him, her husband. Bein
the sort of man he was, he wouldn't have been able t
understand that her lovers were for her really no mor
than a diversion, a physical appetite perhaps, or a so
to her ego. Playthings, really, I suppose. For him
sexual relationship meant commitment and he couldn
have begun to understand that she could be committe
to her husband while enjoying an affair with someon
else."

"You really think she did feel deeply for him, then!

"Yes, I do. Mind, I don't think even she was awar
just how deeply until he was dead. I think that it wa
this realisation that hit her so hard, coming too late, a
it did. Anyway, the result was that, whereas I suppos
he expected her to deny, bluster, appear more an
more guilty as each new bit of incriminating informa
tion came along, in fact she reacted in precisely th
opposite manner. She insisted from the start that
couldn't have been suicide and, if it had been murde
seemed hell-bent on incriminating herself. She wou'
have had to be the most efficient murderer in th

annals of crime to have made such a mess of her story.
It was as full of holes as a colander, and the discrepancies were so pointless, so incomprehensible. No, I don't
think either of them had any idea how much she cared
for him."

"Sad, wasn't it—that he died not knowing, I mean."
Joan was silent for a while, thinking; idly picking up
handful after handful of sand and watching it trickle
away through her fingers.

"So," she said at last, "how did you cotton on, in the
end? It was to do with the mis-spelling of Andrew's
name in the suicide note, you said?"

"Yes. Well, it wasn't just that. All week . . ."

"Just a minute," Joan said suddenly. "Sorry to interrupt, darling, but what about the other note, the one
you found in Andrew's bedroom? Did you find out any
more about it?"

"No. I'm still convinced that there was nothing between him and Gemma. But the trouble was that I
couldn't be certain without either tackling Andrew himself or Gemma—and I didn't want to do that and risk
embarrassing the boy if the whole thing was no more
than a fantasy. I felt that to know we knew how he felt
about Gemma would just have caused him unnecessary
distress, and he had enough to cope with as it was."

"I agree. Poor boy. He must feel completely lost,
now. What will happen to him, do you know?"

"It's been arranged that he'll live with his grand-
mother—well, adoptive grandmother, really. Mrs Blaidon."
Thanet gave a reminiscent smile. "You'd have liked her.
And she seemed fond of Andrew."

"I should think that's far and away the best arrangement in the circumstances. Anyway, do go on with what
you were saying."

"Where was I? Oh, yes, explaining how I finally
came to see what had been going on. Well, as I said,
although it was the mis-spelling of Andrew's name in
that first note which eventually put me on the right
track, there was much more to it than that. All week

the clues came along so neatly—Gemma's guilt seemed
too obvious, the explanations too pat. And all along I
felt uncomfortable, uneasy. I knew something was
wrong, but I couldn't put my finger on it. I felt as
though I was being nudged further and further along a
road I didn't want to follow . . . as if someone was pulling
the strings and there I was, dancing against my will.
Like a puppet."

Joan grimaced. "A puppet for a corpse. What a macabre
notion."

"A delightfully graphic way of describing it, darling.
But yes, that was it, exactly. Though, as I say, I didn't
realise it for some time. I just had this feeling of
resentment which people get when they're being manipulated into something against their will."

"I know what you mean. Like me and Mrs Markham."

"Well, as a matter of fact, I think Mrs Markham had a
lot to do with my understanding, in the end, of what
was happening."

"What do you mean?"

"Well, the night I finally worked it out, we'd had that
discussion about driving her down here today, do you
remember? Though I must admit," Thanet added,
gazing around at the sunlight sparkling on the water,
the near-deserted beach and Bridget and Ben rushing
to and from the water's edge with buckets of water for
the moat, "it wasn't such a bad idea after all. The point
is, she'd been in my mind all week—Mrs Markham, I
mean—the way she had you dancing attendance on her.
To be honest, I think now, looking back, that one of the
reasons why I became increasingly angry with you for
allowing her to manipulate you like that was because
subconsciously I was aware that precisely the same
thing was happening to me, and I didn't like it one little
bit. I think I was taking out my anger and frustration at
my own situation on you. Anyway, to get back to how I
came to work it out, if you remember I'd just learnt
that afternoon that Pettifer had been sterile and as I
said this discovery had turned my previous thinking

about the case upside down. The final thing which made it all click was, believe it or not, a game I was playing with Ben."

"With Ben?"

"Yes. In the early hours of the morning, when you were snoring your head off."

"I wasn't!"

"All right, calm down, I was teasing. Anyway, I forgot to tell you, but Ben woke up in the night wanting to go to the lavatory. When I put him back to bed he said he wanted to play another game—little monkey, wasn't he, trying to wring the last ounce of concession out of being unwell. But he was still very hot and I thought he'd get off to sleep again more quickly if I agreed. We played 'Spot the Deliberate Mistake.'"

"Yes, he's very good at that, isn't he?"

"I know. Well, he was asleep before we'd finished but I decided I'd wait a few more minutes to make sure he'd gone off properly. I dared not move in case I disturbed him so I just sat there, staring down at this puzzle with all this stuff about the Pettifer case and Mrs Markham floating around in my mind—and suddenly, simultaneously it seemed, I thought, *Deliberate Mistake* and *My God, that's what's been happening to me*— meaning the manipulation, of course. And that was it. The whole thing just fell together. Suddenly I saw it all—the deliberate mis-spelling of the name, the reason why Pettifer had gone on pretending ignorance of his wife's infidelity, the way he'd planned his revenge— everything, that is, but the reason why he had chosen to die. For that, I had to wait until next morning. But even before I heard about his illness I was convinced I'd hit on the truth, however incredible it might seem."

Thanet laughed. "You should have seen Mike's face when he finally worked it out for himself. He thought I'd finally flipped."

"You say 'worked it out for himself,' but did he really?"

"Well, as I said, I did have to give him a gentle push

211

from time to time, when he stopped. But he got there, in the end. That's why..."

"All right, I know. That's why you felt such a fool, etcetera, etcetera. But the fact is, darling, I doubt if he would have, without your help."

"But..."

"No, listen. You yourself gave the reason why. Even when he'd reached the correct conclusion, he couldn't believe that it was true. I think that it's because he can't yet think beyond the likely that he has never yet solved a major case before you. He's got some kind of internal barrier in his brain which prevents him from going down paths which subconsciously he can see are going to lead to unacceptable conclusions. Whereas you tend to let your mind run free... Why are you staring at me like that?"

A slow smile spread across Thanet's face. "You know, you could well be right."

"Well, don't sound so surprised! I'm not a complete moron, you know. How condescending can you get!"

Thanet mimed contrition.

"Why are you making funny faces, Daddy?" It was Bridget, watching him with interest.

"Mummy made a joke," Thanet said, with a teasing glance at Joan.

"Come and see our castle." Bridget tugged at his hand.

Reluctantly Thanet rose, helped Joan up. Dutifully they admired the children's creation.

"Make me a sand-car now, Daddy," Ben said. "Big enough for me to sit in?"

"Me too, Daddy, me too," Bridget chimed in.

"Sounds a long job," said Thanet. "Mummy and I have been sitting down so long we want to stretch our legs. A little walk, first, then we'll make your cars."

Bridget and Ben raced away, wheeling and curving across the wide, empty expanse of sand. Thanet and Joan followed more sedately, holding hands.

"You know, I feel sorry for Mrs Pettifer," Joan said at

last. "For you the case is over now, finished, but for her . . . well, I don't suppose it ever will be."

"That's one of the depressing things about serious crimes, the long-term effect they have on the innocent people connected with them."

"You'd call her innocent?"

Thanet shrugged. "Innocent or not, she's going to have to pay in her own way, I think."

"What do you mean?"

"Well, Mike and I couldn't agree on this. He thought she ought to have been told—about the baby, about what her husband tried to do to her."

"But why?"

"I think he thought that she was getting off too lightly, that she ought to be brought to a realisation of her responsibility in the matter."

"But you disagreed."

"Yes. For one thing, it's outside my brief. I see myself as an instrument of justice, not a dispenser of it. And then, as I said, I think she will pay in the end. For one thing I think she was genuinely shaken to find out how much she cared for her husband and she's going to have to come to terms with her regrets that her attitude to him wasn't different while he was still alive, as well as the sense of loss I think she's genuinely feeling. And, although at the moment she's relieved to find that there was a genuine reason for his suicide and feels absolved of any personal guilt, sooner or later she's going to see it rather differently. She's going to realise that what must really have tipped the balance for him was that, knowing how she felt about sickness, he simply couldn't face the prospect of eventually becoming an object of repulsion to her. And I'd guess that at that point she's bound to begin to feel a measure of guilt. Perhaps she'll go on feeling it for the rest of her life. I don't know. Maybe I'm wrong. Maybe I'm overestimating the strength of her feeling for him, her degree of sensitivity, the power of her conscience. But I don't think so."

Bridget and Ben were racing back towards them.

"Can we go back now, Daddy? Can we make the cars?"

"Race you!" he challenged.

They all set off at a run, Thanet and Joan deliberately holding back, allowing the children a sense of victory.

Thanet picked up a spade. "I can't do both at once, though, can I? Perhaps . . . ?" He raised his eyebrows at Joan, who had flopped down upon the sand, puffing.

She pulled a face. "And I thought I was going to have a lazy day."

But he could see that she didn't really mind.

"Come on then," she said, getting to her feet. "Daddy's biggest, so he can help Ben, who's smallest. And you and I will work together, Sprig."

Enough of the dead, thought Thanet. Life is for the living.

Sand went scudding in all directions as they set to work with a will.

ABOUT THE AUTHOR

DOROTHY SIMPSON, winner of the prestigious Silver Dagger Award, is the author of seven Luke Thanet mysteries, most recently ELEMENT OF DOUBT, LAST SEEN ALIVE, CLOSE HER EYES, and SUSPICIOUS DEATH. A contributor to *Ellery Queen's Mystery Magazine* and *Alfred Hitchcock's Mystery Magazine*, she lives in Kent, England.